To Win Her Trust

A Players Series Novel

Mackenzie Crowne

LYRICAL PRESS
Kensington Publishing Corp.
www.kensingtonbooks.com

First Electronic Edition: January 2015
eISBN-13: 978-1-61650-739-8
eISBN-10: 1-61650-739-X

First Print Edition: January 2015
ISBN-13: 978-1-61650-740-4
ISBN-10: 1-61650-740-3

Printed in the United States of America

Can she trust this player with her heart?

Ever since experiencing a childhood trauma, reclusive artist CC Calhoun has suffered from panic attacks. But when a fateful kiss from handsome wide receiver Kevin "Tuck" Tucker is enough to stop one of those episodes cold, she wonders if guarding her heart has been the right choice. Will going on a test date with Tuck open her to trusting someone for the first time in years? Or will she wind up being just another notch in the football player's bedpost?

Tuck has a reputation for charming women into bed, but after his kiss with CC, he's left aching for more. When he proposes a second date, his attraction to the sexy blonde looks like the makings of true love—something he's never quite believed in—until now. But when Tuck discovers CC's childhood secrets, will the pro athlete be tough enough to stay by her side—or will he betray her hard-earned trust?

Books by Mackenzie Crowne

The Players Series
To Win Her Love
To WIn Her Trust
To Win Her Heart

Published by Kensington Publishing Corporation

Dedicated to my fellow football chicks who, like me, love the game and believe in happily ever after.

Chapter 1

"Hey, Romeo! Would you mind hurrying this along? Some of us have appointments to keep."

CC Calhoun darted a glance over her shoulder at the next customer in line. Lips twisted with displeasure, the disgruntled blonde huffed her impatience. CC offered the woman a pained smile and faced forward once more. The Romeo in question broke off his flirting with the pretty coffee clerk and straightened from his negligent slouch against the counter. On a lazy pivot, he turned. Shaggy, sun-streaked blond hair stuck out from beneath the faded ball cap worn low on his forehead. Dark lenses concealed his eyes—until he dipped his head enough to study CC over the rim of his glasses.

She blinked and suppressed a helpless shiver. *Geez.* Even *she* could understand why the clerk had been buying his ridiculous excuse for not calling. Topping six feet by several inches, his tall frame was the stuff of women's dreams, with wide shoulders and a muscled chest wrapped up perfectly in a dark blue T-shirt. Time-washed jeans rode low on his lean hips and molded to thick thighs and long legs. Despite the slight bump in his nose and the jagged scar bisecting his right eyebrow, his cobalt blue eyes were enough to melt a woman's circuits. The dimples creasing his all-American, bad-boy-next-door face only added to the mega wattage of his grin.

With an abbreviated bob of her head, she indicated the woman at her back who'd voiced the complaint and interrupted his flirtation. Romeo didn't take the hint. The heat of a flush warmed CC's cheeks, and she fought the urge to squirm as his gaze traveled down to her feet and up again to zero in on her face. She swallowed and punched a thumb over her shoulder.

The scarred brow arched, and he cocked his head in silent question. She bared her teeth in a taunting smile and nodded. Unfazed, he shifted his gaze to a spot over her shoulder, and she waited for him to turn the charm on the impatient blonde. Men like him were experts at that type of thing, after all. A slow smile, a knowing look, and even the most grievous of crimes would be forgiven and forgotten. He didn't disappoint.

Straight, white teeth flashed in a smile capable of lighting up Times Square. Eyes bright with a you-know-you-can't-resist-me twinkle, he addressed the annoyed woman in a sharp New England accent. "Sweetheart, why don't you step right up and cut the line? I'm sure the rest of us won't mind."

The woman's derisive snort didn't prevent her from taking him up on his offer. Her three-inch heels clicked out an angry beat as she stepped around CC to the counter and demanded a large, black coffee. Romeo received a pointed glare as she spoke into the smart phone pressed to her ear. "I'll be there in five minutes. A Beantown Gigolo threw me off schedule."

Several of the customers behind CC snickered, and she braced for a heated exchange. This was New York. Murders had occurred for much less than a snarky insult. To her surprise, his smile widened, accompanied by a soft chuckle.

The flustered clerk splashed coffee into a to-go cup with impressive speed. She set the order down in front of the blonde, who tossed down a ten and scooped up the cup. With a perfectly manicured fingernail, she flicked the dark sunglasses down her pert nose. She pinned Romeo with piercing gray eyes, and her cultured tone cut with the sharp edge of sarcasm. "You're cute, *sweetheart,* but do us all a favor and save the seducing for your own time."

More snickers sounded, and CC twisted her lips against a helpless smile. She'd chosen to live in Manhattan because of the anonymity factor, but sharing the city with close to eight million people also provided some entertaining side benefits, like the frankness of her fellow citizens. New Yorkers had no patience for polite acceptance of the unacceptable and weren't afraid to say so.

All eyes followed as the snarky diva brushed by the line of waiting customers to flounce out into the early morning sunlight. CC sank her teeth into her bottom lip as the woman approached Walter. Berating a flirt was one thing, turning her impatience on an innocent dog was another altogether. Preoccupied by his attempt to chew through the parking meter to which he was tied, the Rottweiler paid her no mind. CC's shoulders slumped in relief when the diva hailed a cab without giving her dog a single glance.

"Ouch." The low complaint rumbled in her ear. "Some women just don't appreciate romance."

CC jolted and spun around.

Romeo's boyish grin reignited the burn in her cheeks, and she drew a bracing breath. A lifetime of painful lessons normally provided a healthy immunity to handsome flirts, but faced with his crooked smile, even the most cynical of women would suffer a rush of giddiness. Thankfully, those lessons also taught her how to handle overblown egos.

She flattened her lips in a smirk. "Maybe she found your excuse of a dog eating Lisa's telephone number as ridiculous as the rest of us."

He didn't bite on the insult. "Lisa?"

She rolled her eyes. Typical. The guy didn't even know the name of the woman he'd been schmoozing. She jerked her chin toward the counter. "Lisa. The clerk you were flirting up."

Behind him, color spread across Lisa's high cheekbones. She thumped a large cup to the counter. "Your order is ready. *Keith.*"

He winced and dipped his head closer to whisper, "Does she look as mad as she sounds?"

CC popped her head to the side to check, then offered him a bland smile. "She looks like she's imagining you wearing your order."

"Not a good sign." He shook his head and straightened. "Is she a friend of yours?"

The unexpected question made CC frown. "No. Why?"

"You know her name."

Apparently brains hadn't been included in his gift-from-God package. "She's wearing a name tag."

"Well, damn. How'd I miss that?"

Considering Lisa's impressive chest, CC had a pretty good idea how he'd missed the bright red badge clipped to the clerk's crisp white shirt. "Maybe if you'd been looking a few inches higher…"

Dimples bracketed his sharp grin.

Horror and stunned disbelief heated her cheeks to a flash point. *Crap. Did I say that out loud? And since when do I insult complete strangers— or even* talk *to them? I must be coming down with something.*

Lisa cleared her throat. "Next?"

Another wince. CC took solace in his discomfort. *Serves you right, pal.*

Wry acceptance did nothing to diminish his handsome features. He shrugged and surprised her by spinning around to face Lisa. Handing over payment, he picked up his order. "I truly am sorry. Please forgive me?"

The genuine regret in his low voice was as unexpected as the apology itself.

In CC's experience, most men in his position—and women, for that matter—would be too embarrassed to bother with an apology, despite one being warranted. He didn't seem the least bit concerned over doing so in front of half a dozen witnesses. A surprising seed of respect bloomed in her belly, then immediately withered when he reverted to form.

"And, sweetheart, I still say your smile packs more of a wallop than your double espressos." With that, he turned, winked at CC, and sauntered toward the exit with a carefree whistle.

She refused to allow her gaze to follow the attractive backside of a man who'd been given a surplus of male confidence. Lisa wasn't of the same mind. Disappointment softened the anger in the clerk's eyes as they trailed him out the door. CC shook her head. Some women didn't recognize when they'd dodged a bullet.

Two minutes later, coffee in hand, she stepped out onto the sidewalk. Walter spotted her and lunged, startling a passing group of teenage girls. His leash snapped tight. Undaunted, the eleven-month-old pup spun in a happy circle. Hind end wiggling with excitement, he danced around the wary teenagers, entangling one of the girls in the heavy canvas strap of his leash.

A reckless endangerment lawsuit flashed through CC's mind, and she rushed forward to grab his collar. "He's harmless." She tugged the dog back, and freed from the tether, the frightened girl skittered away, casting nervous glances over her shoulder as she hurried down the sidewalk with her friends.

CC scowled at her exuberant dog. Oblivious to the averted disaster, his body quivered with juvenile exhilaration as he gazed up, wearing a doggy smile.

"Damn it, Walter. What am I going to do with you?"

I was only playing. No need to curse.

She frowned at his imagined answer, delivered in Antonio Banderas's sensual accent. Normally, the whimsy of applying Zorro's sultry tones to her dog amused her…. "God. I have *got* to get a life. Come on, boy. Let's go home."

Ninety-five pounds of leaping, overgrown puppy were impossible to control with only one hand. Like a four-legged wrecking ball, the dog sprang. Large paws thumped against her chest. Coffee flew and CC's world tilted.

Staggering under Walter's weight, she stumbled backward and slammed into a human brick wall. A low grunt sounded in her ear. Walter lunged again and the back of her head collided with a solid chin. She had no time to be shocked at the large hand sliding up her rib cage and clamping onto her left breast. The brick wall toppled and took her along in the process.

A rough *oof* burst from her lips, but the jarring landing she expected didn't occur as she came to rest with her butt cradled by a very male lap. Long, denim covered legs stuck out from beneath hers. The odd combination of sawdust, coffee, and something sweet, yet spicy, teased her nostrils, making them flare. She squeezed her eyes shut briefly, then turned her head and stared into the Beantown Gigolo's laughing face.

Walter's warm tongue swiped at her cheek and kept her from making a bad situation worse by babbling incoherently. Angling her face away, she recaptured his collar. Strong arms tightened around her and alerted her to the hand still cupping her breast. Before she could slap at the long fingers curled around her flesh, a soft hiss blew in her ear.

She twisted around to meet the blue gaze so close to hers and the hiss became a soft groan. He shifted his hips, drawing her attention to the swelling erection pressing into her left butt cheek. A horrified gasp escaped her lips, and he tightened his hold.

Seemingly unconcerned by his body's reaction, warm humor twinkled in the gigolo's eyes. "Not that I'm complaining, but we should probably get up. We're drawing a crowd."

She glanced around. He was right. Half a dozen pedestrians had paused in their early morning travels to witness the spectacle they presented. The urge to flee from prying eyes clawed at her like wicked talons, overshadowing her embarrassment at the drag of his palm releasing her breast as she scrambled from his lap. She rolled to her knees and shot him an accusatory glare. He wiggled his fingers as if he only now realized where they'd rested, but the twinkle in his eyes said just the opposite.

He gripped her elbow and helped her to her feet. To her further agitation, he didn't let go.

"You okay? Nothing broken?"

She shook her head as her gaze flew from one stranger's face to another. Terror, insidious and painful slithered through her. The years dropped away, and memories of other clamoring crowds rushed her. She fought against the all-too-familiar suffocation compressing her lungs, forcing herself into a shallow pant.

Breathe, CC. You aren't nine, and these people have no idea who you are.

Neither the reminder nor the breathing technique helped. Her lungs constricted beneath an iron band of dread. She tightened her grip on Walter's collar, prepared to force her way through the human wall of interest to make her escape. Desperate, her gaze darted to the fingers wrapped around her elbow, then bounced up to the face of the man holding her captive. Between the hat's brim and the glasses, his brow beetled together.

He surprised the hell out of her when he turned on their audience and his sharp command held the steely edge of menace. "Nothing to see here, folks."

One by one, the nosy pedestrians began to wander off, and she clamped down on her bottom lip to suppress a whimper of relief. Taking advantage of his preoccupation, she turned to go. The long fingers still wrapped around her arm brought her up short.

He softened his hold but didn't let go. "Hold on a second."

Teeth clenched, she squeezed her eyes shut against the ominous black halo hovering at the edges of her vision. She gulped convulsively as her oxygen-starved lungs trembled on a spasm.

"Hey, what's this?"

With a fingertip under her chin, he tipped her face up, and her eyes flew open. A single, sharp gasp provided a shallow breath of air, but not enough. Not nearly enough.

"Hey now," he crooned and stepped closer. "What is it? What's wrong?"

Over the buzzing in her ears, the echoing facsimile of his Bostonian accent came from a distance.

Oh, no. No, please. Not here. Not now.

Her circle of vision shrank. Warm fingers brushed over her arm. Confused alarm tightened his features. "Don't faint on me, baby. You're fine. Everything's going to be fine."

A helpless shake of her head was the best she could manage. She opened her mouth and gulped like a grounded fish.

"Aw, hell." He dipped his head and covered her mouth with his.

Shock did the job her breathing technique couldn't. Suddenly, a sweet, healing breath filled her lungs. Tasting of coffee and spice, he sucked and nibbled at her lips, and her eyelids fluttered shut. Terror fell victim to wonder, and she greedily accepted his unexpected gift of desperately needed air. Awareness broadened slowly, taking her beyond relief to recognition as strong arms surrounded her and his hard body pressed to hers.

He's kissing me. The Beantown Gigolo is freaking kissing me! On the sidewalk. In Manhattan. In broad daylight! Holy hot lips!

She waited for the surge of panic, but pleasure held sway as his silken tongue rubbed against hers, retreated, returned, and retreated again. With a final, gentle nibble of those magical lips, he broke the kiss and lifted his head.

She couldn't prevent the shuddering sigh, didn't even try. Lethargy, heavy and warm, dragged at her. A moment passed before she could open her eyes. Like twin funhouse mirrors, the lenses of his glasses reflected her pale image.

"You okay?"

Hanging suspended in his arms, she blinked at him. Was she okay? How was she supposed to answer when she had no idea? He'd scrambled her brain, managing something she'd never been able to achieve on her own. Her breathing remained erratic and shallow, but she wasn't sprawled on the sidewalk in a dead faint, and her body hummed with undeniable pleasure. Overall, that qualified as more than okay in her book.

"I—" Was that her voice, all breathy and hoarse? "Uh... I'm fine."

He dipped his chin, and above his glasses, his steady blue gaze moved over her face in a slow survey. She swayed as he slid his arms from around her, and he gripped her shoulders with his large hands.

"Glad to hear it, but what about me?"

Guilt ricocheted down her spine. Caught up in the remnants of childhood nightmares and then that unprecedented kiss, she'd forgotten all about their fall. Had he been hurt? The possibility hadn't crossed her mind.

She eyed his squared chin but found no evidence of damage from the impact with the back of her head. Likewise, his body received a quick study. As solid as he appeared, an injury didn't seem likely. Patently refusing to think of one prominently solid body part swelling beneath her butt, she squinted her eyes in suspicion. "What *about* you?"

The clenched line of his jaw softened with his chuckle, and he released her shoulders. "I just sacrificed my body so you wouldn't be hurt, not to mention that little mouth-to-mouth exercise. I deserve a thank you, at least, if not an introduction."

"Sacrificed your bod—" She snapped her mouth shut and pressed her lips together. Rattled, she'd forgotten the kind of man she was dealing with. Give a player an inch and he'd demand a mile. Okay, he was right about the apology. She owed him one. A big one. But an introduction? Not in this lifetime.

"Look, I'm embarrassed, and I don't think clearly when that happens."

He cocked his head and waited.

"Thank you for catching me."

"And?"

"And good-bye." Time to go. Any further conversation would inevitably lead to *why* that mouth-to-mouth exercise had been necessary. She spun away and tugged a lagging Walter down the sidewalk, not surprised when her unwanted savior slipped up beside them. He matched her stride for stride but said nothing.

Half a block later, she couldn't take it anymore. She shot him a sidelong glance. "What?"

"I'm still waiting for my introduction." He ruffled long fingers over Walter's muscled back and grinned. "You may be a violation of the city ordinance, pal. I'm not sure this neighborhood is zoned for livestock."

A smile wanted to form. She squelched the urge. Yeah, the guy was charming and his kiss had magical powers. He was also a player. She sped up her pace, to no avail.

"I'm Kevin Tucker, by the way."

Curiosity got the better of her. "I thought your name was Keith."

"Keith?" Confusion flitted over his bad boy features before a deep rumble began in his wide chest. His humor welled to become a full-throated laugh. Disturbed by the shiver of awareness at his obvious pleasure, she frowned.

"I'm flattered you were paying enough attention to catch my name, but it's Kevin." He nodded back toward the coffee shop. "Lisa was handing me a little payback by getting my name wrong."

"Which you deserved."

"Yeah, I did," he said without hesitation and smiled. "But I'm a victim of extenuating circumstances. A dog really *did* eat the slip of paper with Lisa's name and number."

Her breath expelled in a scoffing huff. "Give me a break."

"Cross my heart." He backed up the claim with a finger slice across his chest.

Suspicious, she studied his innocent expression. "That excuse wasn't just a dating version of my dog ate my homework?"

He shrugged and shook his head. "If you'd ever met Murphy, you'd understand."

"Murphy?"

"An idiot mutt." His chuckle skittered over her nerve endings, making them tingle. "So, I'm Kevin, and you are…?"

She stopped short. He halted beside her.

She sighed. "You're not going to leave me alone until I tell you, are you?"

He faced her and crossed his arms.

"If I tell you, will you go away?"

He hesitated at the request but finally nodded.

"CC Calhoun." She scowled. "Happy now?"

He moved quickly. Snatching up her free hand, his strong fingers kept her from pulling back. He bent to brush a whisper of a kiss over her knuckles, and the fine hair on her arms stood at attention. He straightened, and as though fully aware of the unexpected but completely pleasurable flash fires sparking throughout her body, a small smile curled the corners of his lips. He released her hand slowly.

"A pleasure to meet you, CC Calhoun." Tapping a fingertip to the brim of his cap, he walked away.

Chapter 2

CC crouched over her workbench and ignored her cramped fingers as she twisted the dental-floss-thin wire. Over and over, she wrapped the yards of flexible metal filament around the skeletal base of the piece. An hour passed, then another. Shape slowly took form. A fifth hour neared its end when the finished sculpture finally emerged.

Intent concentration slid away as her critical eye considered every line of her creation. Sophisticated and sleek, the slim figure stood, one delicate, feminine arm outstretched as if in a plea toward the unknown.

She sat back and moaned at the sudden relaxation of screaming muscles. Rolling her head and shoulders, she stretched the bunched tendons in her neck and flexed her fingers to rid them of their stiffness.

Yearning. The title whispered through her mind.

The foot tall sculpture filled her gaze, but as it had numerous times over the past six hours, Kevin Tucker's smiling face formed in her mind's eye. Sweet and spicy, the memory of his scent teased. A sharp snort cleared her nostrils and disbursed the haunting fragrance, but the memory of the man remained.

She tossed the small needle nose pliers onto the workbench and slid from the stool. On bare feet, she padded across her studio to the tiny fridge in the corner. After selecting a bottle of cold water, she twisted off the cap and sipped deeply.

Men like him, with rock solid bodies and tough guy good looks, emitted a mysterious, come-to-me-baby lure that drew women in. He had that certain something. A kind of irresistible force a woman couldn't quite put her finger on but responded to just the same.

No doubt he'd broken his share of hearts. She gulped another sip and scowled. But damn. He sure knew how to kiss.

She rolled her eyes and wandered back toward her bench to eye the finished sculpture. Of course he did. Practice made perfect, and from what she'd experienced this morning, he'd put in plenty of time in his quest for perfection. Kisses like his could take a woman's breath away, or give it back, as in her case.

Faced with the double whammy of finding herself in his lap *and* her rush of memories, the panic attack didn't surprise her. She'd faced them under far less stimulation. What *did* surprise her was the effectiveness of his kiss in cutting it off. Sure, her mother and Kris had experience pulling her back from the edge, if they happened to be around when an attack hit, but a complete stranger?

Years of therapy, breathing techniques, and avoiding potentially stressful situations hadn't come close to accomplishing what Kevin Tucker had with the brush of his mouth. Geez, if she'd known the answer to heading off the debilitating attacks was kissing a man, she'd have tried locking lips long ago.

Yeah, right.

The physics of kissing required a woman to allow a man close enough to touch. For a girl who froze at the mere thought of a man's strong hands holding her captive, kissing wasn't an option, and yet... Her brows crowded together on a thoughtful frown. She hadn't froze when Kevin Tucker's large hands roamed over her arms and then her back. Quite the opposite. Not only had she survived his warm embrace *and* his shocking kiss, she'd found pleasure in both.

The revelation wouldn't leave her alone, and the stunning implications lit a fire of cautious optimism in her belly. With her one year time limit approaching, she'd begun to doubt her ability to fulfill the promise she'd made herself on her twenty-fifth birthday, but now... For the past eleven months, she'd worked hard to overcome the constant, clammy fear she'd lived with for years. Through sheer force of will, she'd achieved a measure of success. Each trip to shop, dine out, or simply pick up a cup of coffee was an in-your-face, screw-you to the kidnappers...*and* her father. She'd made important strides, but had she let old fears rob her of the complete recovery she desired?

Hope hit her like a solid fist and stole her breath. Had she accidentally found a solution to her worst, lingering neuroses? Could she overcome the spidery fingers of dread clawing their way through her hard-won sense of safety whenever a male got too close? Until she did, she'd never be able to claim complete victory.

This morning's events proved she wouldn't fall apart if a man touched her, but what exactly had happened? Had shock over Kevin Tucker's kiss allowed her to not only gain control of her breathing but to accept his touch without shattering into a thousand shards of cowardice? Or had the genuine concern in his eyes been responsible for her astonishing response? Logic said it was a combination of both.

He might be a player, and God knew his kiss was enough to jolt her out of her panic, but his unexpected protectiveness had played a part as well. They were complete strangers, and yet, he'd taken one look and instinctively sized up the situation correctly. Without hesitation, he'd come to her aide and banished her demons with single-minded purpose.

No one had ever done that before.

She ran a fingertip over the smooth wire of the sculpture. The question was, could she recreate the scenario, harnessing the ability to overcome the attacks in the process?

Before she could answer the question, a key turned in the front door lock and drew her attention. She spun around as Kris breezed inside. The tall redhead crossed the foyer into the studio in her typical lazy stroll.

"Are you still at it?"

"Just finished." CC nodded her head at the sculpture. "What do you think?"

Her cousin stopped at her side and pursed her lips. "It's beautiful. Kind of sad, but gorgeous."

"It's *Yearning*."

Toenails clicked against the condo's hardwood floor, and Walter rounded the corner from the hallway. He loped into the studio, then slid to a stop at Kris's side. The jerking stub of his tail telegraphed his pleasure as he bumped up against her thigh.

She rested a hand on his wide skull and stabbed CC with narrowed eyes. "Okay, what's up?"

"What do you mean?"

"You came barreling in here this morning and started twisting your wires like one of those crazy dead artists you idolize." She jerked her chin toward the sculpture. "You always dive for your workbench when you're upset." A militant gleam sparkled in the hazel eyes, pinning her in place. "I heard Curt's message on the answering machine. Are you going to see him?"

A grimace tightened CC's lips. After the unprecedented events of this morning, she'd forgotten all about her father's message. Of course, Kris would blame his call for the frenzied work session. More sisters than cousins, they'd grown up together. While panic attacks and neuroses were CC's legacy of having survived her dysfunctional childhood, Kris tended toward overprotectiveness, especially when it came to dealings with Curt Jensen.

She shrugged. "Probably not."

Disapproval creased her cousin's brow. "Don't let him pressure you. You know how he is."

"And you know me better than that."

Kris smirked and leaned forward to lift a hank of curls at one side of CC's head.

She slapped at her hand. "What are you doing?"

"If you're not upset over Curt, then it must be some kind of crazy artist thing. I'm checking to see if you still need a *pair* of earrings instead of just one, CC Van Gogh." She grinned at CC's snicker. "Hey, you know I've been lusting over your pearl studs for years."

"And you'll be lusting for years to come."

Walter padded off toward the shallow basket holding his toys. Her cousin slouched against the edge of the workbench and raised a questioning brow. "What whipped you into a creative frenzy?"

Though tempted to keep this morning's fiasco to herself, she didn't bother. Kris would only badger her until she spilled the beans. "I had a panic attack outside the Coffee Clutch this morning."

Concern bloomed in her cousin's eyes. "Aw, Cees."

"*And* I met a guy."

"What? Wait a minute." Kris sprang up from her slouch. "*You* met a guy? Like a real guy? Not some pimple-faced bagger in the grocery store who handed your purchases over and said, 'Thanks for shopping with us'?"

She rolled her eyes. "Yes, he was a real guy."

"Way to go, Cees! It's—"

"Not what you're thinking." She climbed onto her stool. "I only mentioned him because something kind of weird happened."

"Weird how?"

She drew a long sip from her water bottle. When she couldn't stall any longer, she looked away. "He kissed me."

"Kissed you?" Kris choked.

She nodded, understanding her cousin's shock. Other than for classes or a rare outing with Kris, up until a year ago, CC barely left the condo. Forget being kissed by a stranger, meeting a pimply-faced grocery clerk would have been a big deal.

"I hate to point this out, cuz, but considering your aversion to guys, letting a complete stranger kiss you goes *way* beyond 'kind of weird.'"

"I didn't *let* him kiss me. He just…sort of did it."

"Why?"

She blinked at the question.

"Don't get me wrong, I'm not saying that's a bad thing. It's about time you put what happened behind you and found yourself a guy, but Cees, a stranger? That's not like you."

A soft sigh lifted her chest. "No, it isn't, and I haven't found myself a guy. In fact, if I hadn't been in the middle of a major attack, I probably would have kneed him in the balls." They shared a grin. "But the weird thing is, I was so shocked at what he was doing the attack just"—she shrugged her shoulders—"stopped. One minute I was fighting off a faint, and the next I was fine. Well, not fine exactly, but I wasn't sprawled on the sidewalk."

"Uh-huh. That's nice." Kris flapped her hand impatiently. "You still haven't explained why he kissed you."

Across the room, Walter's playful growl drew CC's attention. Front end lowered to the floor, his backside wiggled to beat the band. A moment later, he pounced on a mauled shoe. His favorite toy slapped against his jowls as he whipped his head back and forth.

She scowled. "It's all Walter's fault. We had a little…incident."

"Define incident."

Her detailed account of her morning sent Kris into a fit of giggles. She ended with the Bostonian Gigolo's demand for an introduction and his surprisingly agreeable exit once he'd gotten her name.

"He smelled like sawdust and coffee." The water bottle paused at her lips. "And cinnamon!" Water sloshed over her fingers as she dropped her hand to the workbench. Yes, the sweet and spicy edge teasing her memory since he walked away all those hours ago had definitely been a hint of cinnamon.

"Um, Cees. You're scaring me a little."

She wiped her wet hand on the thigh of her jeans. "I'm scaring myself. I just experienced my first kiss, with a stranger no less, in the middle of a crowded sidewalk. What's more, I somehow escaped the worst effects of an attack, and what keeps going through my head? The way he smelled." She frowned. "A man has no business smelling like that."

Kris's eyes widened. Her mouth dropped open, and her lips formed a silent *O*.

A low growl vibrated in CC's throat. "Don't even go there."

Kris rubbed at her arms as if chilled. "You've got to admit, it is a little spooky. Your mom would have a fit if she heard what you just said."

"Oh, please. A woman knows her mate by his scent? What a crock. Mom's Hocus Pocus theories are nothing but the wistful imaginings of an aged hippy. A man's scent is nothing more than leftover fragrances from what he's consumed that day and what he does for a living." She aimed the bottle at her cousin's nose. "The guy is nothing more than a gum chewing carpenter who likes coffee…and flirting. You should have seen him. Flashing dimples at every unsuspecting woman in the place. He's probably been charming little girls since the playpen."

"You say that like it's a bad thing."

She flattened out her lips in a bland stare. "In my experience, that *is* a bad thing, but you're missing my point."

"Which is?"

"He stopped the panic attack. Stopped it cold."

"And?"

"And? Are you kidding me? That's huge! It has me wondering." She rubbed her fingers over her chin. "Would it work with just any guy?"

"Would what work?" Confusion hazed Kris's eyes. "What are you talking about?"

"I'm talking about exploring the possibility of controlling the attacks and getting past my *ick* factor with guys at the same time. My birthday is in less than a month, and I'm running out of time on my promise. Do you think I *want* to be the weirdo twenty-six year old who's never been on a date? I'm sick of being a scared rabbit, and from what I learned this morning, I don't have to be. A complete stranger kissed me on the sidewalk, and the world didn't end. It's time I put that neuroses behind me."

"Oh, man. I have *got* to meet this guy. When are you seeing him again?"

"Who said I was?"

"But—"

"I'm thinking of asking Ronald out."

"Ronald?" Sour disapproval puckered Kris's mouth.

"Why not?" Though her art agent didn't have the kind of billboard good looks that made a woman breathless, his quiet and steady manner offered no surprises. "I won't know for sure if this morning was a fluke unless I test it in theory. To do that, I need to spend some time with a guy. Ronald and I are friends, sort of, and I don't think he's seeing anyone right now. I can't see him objecting to sharing a few dates."

"He's a guy. Of course he won't object, but if you're going to step outside your comfort zone to test this theory, why not do it with Mr.

Cinnamon? You already know he's got the necessary skills to do the job."
She waggled her brows.

"Mr. Cinnamon works from the same playbook as my father. No thanks. Besides, there are millions of people in Manhattan. I'll never see him again."

"Oh, ye of little faith." Kris slipped a slim tablet from the bag on her shoulder. "Anyone can be found if you know what you're doing."

"I'm not interested in finding him."

"I am. What's his name?"

She growled her displeasure but caved under Kris's pointed stare. "Kevin Tucker."

As if dumbstruck, her cousin's brows jumped to her hairline. "Tuck?"

"Tuck what?"

"Not what. Who! *Tuck.* Sexy wide receiver for the Manhattan Marauders?"

CC gnawed at her bottom lip. Not a fan of football, she'd nonetheless heard the name mentioned. One couldn't live in Manhattan and not be aware of the buzz surrounding football's newest franchise, but what would a pro player be doing in a local coffee shop?

Kris frowned when CC didn't respond. "Remember that story a couple months ago about the retired quarterback who found out that lady football blogger was his daughter? Her name was Gracie something. She was the one with the little twin girls who accepted the wedding proposal on TV? They got married a couple of months ago."

"He's *married*?" She refused to name the expanding lump in her belly as disappointment. The man had kissed her, for heaven's sake. The cheating dog.

Kris wagged a dismissive hand. "No. Tuck's not married. She married Tuck's friend, Jake Malone."

CC's head spun at her cousin's convoluted explanation. "Whatever. This guy must be some other Kevin Tucker."

Kris's fingers slid over the smooth surface of the tablet in a blur. "Let's see. There's a Kevin Tucker, city councilman." She rubbed a fingertip down the screen. "Nope, he's from Atlanta. Any chance he's an Australian cliff diver?"

"I don't think so. His accent was definitely Bostonian."

"Okay, our only other options are..." Her eyes went wide, and she looked up, then burst out laughing. "Too Long Tucker, L.A.'s premier adult film star?"

She narrowed her eyes and smirked. "You're making that up."

Kris held out the tablet.

She peered at the naked, anatomically impossible man on the screen. "Oh. My. God!"

Kris cocked her head, and her eyes sparkled with mischief. "I take it that's not him?"

"Holy shit. What is he, half horse?"

Laughter shook Kris's shoulders. She tapped the screen and Kevin "Tuck" Tucker's image appeared in full, living color. All dimpled charm and scruffy blond good looks, he stood on the sideline of a packed stadium. Football helmet tucked under his arm, sweat plastered his thick shock of hair to his head. His blue eyes gleamed at CC from the tablet.

She covered her indrawn breath with a cough. "That's him."

Wide-eyed, Kris gawked at her as if she were nuts. "Why would you waste your time on a dweeb like Ronald when you've got a hottie like Tuck showing interest?" She dropped her gaze to the screen. "Look at him. He's gorgeous."

She scowled at the grinning face staring back at them. As tempting as the idea was, *Tuck* simply wouldn't do. No, Ronald was a much safer choice.

It crossed her mind she'd never been particularly aware of her agent's scent. She shut her eyes and concentrated, but, try as she might, she couldn't associate any fragrance with Ronald, enticing or otherwise. Her eyes snapped open.

God, what was she doing? Scents and mates and contemplating dating a friend in order to cure her neuroses? *I'm as crazy as Mom. Next thing I know I'll be chanting along with her and her kooky friends as we celebrate the summer solstice.*

She swallowed. "Ronald isn't a dweeb. He's a nice man. Anyway, I didn't say I was going through with testing the theory, just that I was considering it."

She jolted at the sudden jangling of her cell phone as her mother's ringtone filled the room.

"Spooky." Kris gave a mock shiver. "We were just talking about her, and there she is. It's like she's…psychic or something."

CC bared her teeth in a cutting smile before answering the call. "Hi, Mom."

"Hi, baby. I called to see how the two of you are doing."

"The same as always." She rolled her eyes at Kris. "We haven't been raped and murdered in the big, bad city."

"That's nothing to joke about, CC. I worry about you girls, there all alone."

"We're not alone. We have each other, and Walter. We're fine. We keep the doors and windows locked, and though I can't vouch for Kris, you know *I* don't talk to strangers."

Well, not until recently, that is.

Natalie Calhoun's sigh was long-suffering. "Your father's going to be in Manhattan at the end of the month."

"I know. He left a message on my machine."

"But you didn't talk to him. Why don't I give him your cell number?"

"Mom." She squeezed her eyes shut and pinched the bridge of her nose. "Don't do that. Please."

"When are you going to forgive him, baby? It's harmful to the spirit to carry around old bitterness. You need to let it go."

Bristling at the old argument, she opened her eyes and gave her pat answer. "I'm not bitter. I'm doing what I need to survive."

"You're still suffering from attacks." It wasn't a question, so she didn't bother offering a denial. "He's sorry, CC, and he's not getting any younger. If you don't forgive him soon, you might lose your chance."

This, too, was an old argument, one she didn't buy into for a moment. Curt Jensen would never die. He'd lie, cheat, steal, or sell his soul to the devil, the way he'd sold out his own daughter to insure his rock-star immortality.

Her mother never could see the truth when it came to the only man she'd ever loved. Curt might be getting older, but he hadn't changed. Neither was he too old to appear on last month's cover of *Rock World* with his latest, barely-beyond-jail-bait lover. The blonde bombshell hanging on his arm in the photo could have been CC's *younger* sister. Pointing that out to her mother would only hurt her, however.

"He'll be there on the twenty-sixth."

"I've got to go, Mom."

Another sigh. "Okay, but please think about it. He really wants to see you. I love you, baby. Kris, too."

"We love you, too."

Chapter 3

Tuck paused in the kitchen doorway of Jake and Gracie Malone's historic Long Island farmhouse. Across the hardwood floor with her back to the room, Gracie worked at the counter. Tall, blond, and stacked, his best friend's bride of two months wielded a wickedly sharp knife as she sliced and diced the makings of a salad with the precision of a Paris-trained chef.

Unaware of his presence, she sang along with the show tune belting out from her docked phone on the counter at her elbow. She paused in her chopping, raised the knife over her head, and struck a dramatic pose. He winced when, reaching for an impossibly high note, she proved that although she had the looks and the attitude for a Broadway career, her singing ability was a nonstarter.

He arched an appreciative brow as she rotated her hips in a hoochie mama swivel, then brought the knife down to hack at a mushroom in time to the up-tempo beat. Grinning, he shook his head. There'd been a moment last fall, a very brief moment, when despite Jake's obvious feelings for the lady football blogger, Tuck had considered going after Gracie—and not just for a quick fling. Thankfully, he'd come to his senses before Jake resorted to physical violence and in the seven months since, she'd become that rarest of things, a true female friend.

Unfortunately, that brief moment of lapse, when he'd looked at her and seen the potential for something more than his typical wham bam relationship with a woman, left behind a festering sense of unease. Since meeting CC Calhoun, unease had slid into full-blown concern.

Damn it, he wasn't a one-woman kind of man. Never had been. When it came to chicks, he didn't do long term. Hell, why should he when half the world's population was female, and with very few exceptions, his for the taking?

Not that he didn't hope to settle down someday. Growing up the way he had, he understood the importance of a loving home and family. He also knew how rare a truly happy marriage was, especially where fame and fortune were involved. Bottom line, if he were ever to take the plunge into the marital pool, he wanted what his parents had and would accept no less. He wanted that one perfect woman who would be the other half of his whole, the way his mother was to his father. Unfortunately, if such a woman was out there, he hadn't found her. He'd begun to think she didn't exist. Then he'd met CC Calhoun.

He rubbed a hand over the uncomfortable tingle stinging the back of his neck. They'd spent less than five minutes together. He had no fucking business thinking of her along those lines, but the idea of never seeing her again was making him nuts. Which was the reason behind his visit. Gracie was one of the most grounded women he knew. She'd talk him down from the ledge.

He stretched his neck to peer down the hallway. No sign of Jake. No Mary, the housekeeper, or the twins either. Where the hell was everyone?

Making his steps silent, he tiptoed forward. Murphy, Gracie's sixty pound idiot mutt, bolted from beneath the kitchen table. His claws scrambled for purchase and clattered against the hardwood floor. The racket nixed Tuck's plan to sneak up and lay a smacking kiss on Jake's bride.

As Gracie spun around, clutching the deadly sharp knife in one hand and a carrot in the other, Tuck kept a watchful eye on the dog. He'd already experienced the Border Collie's testicle-crushing, head-butt greetings on more than one occasion and wasn't interested in a follow-up encounter. He pivoted sideways and splayed a protective hand over his crotch for good measure. Murphy surprised him by skidding to a stop and plopping to his butt at Tuck's feet.

When the dog politely offered a paw, he lifted his head and shot Gracie a quizzical brow. "What'd Jake do, snip his balls?"

Gracie laughed and dropped her hips back against the counter. "He enrolled him in doggy finishing school."

"Smart man." He shook the dog's paw, then scrubbed at his side.

She chuckled. "If you're looking for Jake, he and the twins went to visit Dad." Her grin softened into a bemused smile. "It still gives me a thrill to call Tom, Dad."

Tuck straightened and returned her smile. "It's the same for Tom. I didn't think a man his age was capable of blushing, but I was wrong. He colors up like a teenager whenever he mentions your name." And the retired superstar quarterback had mentioned Gracie a *lot* in the months since he, along with the rest of the world, learned she was his biological daughter. Their surprise familial connection had quickly become the story of the year, and Jake's fifty yard-line marriage proposal to Gracie only added flame to the press firestorm.

Gracie's smile went dopey, and Tuck crossed the room to snag a slice of cucumber. Popping it into his mouth, he considered her while he chewed. "I actually came by to see you."

She shook her head and grinned. "Jake and I are still technically on our honeymoon. I doubt he'll be happy if I run off with you to Bermuda."

He bared his teeth in a leering smile. Gracie and her groom might be sickeningly happy together now, but their happily ever after hadn't been a foregone conclusion when they faced each other as adversaries vying for guardianship of the twins. The bizarre custody battle over Jake's half sisters and Gracie's nieces had offered Tuck countless opportunities to jerk his friend around. He'd taken full advantage by showing up at the farm and trying to convince Gracie to run off with him. The game, however, lost its appeal the moment Jake slipped his ring on her finger.

Just as Tuck didn't do long term, neither did he poach... And women *didn't* get under his skin. How, and more importantly, *why* had CC? He frowned.

Gracie's smile slipped. "What's wrong?"

He wiped his face clear of emotion. "Why do you think something's wrong?"

"You look... Oh, I don't know." She rotated the knife's edge in a circular motion, indicating his face. "You look off."

Off was an apt description. His disquiet, however, had nothing to do with the disappointment he *should* be experiencing now that his plans to get the luscious Lisa alone and naked were shot. Truthfully, other than a twinge of guilt for how things had played out with the busty coffee clerk, he hadn't given her much thought since the moment he turned around and his gaze landed on the tiny blonde with the old-soul eyes.

What the hell was it about CC Calhoun that kept her popping into his mind hours later? Sure, she had a body designed to bring a man to his knees, but so did a lot of women. She wasn't the most beautiful woman he'd ever seen. Hell, she wasn't even in the top ten, and he made it a habit to steer clear of women with issues. The anxiety attack she'd suffered on the sidewalk was a definite issue, but something about her...

Damn it, this was nuts. What was he doing here? *I'm here because the phrase "love at first sight" suddenly doesn't seem so far-fetched.* A cold chill raced down his spine, and his stomach muscles clenched painfully. He scrubbed a shaking hand down his face.

The knife in Gracie's hand clattered to the counter at her hip. "Tuck, you're scaring me."

A mirthless laugh shuddered through his clenched teeth. "You should see things from my perspective. I think I might have just shit my pants."

Her helpless chuckle was short-lived. Worry darkened her eyes. "Are you going to tell me what's wrong or aren't you?"

He chose his words carefully, delaying the inevitable. He'd doled out more than his share of trash talk over Jake's meteoric fall for the lovely blogger and knew from experience, payback was a bitch. "How did you know Jake was the one?"

"The one what?"

"You know. *The* one."

Her blank stare held for a good five seconds. Then she flattened her lips in a disapproving line and turned to pick up her knife. She returned to her dicing. "You're an ass, you know that? I thought you were sick or something!"

He propped a hip against the counter and lowered his head to meet her gaze. "Gracie, I'm asking you about *the* one. You don't think that qualifies as sick in my book?"

She blinked. "Wait. You're serious?"

Pushing straight, he jammed the fingers of both hands through his hair. "Hell, I don't know." He shook his head to clear it. "Jesus, maybe I *am* sick." He jerked his chin toward her ever-present laptop on the table. "Google brain tumors, will you? See if a lack of oxygen in the bloodstream can cause an otherwise sane man to start thinking crazy thoughts."

She started to laugh. Hoots of glee echoed through the large room. Disgusted, with both himself *and* her, he stalked to the refrigerator for a beer. When he turned back, she'd set aside the knife and slowed to a snicker.

"Kevin Tucker, master of the three-day relationship, is asking about *the* one?" A scoffing sniff escaped her nose and off she went again into gales of laughter.

He pinned her with the steely-eyed stare that made even the meanest defensive linemen take notice. She laughed harder.

He scowled. "I didn't say I'd found *the* one. I was just asking out of curiosity."

She fanned her face with one hand and was only partially successful at controlling her mirth. "Uh-huh." She continued to snicker. "Who is she?"

He brought the beer bottle to his lips for a long slug. "Her name is CC."

"And?"

"And she's blond." Butterscotch curls framed the classic lines of her face. "Green eyes. Serious and a little shy." Even widened in panic, a man could gaze into those Irish green orbs and forget what he'd been about to say. He held the bottle level with his collarbone. "About five four." Slim and sleek with several very nice exceptions. The memory of a plump breast spilling over his palm made him smile for the first time in hours. "And built."

Gracie smirked. "Of course she's built. *Who* is she?"

"I have no idea."

She turned to the fridge, grabbed a beer for herself, and shoved him toward the table. After pushing him into a chair, she sat across from him. "Okay. Details."

He spared nothing. A survivor of New York City's housing authority, Gracie recognized bullshit when she heard it and wasn't afraid to say so. Besides, she understood him better than he did himself, most of the time, and, at the moment, he needed all the understanding he could get.

She got a kick out of the Beantown Gigolo remark and at learning Murphy had eaten Lisa's telephone number when Tuck borrowed him for a romp in the park last weekend. She rolled her eyes upon hearing how he'd waited for CC outside the coffee shop and laughed outright when he detailed how he and the built blonde ended up on their asses in front of the morning rush hour crowd.

"A panic attack?"

A shrug lifted one shoulder and he sipped his beer. "Sure seemed like it to me." At least at first. Whatever the cause of the attack, she hadn't looked panicked by the time he'd finished kissing her. She'd looked flustered, a little embarrassed, but there was no missing the pleasure in her incredible eyes.

"When are you seeing her again?"

He sighed. "I have to find her first."

"Find her? As in you didn't get her number?" Gracie widened her eyes. "What? She wasn't bowled over by your golden boy charm? You must be losing your touch." She sprawled back and grinned. "I guess there *is* a first time for everything."

He sniffed in offense. "My failure to get her number has nothing to do with losing my touch." He rose to toss his bottle in the trash and retrieve another. "She was justifiably embarrassed, and she'd just watched me trying to make a date with the coffee clerk." Dropping back into his chair, he frowned. "She wasn't impressed when I switched targets."

The bottle stilled inches from his mouth. Of course! The sudden explanation for his confusion of the last few hours loosened the noose strangling his windpipe. Though others might disagree with the notion, he didn't consider himself particularly vain where it came to the fairer sex. Women simply came easily to him. Always had. A smile, a little conversation, and he was in.

Not so with CC Calhoun. He'd never had a woman shut him down as casually and completely as she had, and the rejection stung. No wonder his thought processes were fucked up. When bruised, the male ego acted irrationally.

"Can you blame her?" Gracie tipped the lip of her beer bottle his way. "Karma, baby. That trail of broken hearts you've left behind has come back to bite you in the ass."

He grunted. Karma or not, he *would* see CC Calhoun again. He didn't have a choice. Staring into her panicked eyes, he'd been rocked by the gut-deep impression that the moment *and* the woman were more important than any other he'd faced in the past. Now that he was thinking more clearly, he was inclined to chalk the bizarre notion up to his irrational ego, but he had to be sure.

He knew women. Knew when one was playing hard to get and when one didn't want to be bothered. CC fell in the latter category, and yet her reaction to his kiss said the opposite. There'd been definite interest in her haunting eyes, despite the fact she didn't seem to have a clue who he was. Oh, yeah. He'd see CC again, whether she liked it or not.

He'd never had to resort to stalker tactics to find feminine companionship, but to disprove the whole love at first sight theory? What the hell? Gracie was right. There was a first time for everything.

He eyed Murphy, sitting like a perfect gentleman at Gracie's feet. A slow smile pulled at the corner of his lips as the germ of an idea formed. "A smart man makes his own karma. What's the name of that dog finishing school?"

Chapter 4

Tuck trotted down the steps of city hall with an easy whistle. It paid to have contacts in the halls of power. Especially wine snobs with an obsession for rare vintages. He grinned and patted the front pocket of his jeans where the slip of paper with CC's address rested. Best two hundred bucks he'd spent in a long time.

Tracking her down had proven ridiculously easy. How hard could it be to convince her to spend some time with him? Last night, he'd had a really dirty dream about her, and while he appreciated his mind's ability to fill in the little details he'd been fantasizing about since meeting her, he preferred waking up to the real thing instead of sweaty and uncomfortable. He meant to get his hands on her for more than just an accidental touch. Then, once he'd had his fill, he'd finally be able to exercise the sexy little blonde from his mind.

The ball cap, pulled low on his forehead, did its job of disguising him from the occasional fan looking for an autograph. He hailed a cab, winking at a passing pair of matronly women out for a stroll on a warm summer morning. One of the old girls winked back, and he threw back his head and laughed. He was still chuckling when he climbed into the battered vehicle. Damn, he was pitiful, grinning like a teenager who'd gotten the homecoming queen's number, but he couldn't bring himself to care.

With training camp less than a month away, his time was his own, and he meant to use it wisely. He couldn't think of a better way to fill that time than seducing CC Calhoun.

Anticipation thrummed through his veins. As much as he enjoyed the grueling schedule of the football season, the long hours didn't leave much time for extra-curricular activities. Consequently, the type of women he normally saw didn't exactly play hard to get. One-night stands and friends with benefits were fine with him, but a man appreciated a challenge now and then. If CC's reluctance the other day was any indication of what he faced, he'd have his work cut out for him, which suited him fine. It had been far too long since he'd experienced the thrill of an actual chase.

He directed the cabbie toward the lower east side. Five minutes later, the cab pulled to the curb in front of CC's building. He tipped the man and stepped out to eye the well-tended brownstone. Though Gracie scoffed when he'd detailed his intentions, the plan he had in mind would work. The overpriced certificate in his pocket gave him the excuse he needed for showing up at CC's door. After all, what woman would pass up a week of free obedience training when she had to deal with an exuberant Rottweiler every day?

He owed the mutt a thank-you. Her dog had presented the perfect opportunity to approach CC outside the coffee shop. As he'd watched the oversized pup dancing around the group of teenage girls, he was reminded of the day he'd met Murphy, and the echo of remembered pain contracted his balls. A wise man would have taken the discomfort as an omen and stayed clear of the potential carnage, but he couldn't regret stepping in to save CC.

He grinned. Landing on his ass had never been sweeter.

As chance would have it, providence offered him an unfettered moment to appreciate the target of his seductive plans. CC's door opened, and dragged by her dog, she stumbled onto the wide front stoop.

"Damn it, Walter. Stop!"

Tuck grinned. For such a small woman, she made quite an impression. The other day's faded jeans had cupped a sweetheart ass that made his mouth water. The short sundress, flowing over her slim form, might have robbed him of the tantalizing view of her sweet backside, but the length of exposed leg more than made up for the loss.

Toned and shapely, her calves and lower thighs made his fingers itch to ride the smooth columns up and over the rounded globes he remembered. The fantasy had the same effect as when he'd cradled her in his lap, and he slammed the mental door shut on the image. From her behavior the other day, she wasn't going to be happy to see him. The last thing he needed was to show up on her doorstep with a boner tenting the zipper of his jeans.

For a little added insurance, he adjusted his step to a slow, stilted gait and hobbled up the walkway toward her. When she looked up and saw him, she stiffened. Disbelief flashed in her eyes.

"What are you doing here?" Walter nearly wrenched her arm from the socket. The leash snapped taught as he bolted forward. His body wriggled in happy welcome.

Tuck offered her his most winning smile. "I was in the neighborhood?"

"Nice try." Walter attempted another lunge. She held him fast. "Let me rephrase that. What are you doing in *my* neighborhood?"

"Looking for you."

He chuckled at her suspicious scowl. Yep, he had his work cut out for him. First things first. Time to play the guilt card. He moved a little closer, increasing the limp he'd affected, and hoped he wasn't overplaying it.

Her gaze dropped to his legs. "You're limping."

"Yeah, I am." He blasted her with a wicked smile. "I had a little accident the other day."

Her scowl immediately became defensive. "I didn't ask you to jump into the middle of things. If you're hurt, it's your own fault."

The vehemence of her response surprised him. He raised a brow and glanced at Walter. The dog's rear end wagged so vigorously he was amazed the animal managed to remain on his feet.

"I'll tell you what." He met her gaze and kept his smile in place. "I promise not to sue, if you promise—"

"Ha! Try it, pal. I'll countersue you for public molestation."

He chuckled. She had a point, and wouldn't that spectacle go over well with the league front office? "You didn't let me finish."

Suspicion darkened those eyes he'd stared into in his dirty dream, but she didn't interrupt again.

"I promise not to sue, if *you* promise to accept my gift."

Long, dark blond lashes fluttered when she blinked. "What gift?"

He tucked a hand in his back pocket, retrieved the small envelope, and held it out. "Go ahead. Take it." When she refused, he dipped his head closer. "Did I mention I have a really good lawyer?"

She hesitated a moment, her lips flattening further, then snatched the envelope from his fingers with ill grace. Her brows puckered as she read the embossed label. "Paws Finishing School?"

"It's a certificate for a week-long obedience program. I thought Walter could use some lessons in manners."

Her gaze flicked to her dog, who was attempting to stretch his leash far enough to lift his leg on her neighbor's rose bush. "He could definitely use some lessons in manners, but"—she held out the envelope—"I can't take this."

Tuck shoved both hands into the front pockets of his jeans and grinned. "A really *great* lawyer."

She sighed. "Look. I appreciate the thought, and to tell the truth, I've been planning to enroll him somewhere, but—"

"Perfect. Now you're all set."

"But I can't let you pay for it. Why would you, anyway?"

He waved off her question. "It's no big deal. I won the certificate at a silent auction." A big fat whopper if he'd ever told one, but the white lie was for a good cause. "I don't have a dog, so if you don't take it, I'll just give it to someone else."

"What about that idiot mutt you mentioned?"

He smiled. "Oh, he's not mine. We just hang out sometimes."

She cocked her head. A butterscotch curl escaped the knot of hair gathered at the top of her head, sliding over her forehead to wrap around her chin. His fingers tingled with the desire to tuck the glossy lock behind her ear, just for the chance to touch her.

"Why would you bid on a dog obedience program when you don't have a dog?"

Prickly *and* beautiful. Major turn-on. His cock twitched. "It was for a good cause."

His own.

He jerked his chin toward the envelope. "Paws Finishing School has a four month waiting list, but that certificate moves you to the front of the line." And Gracie had laughed her ass off at the outrageous sum he'd had to pay to convince the instructor to include Walter in this week's class. "Class starts tomorrow morning."

"Tomorrow?" Her eyes went wide.

Yep. Eyes that can make a man forget what he is saying.

He sucked air through his teeth. "Yeah, I know. Short notice. You'll need to arrange to be there, at least for a few of the lessons, but I can take him to the first one for you if you've got scheduling issues."

"No!" Her full lower lip creased beneath the nervous scrape of her straight, white teeth before she cleared her throat. "I mean, no, my schedule is flexible."

Instead of leaning forward and kissing her senseless like he wanted, he pressed his case. "Just think, no more pulled arm muscles. No more getting knocked on your ass." He grinned at her narrow-eyed stare. "Take the certificate, CC. I might not be the kind to sue over a little rambunctious play, but others may not be as forgiving."

She pressed her lips together in a tight line, but after a long moment, she nodded. "Thank you."

"You're welcome." He bent to scratch Walter's neck. "Where are the two of you headed?"

She sighed, her exasperation clear in her jerking movements as she hefted the canvas bag in her free hand. "I have some library books to return."

"The library, huh?" He straightened. "It so happens I'm headed that way. I'll walk with you."

She eyed him suspiciously. "I have the feeling you'd say that even if you weren't."

When she was right, she was right. His condo was in the opposite direction. He smiled.

"And if I say go away?"

"Come on, sweetheart. Cut me some slack. I'm wounded, remember?" Doubt blared at him from her steady stare. "I'll watch Walter for you while you go inside. Don't want him chewing through his leash and causing another incident, do you?"

She opened her mouth as if to refuse, then snapped it shut again. Jerking her head in a *come on then* motion, she whirled to her right and walked away. Tempered satisfaction coursed through him. Although the first victory in their little skirmish belonged to him, the war was far from won. Still, she hadn't told him to go to hell.

He grinned and slid into an easy stride at her side.

She shot him a sidelong glance. "Can I ask you a question?"

"Anything you want. I'm an open book."

She quirked a disputing brow. "Are you always this pushy?"

"Pushy?" He slapped a hand to his chest, fingers spread. "You wound me."

A delicate scoff flared the nostrils of her pert nose. "I wouldn't worry too much. You seem to be a quick healer." Her gaze dropped to his legs. "Your limp is practically gone already."

He chuckled. "Noticed that, did you?"

The ghost of a smile teased her lips.

Tucker two, gorgeous blonde zero.

"I knew you were faking, and it's a good thing. I'd hate to think Walter destroyed your lucrative football career, *Tuck*."

"You know who I am?" Disappointment warred with pleasure. He'd been looking forward to spending time with her without the specter of his fame hovering over them. Then again, if she'd gone looking for information on him, that was a good sign.

"*You* told me who you are."

"No, I told you my name. I didn't think you recognized it."

She glanced away. "How could I not? I get the paper. I…read an article linking your name with that Gridiron Love Child story the press was so excited about this spring."

His shoulder muscles bunched painfully. More than likely, she'd read more than one. The press had had a field day with Gracie and Tom in their crosshairs. Jake hadn't fared much better, nor had Sharon, Tom's wife. Watching his friends suffer under the scrutiny of ambitious journalists made Tuck's blood boil. In the way of scandals, the story was old news four months later, but the gossip lingered. CC had obviously heard some of it.

Disappointment tightened his voice. "I don't dish dirt on my friends."

She slowed her steps. Her chin at a stubborn angle, she met his gaze, and her eyes went as cool as her tone. "I wouldn't ask you to. I value my privacy too much to invade someone else's."

Damn, antagonizing her was the last thing he wanted. "Sorry, sore spot."

"Obviously." She looked away and resumed her clipped pace.

He sighed and caught up. "Most people don't understand the importance of privacy to someone who's had to deal with public interest."

She said nothing and he studied her profile. The tension in her stiffened shoulders spoke volumes.

"But you do." He threw out the guess.

She was silent for several heartbeats. "Yes, I do."

Interesting. Was a brush with public scrutiny responsible for yesterday's over-the-top reaction to the crowd of onlookers? He'd told Gracie CC was shy, but she certainly wasn't showing any signs of shyness this morning. Reluctance yes, but not shyness. He wanted to ask why. The tight line of her lips told him he'd be wise to wait.

"What about you?"

She turned her head. "What about me?"

"It's barely noon, and you're taking a stroll to the library. Don't you have a job?"

The tension eased from her shoulders. Definitely interesting and a mystery he meant to unravel before long.

"I'm an artist." She jerked her head back toward her building. "My studio is in my condo. I make my own hours."

"An artist, huh?" He deepened his voice to a croon. "I'd really like to see your etchings sometime."

Though she rolled her eyes, they sparkled with humor. Point three to him. He was on a roll.

"Do you paint?"

"Some. Mostly I sculpt."

"I was teasing about the etchings, but I would like to see your work."

Her gaze cut to his. "Are you an art lover?"

"I'm a guy. You said your studio's in your condo." He grinned. "Two birds, one stone."

Her quiet chuckle sent a spear of heat straight to his dick.

"You really are a Beantown Gigolo."

He rolled his shoulders in a shrug. "I've been called worse."

"I'll bet you have. You're not getting anywhere near my *etchings* or my condo."

He widened his eyes in easy innocence. They'd see about that.

They reached the library, and she paused at the foot of the steps. The humor of moments ago disappeared beneath her steady regard. "How did you find me?"

The utter seriousness of her tone indicated her apprehension at his answer, but he wasn't about to admit he'd bribed a public official. "A smart man knows how to keep a secret."

Disappointment clouded her eyes, but she shrugged, as though his answer didn't surprise her. "You must have something else to do besides babysit Walter."

He snagged the leash from her hand. "Go return your books. Walter and I are going to enjoy a little male bonding time." He didn't wait for a response, turning his back on her with her dog at his side. "Come on, Walter. See that fine looking poodle with the long legs across the street in the park? She was checking you out when we walked by. Stick with me, buddy. I'll score you an introduction."

A laughing sigh reached his ears, and he grinned. *Point number four.*

Fifteen minutes later, he sat sprawled on a park bench. Walter lay at his feet, eyes closed, snoring softly. In Tuck's opinion, watching a fine looking woman walk your way was one of life's little pleasures. Add sparkling green eyes and an open smile on a full mouth, and a man would be hard pressed to come up with anything sweeter. CC Calhoun, crossing the park with her wispy dress fluttering in the breeze, was a sight to behold. She didn't stroll or strut—like some women. Instead, her hips swished in a precise clipped roll. Her purposeful gait was about as sexy a walk as he'd ever had the chance to ogle. She moved from point *A* to *B* without veering off the path she'd set for herself. It would take a determined man to throw her off course, and he was just the man for the job.

Her stride matched her attitude. From the little he'd gleaned of her, she was a serious, no-nonsense woman with a backbone of steel and just enough flashes of humor and sass to keep a man interested. Love at first sight? The jury was still out, but damn, he liked her.

She approached the bench. Walter snuffled as he woke suddenly and leaped to his feet to greet her. Brushing a palm over the dog's wide skull, she eyed Tuck. "For a minute there, I was afraid you'd killed him."

"I thought about it, but I'm scared of his owner. I hear she's as mean as a snake."

"Uh-huh." Her smile widened and she straightened, glancing around. "What happened with the poodle?"

"She was a snob."

Her searching gaze flicked back to meet his, and she arched a brow.

He shrugged. "Walter wasn't impressed. She had hairy ankles."

"Hairy ankles?"

"You know." He twirled an index finger in the air. "Puffs of hair on her ankles and tail."

Her lips quirked toward a smile, but she twisted them into a smirk. "I think that's called a pom-pom cut."

He grinned. "Yeah, well, it grossed Walter out. Right, buddy?"

The dog pressed against Tuck's thigh in a bald demand for attention. Tuck obliged. "He took off to chase a butterfly. She left in a snit."

"Snit?"

Her tinkling laugh brushed over his nerve endings like a live wire.

She shook her head. "Where exactly are you from?"

"Southie. South Boston."

"I didn't realize *in a snit* was a common New England phrase."

He smiled and stood. "It's not, but Maryanne Tucker, my mom, is from Jackson, Mississippi. Once, when I was six, she washed my mouth out with soap when she heard me say 'pissed off.' The phrase offended her sensibilities." He chuckled at the memory. "'In a snit' seemed like a healthy alternative. Mom agreed."

She grinned, and he tapped at the prominent bump on his nose.

"Unfortunately, my friends didn't. At first. I changed their minds."

She snickered, and moving closer, he ducked his head to meet her humor-filled gaze. "You're a cruel woman. Laughing at a man's battle wounds."

"I'm laughing at the irony of you having had your nose broken in a fight over the word snit."

He fought off a laugh with a smirk. "I've been in fights caused by much less. You don't survive childhood in Southie without a few scars."

She shook her head. "Boys are idiots."

A wry grin tugged at his lips, and he rubbed at the bump in his nose. No way in hell would he admit the deformity came courtesy of Angie Connors. The rough and tumble neighborhood he'd called home produced tough boys, and the girls were no slouches either.

All in all, he couldn't complain about the progress he'd made, but she'd regrouped by the time they arrived back at her condo. Her excuse of having a doctor's appointment, with her gynecologist no less, was a bald-faced lie, and they both knew it. He let her go, promising himself they'd tangle again soon. As he watched her disappear inside, he smiled.

Chapter 5

"Ronald! I wasn't expecting you."

CC's heart skittered erratically upon opening her door. For the past forty-eight hours, she'd gone back and forth, debating pros and cons as she wrestled with the idea of requesting Ronald Bartolini's help to test her theory. On the one hand, she risked their very satisfactory business association if things went badly. On the other, things *could* work out just fine, and her odds of success were better if she stepped out of her comfort zone with a man with whom she was at least somewhat comfortable.

She'd been briefly tempted, when Tuck appeared on her doorstep yesterday, to throw caution to the wind and take advantage of his obvious interest, but no. She wouldn't repeat her mother's mistake by tangling with a playboy, even if the relationship was just temporary. Playboys were selfish, pushy, and nothing but trouble. Kevin Tucker wouldn't do. If she was going to take this crazy step, Ronald was the safer choice.

With her choice standing in front of her, however, nerves urged her to forget the entire thing. Yet, how could she live with herself if she didn't at least try? She'd made herself a promise, damn it, and time was almost up. Crazy she might be, but the possibility of controlling the panic attacks, while grasping at the chance for a relatively normal life, was too tempting to dismiss out of hand.

She eyed Ronald critically. Chin high, shoulders straight, his natural confidence made him appear taller than his actual five-foot-nine-inch height. His conservative, slate-gray business suit matched his serious personality. Not a strand of his short, coal black hair was out of place. His dark complexion spoke of his Italian heritage, as did the Roman nose below chestnut eyes. Those eyes smiled warmly as he blocked Walter's enthusiastic greeting with the briefcase he carried.

She grabbed the dog's collar and pulled him back.

"I have an appointment down the street, so I thought I'd drop this by on my way." He held up an envelope. "Putnam Gallery sold two more pieces by Anonymous. You're gaining a following. It won't be long before the masses start clamoring for the artist's name."

"Ronald."

He passed her the envelope. "I know. I don't *understand* your need to keep your name private, but I know. Still, it's my job to advise you on your career."

"Consider me advised."

He chuckled at her dry tone, but then his gaze snagged on a spot beyond her shoulder. "New piece?"

He brushed by her to cross the room in four determined strides. She didn't bother answering. Experience had taught her he wouldn't hear a word she said. When it came to art, everything else faded into the background for Ronald. He knew talent when he saw it. Two of the reasons he was such a success at his chosen career.

Circling her workbench, he bent at the waist, twisting his head this way and that. He studied the piece from every angle before straightening. "What's it called?"

She left the door open and followed, then stopped at his side. "*Yearning.*"

He nodded and slid a slim smartphone from his pocket. He caught her eye. "May I?"

She nodded and he snapped several pictures. "I'd be remiss in my duties as your agent if I didn't demand you build a show around this one." He shifted his dark gaze to her. "Your work needs to be shown."

She held up the envelope, flapping it back and forth. "My work *is* shown, and you can demand all you want. No shows."

He sighed. "You're the boss, but it's a shame. A pure shame." He jerked his chin toward the sculpture. "Shall I take this with me? Putnam requested replacements."

"No. I'm not ready to part with it yet." She pulled a sealed box from beneath her workbench and handed it to him. "Angela at Putnam called yesterday with her request. I packed up several finished pieces. She's expecting them."

He eyed *Yearning* with a disappointed frown. "Promise me you won't give *this* one away."

She smirked. Against his wishes, she'd instructed the galleries she contracted with to call her directly when a customer inquired after a piece but couldn't afford the asking price. It drove Ronald crazy her sculptures occasionally found their way into the hands of an appreciative stranger at reduced cost, but she believed art was meant to be shared. Since she made sure Ronald always got his full commission, he couldn't complain over much.

"I mean it, CC. This is some of your best work. I'll buy it before I watch you hand it over to one of your cheapskate fans."

She laughed. "You're an art snob, Ronald, you know that?"

"CC—"

"I promise." She held up her hand as if taking an oath. "You'll have first dibs before I give it away."

"See that I do." He pinned her with stern eyes but couldn't hold his scowl. A wry smile curved his lips. Tucking the box under one arm, he checked his watch. "I'd better go or I'll be late."

He turned for the door, and she gnawed at her lower lip. Should she? Could she? Her feet moved without conscious thought. "Wait, Ronald."

He paused in the open doorway to face her. His black brows arched expectantly.

She shuffled to a stop several feet from him and the door. "I…uh." She sucked in a steadying breath. "I was wondering…."

He dipped his head. "Yes?"

Just do it. The worst that can happen is he says no.

"I was wondering if you were seeing anyone." There. Casual curiosity. Easy breezy.

Though he raised a brow at the unexpected question, he smiled. "As a matter of fact, I just met a new woman."

"Oh." *Well, crap.*

"Why?" His smile turned teasing. "Were you hoping to fix me up?"

Her cheeks blazed with heat. Ugh. Why hadn't she kept her big mouth shut? She cleared her throat. "Something like that."

"Who is she?"

"Ah. No one. Forget I asked. I didn't realize you were seeing someone." She shook her head, waving her hand, but her attempt at a dismissive laugh resembled a maniacal yelp.

He shifted the box in his arms and his smile died. "What's going on?"

"Nothing."

"CC?"

Would he go away if she shoved him over the threshold and slammed the door in his face? Nope. Knowing Ronald, that would only increase his curiosity and prolong her agony. Walter started whining and attempted to squeeze by her agent to get out the door. She held the dog firm.

Biting her lip, she met Ronald's waiting gaze. "You promise not to laugh?"

He responded with a demanding stare.

"The truth is, I was asking for myself."

His mouth gaped open comically, and he took an unconscious step backward out onto the stoop. He snapped his mouth shut. Distressed confusion flooded his eyes.

The desire to sink into the floor ranked right up there with the pressing need to slug him. Damn it. He might not be laughing, but did he have to look like she'd just grown a third eye?

"Forget I asked." She gripped the doorknob, preparing to shut him out, and lifted the envelope in her free hand. "Thanks for dropping this by."

"I'm sorry, CC, but you shocked me."

She drew her lips into a thin line, and his eyes filled with desperate apology.

"In all the time I've known you, you've never... I've never known you to date."

"That's because I haven't."

"Well." The box under his arm lifted along with his one-shouldered shrug.

"Look. This has nothing to do with you personally. Really. It's just that..." Unwilling to explain about her test when he obviously found the idea of dating her horrifying, she mentally scrambled about for an excuse that didn't make her sound like a complete lunatic. "It's just that, I graduated from art school almost three years ago. Since then, I've been focused solely on my art. It's time I changed that. Who better to help me slide into the New York dating scene than a friend?"

His prominent Adam's apple bobbed as he swallowed. "I uh... I don't exactly have an exclusive agreement with Janet. I guess I could—"

"Oh, don't." She slapped the hand holding the check over her eyes. "Please. Don't say another word. I'm horrified enough already."

"Damn. I feel like a heel."

Yeah, well, that's better than feeling like an idiot. She dropped her hand and met his gaze and wished she hadn't. If the distress in his eyes turned to pity, she was going to slug him for real. "Don't. It was just an idea. A stupid one. Go, before you miss your appointment."

"Maybe I should—"

"Go, Ronald." She narrowed the opening of the door, willing him to go away. "I'll talk to you later."

He hesitated. "I really am sorry."

She growled low in her throat.

"Okay, I'm going." Wearing a guilty grimace, he spun around and escaped down the walk. She'd never seen him move so fast.

She shut the door and slumped against it. The repeated thud of her head against wood was loud in the silent condo. Walter nuzzled her arm. She scowled at him. "Walter. Your mother is an idiot."

Ronald Bartolini is a stiff. You don't want him, anyway.

Zorro's sensual accent failed to amuse. She moaned. "God. If I ever look like I'm going to do something that stupid again, bite me, will you?"

He cocked his head, and she rubbed his satiny ear between thumb and forefinger. Man, she hadn't realized how lucky she'd been in avoiding the dating scene all these years. Working up the courage to ask a person out on a date was nerve-racking, but extricating yourself from the embarrassment of a "no" was worse. Why did people bother?

A knock shook the door at her back, and she squeezed her eyes shut. "Oh, go away and let me die in peace!"

"We can't have that."

Her eyes flew open at Kevin Tucker's muffled reply. A stark whimper escaped her lips. She jammed the knuckle of her index finger between her teeth and bit down, hard.

"Open up, sweetheart." A long pause…then a singsong promise. "I'll give you mouth to mouth."

Walter danced in excited circles. CC swallowed at the bubbling in her belly and refused to name it as matching excitement. *It's a case of indigestion. That's all.*

Oh, God. Can this morning get any worse?

She pressed a finger to her lips and glared at her grinning dog. Maybe if she ignored Tuck's insistent knocking, the persistent flirt would give up and go away. Then she could deal with the embarrassment of Ronald's rejection and figure out how she was going to face him again.

She lasted a full thirty seconds before pushing off the door with a frustrated growl. Her fingers shook as she grasped the knob and yanked open the door. Walter rushed outside, puppy yelps piercing the morning quiet. Typically gorgeous in faded jeans and a stark white T-shirt, Tuck dipped to a squat. He rubbed vigorously at the dog's neck. His unruly mop of blond hair stuck out from beneath today's baseball cap, the golden streaks gleaming in the bright sunlight. She crossed her arms and glared at her uninvited visitor's gilded head.

"Apparently, no one's ever told you stalking is against the law."

He met her gaze on a full-throated laugh.... And there went her breathing.

The air backed up in her lungs, and though she had no business doing so, she couldn't help herself. She smiled. "What do you want, Tuck?"

"Well, now." His eyes twinkled with mischief. "That's a dangerous question. Do you really want to hear my answer?"

Tingles of excitement rippled down her spine. "Probably not."

"That's what I figured, but one of these days, I'm going to tell you flat out."

The smile died on her lips. Hmmm. What was a woman to say to that?

He rose to his full height. His wide palm thumped Walter on the side as the dog leaned against his thigh. "I'm here to take my buddy to his first lesson."

"Lesson? Oh, the obedience class. I told you I'd take care of that."

He scratched at his stubbled chin with long fingers. "Shit, I must have misheard you."

She lifted a disbelieving brow. "Do you ever take no for an answer?"

He didn't respond, but then, he didn't need to. His answer was there in his wickedly glittering eyes and popping dimples. No doubt he was used to getting his way. The man was a bulldozer. A sexy one, but a bulldozer just the same.

"So, who's the stiff?"

"Stiff?" She dropped her arms to her sides and whipped a shocked glance at Walter. His tongue hung from his mouth as he leaned against Tuck's thigh. She met Tuck's clear gaze once more. Geez, a mind-reading bulldozer?

He nodded over his shoulder. "The suit with the briefcase and the box."

"Why would you call him a stiff?" Her voice held a distinctive squeak.

He dipped his head, bringing his eyes even with hers. "Any man who'd turn down the opportunity to spend time with you has to be a stiff."

Her jaw dropped open. *Oh, kill me now.*

"Your door was open. I heard voices and didn't think it would be polite to interrupt." Devilish possibilities simmered in his dark blue orbs. "Sweetheart, if you need a man to help you slide into the New York dating scene, you've found him."

Her search for an intelligent response ended in colossal failure. She stuttered incoherently, a circumstance he clearly found highly entertaining. His grin spread wide. Retreat was in order, but any chance she had of escaping inside was lost when the door of the condo beside hers opened.

Mary Olsen paused with her hand on the knob to eye Tuck suspiciously. If not for the fear of looking insane, CC would have kissed her. Her cantankerous neighbor's presence had never been more welcome.

Almost as round as she was tall, the ancient terror of the neighborhood wheeled her metal shopping basket onto the common stoop, pulled her door shut, and rounded on Tuck. "Who are you?"

"The name's Kevin Tucker, ma'am."

"Any relation to Agnes Tucker? She's a greeter over at St. Martin's church."

"No, ma'am. Not that I know of."

She nodded curtly and harrumphed. "Never liked that woman. Shifty eyes."

CC cleared her throat before Mary could launch into her habit of ripping her fellow parishioners for their numerous faults. "Where are you off to, Mary?"

The old lady slowly dragged her gaze from Tuck's face. "Parsons Market. Cantaloupe is on sale. Gotta get there early before it's all gone. Wanda Parsons never orders enough produce." She tipped her head in Tuck's direction. "He bothering you?"

Hell yes, he was bothering her. Ronald was no longer a candidate for her test, but how was she supposed to focus on her search for a viable alternative with Tuck's tempting offer dangling before her like a six-foot-four bar of rich, dark chocolate? For that matter, how was she supposed to put the memory of his kiss out of her mind if he kept showing up?

Her gaze clashed with his. The challenge in his waiting smile nearly made her nod her head in affirmation of the old lady's question and leave him to deal with the consequences. He might be a bulldozer, but Mary Olsen was a steamroller. She'd flatten him without blinking an eye.

CC shook her head instead. "Everything's fine."

Mary stabbed him with a steely stare. "You sweet on our CC, Mr. Tucker?"

"Mary!"

Her neighbor ignored her horrified outburst, holding Tuck's amused gaze.

"I admit I am. Can you blame me?" He winked at CC. "She sure is pretty."

Mary pointed a gnarled finger at his nose. "She's a good girl. Always helps out her neighbors. You do right by her, or you'll answer to me."

He nodded solemnly, but his eyes danced with humor. "Yes, ma'am."

Disgusted with both of them, CC found her voice. "Will you excuse us, Mary?" She speared Tuck with a don't-you-dare-cross-me glare and jerked her head toward her open door. "I need to speak to you for a minute. Inside."

He nodded, then turned his dimpled smile on her nosy neighbor. "A pleasure, ma'am." He dropped his voice to a conspiratorial burr. "It so happens I've been in Parsons Market and Wanda told me personally if I ever needed anything, I should ask. You tell her I asked you to pick me up an order of her best cantaloupe. She'll fix you up."

Mary harrumphed, but her eyes gleamed with anticipation. CC shook her head. Of course Wanda Parsons promised him special treatment. Like Mary, the grocer was a woman and a chatty one at that. How many times had she greeted CC personally as she walked through the door? No doubt he'd had Wanda eating out of his hand the moment he arrived in her store.

Mary faced CC and a rare smile twisted her lips beneath the thick coat of dark red lipstick. "It's about time you found yourself a handsome young man, young lady." Her empty shopping cart clanged behind her as she toddled down the brick sidewalk.

CC refused to look at him. Patting her thigh, she turned and went inside with Walter at her heels. Tuck followed then shut the door behind him. She spun around to find him glancing around her home. He propped his hands on his hips and faced her.

She jabbed a finger in his direction. "Don't say a word."

"Aw, don't pout." A dimple popped in his slow smile. "Can I help it your neighbor has good taste?"

"I mean it. Just shut up for a minute and let me think."

He grinned and surprised her by complying. Relaxing into a hip-cocked stance, he raised a blond brow and waited.

Chapter 6

CC's teeth gnashed at the soft skin of her bottom lip as she held firm beneath his steady gaze. If the last two days were any indication, he was already going to be a problem. Now that he'd overheard her crazy proposition....

A little bit of research and she knew more about the Marauders' sexy wide receiver than she wanted to. She hadn't been the least surprised at the countless articles proclaiming his class-A, lady-killer status. If the reports were correct, he'd left a crisscrossing trail of broken hearts across the country and beyond. Not the type of man to waste his time chasing after a woman who'd made it more than clear she wasn't interested. So, what was up with the heavy-duty pass?

Under normal circumstances, she'd enjoy handing a player like him a resounding defeat, but with Ronald out of the running, her list of candidates had shot from one to zero. Why shouldn't she use Tuck's stubborn refusal to take no for an answer to her advantage? There was no denying he was attractive, and after Ronald's rejection, her ego could use the boost.

Physically, Tuck couldn't be more perfect for her needs, and emotionally, she had nothing to worry about. She had an advantage there. For the first time in her life, she was thankful for a childhood spent in the shadow of Curt Jenson. If anyone knew how to deal with an overblown, egotistical ladies' man, she did.

A couple of weeks were all she required. Tuck's ego would be soothed, and she'd have her answers, hopefully crossing one more item off her list of fears just in time for her deadline. A win-win situation as far as she could see. First, however, she needed to explain a few things, and *he* was going to agree to some ground rules.

At Tuck's side, Walter whined. His dark chocolate gaze met hers. *Do I need to bite you?*

She snorted. Clearing her throat, she ignored Zorro to arch a brow at Tuck. "I have a proposition for you."

* * * *

"A proposition, huh? Seems to be a lot of that going around this morning." Tuck bit back a grin at the frown wrinkling her brow. He wasn't sure what was going on, but his timing couldn't have been more perfect. The little darling was in the market for a man, and the fool with the briefcase had left the field wide open.

"The conversation you overheard with Ronald isn't what you think."

"Ronald?"

"My agent."

"Ah, the stiff."

She lifted her chin in offense. "Ronald is a nice man."

"Uh-huh. What part of that conversation didn't I understand? Because it sounded like a case of the stiff turning down your sweet request for a date."

"He happens to have a girlfriend." Challenge sparkled in her eyes. "You obviously began eavesdropping *after* he mentioned that."

"No, I heard that part. I also heard he just met the woman, and they don't have an exclusive arrangement."

"Some men are gentlemen."

He smiled and rolled back on his heels. "Don't fool yourself, sweetheart. When it comes to women, no man is a gentleman. Some are just slicker than others."

"You'd know all about that." He grinned at her grumbled tone. She slashed a hand between them. "We're getting off track."

"I didn't know we were following one."

"I am and if you'd be quiet for a minute, I could get back to it."

"Go ahead. I'm listening."

She huffed a sigh. "As I said, I have a proposition for you."

"Whatever it is, I'm in."

She blinked. "That's it? No hesitation or questions?"

"Oh, I'll get to them, eventually, but when a beautiful woman starts a conversation with 'I have a proposition for you,' a smart man doesn't question his luck."

The immediate blush coloring her cheeks pleased him to no end, as did her sexy habit of chewing on her bottom lip. He wanted to suck that plump flesh into his mouth and sink his tongue deep, just as he wanted to sink another body part even deeper. He tucked his hands into the front pockets of his jeans and rolled his shoulders.

The challenge faded from her eyes, replaced with uncertainty, but she forged ahead. "You may have noticed I have a problem with, uh... elevated anxiety."

The admission surprised him, considering her comment the other day about privacy, but with his plan for seduction about to take a major step forward, if she wanted to share details he hadn't asked for, he was happy to oblige. Since she was the one to bring up the issue, he saw no reason to mince words.

"Elevated anxiety? What I saw looked more like a full-blown panic attack."

She nodded. "Yes, well, I have a form of agoraphobia. I've suffered from it most of my life."

"Why?"

"What do you mean, why?"

"You nearly fainted in my arms, all because a handful of strangers stopped to look at you. I'm no expert, but anxiety that intense has to have a root cause. What brought about the attacks?"

She stiffened and her face went blank of all emotion. "For the purpose of my proposition, the root cause of the attacks isn't important."

The coolness in her voice was a roadblock he couldn't afford. Not when he was finally getting somewhere. He curled his lips in a boyish grin. "Aww, but I'm curious."

"Then you're destined to be disappointed because it's not up for discussion."

"What if I insist?"

She matched his cross-armed stance. "What if I insist you go and never come back?"

He chuckled and backed off. For now. "Fair enough, but if the subject isn't up for discussion, why mention it?"

"I didn't mention the cause, you did. I brought up the attacks themselves or, more precisely, the attack I experienced yesterday, which directly correlates with my proposition."

"Which is?"

"Since Ronald obviously isn't available, I'm wondering if you'd be interested in...dating me? Temporarily, of course."

His gut muscles clenched in anticipation. A *huge* step toward victory. He cocked his head. "Well, now. Can you give me a second to think about it?"

She met his teasing grin with a blank stare.

"That's a question you don't need to ask."

"Yes, I do, and before you answer, there are a few things you should know."

He quirked a brow. "If you tell me you used to be a man, you'll break my heart."

"I'm serious."

"So am I." He laughed when she huffed an impatient breath, and he touched a fingertip to her brow. "Sorry, I couldn't resist. You get the cutest little wrinkle between your eyes when you're aggravated."

She batted his hand away. "If you aren't going to take this seriously, then we may as well forget it."

"Aww now, I said I was sorry. Go ahead. What is it I need to know?"

"First stipulation." She held up her index finger. "I said temporary and I mean it. I'm talking a few dates. Three tops."

"That's precise. May I ask why the arbitrary number?"

"I'm not interested in long term."

He nodded. "Okay, I can appreciate that, since I'm not either. What is it exactly you *are* interested in?"

"Understanding."

"Excuse me?"

"I want to understand how you managed to stop a panic attack in its tracks because, believe me when I tell you, that's never happened before."

He shook his head. "I'm confused. If you wanted to know how *I* stopped the attack, why were you propositioning Ronald? Why not come straight to me?"

"I figured it would work with any man, and I like Ronald."

Definitely confused. "It?"

"The kissing thing. I've never considered that approach before, but I can't argue with the results." The sexy wrinkle deepened when she frowned. "That brings me to stipulation number two. Our dates need to involve some kind of gathering where I can test my theory amongst a group of strangers."

He wanted to stop her there and get to the bottom of that "kissing thing" comment. What did she mean she hadn't considered that approach before? But she was on a roll. He couldn't wait to see where she led them. "What's this theory?"

"It's twofold, actually." Like a professor in front of her class, she warmed to her subject. "You shocked the breath right back into me when you kissed me, but I've been thinking, maybe the shock isn't what allowed me to calm down. Maybe the difference was I was concentrating on something other than the crowd for a change. It makes sense, don't you think?"

Her mouth twisted and her bright eyes clouded over in blind concentration, as if she were working out the issue. She didn't wait for him to reply. "And then there was the way you sent the crowd on their way. No one's ever done that for me before. With very few exceptions, whenever I've had an attack, I've been on my own."

A memory of the wild fear in her eyes flashed in his mind, and an odd band of discomfort squeezed his chest. "What about your family? Couldn't they see what was happening?"

She lowered her lashes, shuttering the flash of wariness in the soul-deep depths of her eyes. Dismissing his question with a wave of her hand, she changed the subject. "As you can imagine, agoraphobics tend to keep to themselves, and that's part of my problem."

There was more to her sudden desire to jump into the New York dating pool than met the eye. As a student of the human experience, he enjoyed discovering the twists and turns that made a person who they were. Uncovering CC Calhoun's path to the fascinating woman she was would be a pleasant side benefit to getting her into his bed. Her theory might be wacky on the surface, but he had to admit, she made it sound logical in backward kind of way. As for testing the concept? He wasn't about to look a gift horse in the mouth.

"I'm happy to help you test your theory, but your three-date cutoff may trip us up. That doesn't give us a lot of time. What happens if you don't have an attack?"

"That shouldn't be a problem."

"You have them that often?"

"Not usually, since I tend to avoid situations that trigger them. To tell the truth, I avoid most public situations. I'm not a recluse. I do venture out, like my daily trip to the coffee shop, visits to the gym, the library, that kind of thing, but for the most part, I keep to myself. I'm working on changing that."

Short bristle scratched his palm as he dragged it over his chin. "I don't want you to take this wrong, or think I'm not interested, because nothing could be further from the truth, but if all you're interested in is recreating what happened in front of the coffee shop, we could take Walter down to the end of the block right now."

"We could do that, but what's the point of learning how to handle the attacks if I continue to keep to myself? I'm talking about making a life change here, one that eventually leads to the kind of life normal people take for granted. I want to go where I want, when I want, without worrying about falling apart in front of strangers. To do that, I need to learn to be comfortable around men. I have to start somewhere, and since you insist on showing up on my doorstep without an invite, that somewhere might as well be with you."

Unease ratcheted down his spine. Uncomfortable around men? What the fuck? "Why are you uncomfortable around men?"

She stiffened at the question but held her ground. "That's another subject not up for discussion."

Anger gurgled in his gut. "Did someone hurt you?"

She lifted her chin. "Not in the way you're thinking. I don't like to talk about my past. If that's going to be a problem, you might as well go right now."

Relief made him dizzy. The thought of some faceless man forcing her... He heaved a cleansing breath. "Fair enough, but you said you needed to start somewhere. Does that mean what I think it means?"

She raised a questioning brow.

"You've never dated anyone?"

She shook her head.

"Ever?"

Another shake.

"That would make you a..."

"Virgin." Her squinted eyes dared him to comment.

Fuck!

His eyes slid shut. Sweat broke out on his brow. His libido howled in frustration, mourning the instant death of his lascivious plans for her seduction.

"I don't see why my lack of a sex life would be a problem since—"

"Of course you don't." He opened his eyes to meet her gaze. "Sex complicates things, CC. Especially for a...when you're a..." He held out a flat hand and indicated her body. "You know."

The heat of her sudden smile stroked over him like caressing fingers.

He bit back a groan. "Why are you smiling? *I'm* about to cry."

Her smile became a chuckle. "You can't even say the word."

"And you find that funny?"

"Hilarious."

He ground his teeth hard enough to chip enamel.

"Actually, I'm kind of relieved."

He coughed a pained laugh. "I'm glad one of us is." Damn it, he should go. He needed to pick a fight or at least punch something. A few minutes abusing the heavy bag in Max's gym might ease his need to put a fist through the wall. Damn it all to hell. A virgin. A fucking virgin. Huh! He could *too* say the word. He simply didn't want to. Not when just thinking it made every fantasy he'd built around seducing the little blonde shrivel and die.

Fuck, bad analogy. He shifted uncomfortably. "This isn't going to work. You're a beautiful woman, but…"

"But what?"

"I don't…despoil virgins."

She had the audacity to laugh, and her sunny humor was so completely seductive he couldn't help his smile—until her cool fingers patted his cheek.

"There. That wasn't so hard. Was it?"

He retreated a step. The hand he scraped over his jaw shook, and he quickly dropped his arm to his side. "You're not thinking clearly. You teased me about being a gigolo the other day, and you weren't far from the truth. I've been with a lot of women. Enough to know a woman like you needs a different kind of man."

She crossed her arms, but the shadow of a smile remained in her eyes. "Is that why you tracked me down and showed up at my door?" Her brow puckered. "How *did* you track me down?"

Oh, no. They weren't going there. "My point is, you need a man who's in it for the long haul. That's not me."

"I guess you didn't hear my first stipulation. I'm not interested in long term."

Tuck scoffed. "You say that now."

"Yes, I do say that now because it's the truth." The sneer curling CC's lips surprised him. "Long term is for suckers. Consider yourself a means to an end, if that helps. I know exactly who and what you are, Kevin Tucker. My father and you could compare notes, so you'll have to believe me when I say you're exactly what I need. You're charming"—she ran her gaze down his body and up again—"okay on the eyes, and you don't know the meaning of permanent."

Put that way, he sounded like the gigolo she'd called him. He'd never been anyone's means to an end before and wasn't sure he liked it. And yet, she still wanted him for her wacky experiment? She watched him in silence, but he didn't have a clue what to say. She sighed, dropping her arms to prop her hands on her hips.

"You're getting all worked up over nothing. I'm relieved to hear you don't *despoil virgins*." Her teeth flashed in a cheeky grin. "That sounds like a line from *Gone With the Wind,* by the way, but if you'd let me finish, you'd know I don't plan to sleep with you."

He forgot all about his intention to walk away. "Maybe you should tell me exactly what it is you're proposing, because I'm not following you. What do you mean you don't plan to sleep with me?"

"No offense, but if I ever do decide to sleep with a man, I won't choose the type of man who disappears before the sheets have even cooled."

As insults went, her barb hit its mark. So he'd slept with a lot of women. Big deal. The type of woman he spent time with understood the arrangement was temporary going in. Unfortunately, being a virgin— he fought a shudder—Little Miss Sunshine wasn't his typical type. She wouldn't understand the finer points of dating in the new millennium. "Is that so?"

She sighed. "I'm being honest. If Ronald had been agreeable, I'd be having this same conversation with him. I realize most men expect some physical contact with the women they date. *I* expect kissing and maybe some petting, but the relationship I'm after will be platonic."

He cocked a brow. "Sorry, sunshine, but the kissing and petting you mentioned disqualifies what you're describing as a truly platonic relationship."

She cleared her throat. "Fine, semi-platonic. My point is, I don't need to sleep with you, or any man, to test my theory."

He shook his head. Dating wasn't the only place she lacked experience. She didn't have a clue when it came to what men expected in even the briefest of relationships.

She shrugged, obviously taking his head shake as a final refusal. "If you can't or won't help me, it's no skin off my nose. There are millions of men in the city. Even if half of them are gay, I shouldn't have trouble finding someone else."

Why her casual dismissal should anger him, when he'd already dismissed the idea himself, he refused to consider. He had no business involving himself with a woman who didn't understand how the game was played. Nothing but trouble in that, but when she spun toward the door, he snagged her arm before she took two steps and dragged her to a stop.

"Hold on a second." He frowned. What the hell was he doing? He should get while the getting was good, but damn it, she didn't understand the kind of trouble she was courting, laying out her proposition to the wrong kind of man. "I didn't say I wasn't going to help you."

She arched a brow. "That's how it sounded to me."

"Let me get this straight. You expect some kissing?"

She nodded. "Necessary to test the theory."

"And petting?"

One shoulder rose in a dismissive shrug. "I'm curious. Sue me."

"No need for that. Curious is good. What if I insist on a practical demonstration, just to be sure I know what I'm getting into, before I agree?"

She cocked her head. Challenge sparkled in her eyes as she repeated his tease from earlier. "Can you give me a minute to think about it?"

Shit. Though his mind screamed mistake, his libido was currently running the show. Permission to kiss the shit out of her with immunity? He couldn't wait to get started. The laughter in her eyes said she expected a smile, but he couldn't quite manage one at the moment. "I can make you swallow those words."

She hummed deep in her throat and damned if she didn't tug on a tiger's tail. "Prove it."

He didn't hesitate, spinning her around by the arm. Wrapping her in his arms, he pulled her close enough to delight his body with the press of her soft curves against his hard angles. He dropped his head, swooping down to take a big taste of what he'd wanted from the moment he first laid eyes on her.

He demanded entrance, pressing his tongue along the seam of her lips until she complied. She opened her mouth. He plunged deep and retreated, only to plunge again. Honey and vanilla, sweet as the day was long, her flavor exploded over him. Her breathing hitched, became uneven, and he didn't care.

No consideration was given for her inexperience or innocence. Frustration drove him as fire licked at his body. This woman had somehow claimed a place in his mind no other woman had occupied. Until he discovered the reason her scent and taste and image wouldn't leave him alone, he had no choice but to go along with her screwy proposition. She'd made a tactical error, however, admitting to a curiosity at the physical consequences of her theory. Those consequences would no doubt burn them both. Little Miss Sunshine didn't have the first inkling of how powerful carnal desire could be, but she was about to learn, because he'd be damned if he'd suffer alone.

With one arm, he clamped her closer and gave her a sampling of that petting she'd mentioned. His free hand found the bounty of breasts that had haunted his dreams. Full and firm, the tight bud of a nipple stabbed his palm through the thin layers of her bra and T-shirt. The blood fled his head in a frenzied race to his hardening cock and left him lightheaded.

She pressed closer, swelling his erection in a painful rush. The innocent roll of her hips both eased and enflamed him at once. The tentative swirl of her tongue over his brought forth an agonized groan. Damn. She might not know what she was doing, but she was a quick study.

He bent her backward over his forearm. The move arched her body into his from knees to chest. Her answering moan seeped through his crazed mind, and he straightened slowly, bringing her up with him. With a final nibble of that sexy, full lower lip, he broke the kiss and lifted his head.

She hung in his arms, a honey-dipped doll. Tousled, butterscotch curls framed the pale oval of her face. A soft slash of pink kissed the perfection of her cheekbones below the fringe of dark blond lashes resting against her smooth skin. Her chest rose and fell with her labored breaths. When her lashes fluttered open, languid passion, deep and true, darkened her eyes until they glistened like emeralds.

Shit. He was in trouble, and whether she knew it or not, so was she. The limitations she'd placed on her proposition were the unschooled demands of an inexperienced woman attempting to maintain control over a situation she wasn't completely comfortable handling. If the need in her eyes was any indication, Little Miss Sunshine was doomed.

His chest bellowed like a thoroughbred after a trip around an oval track, making his voice husky and low. "Still need a second to think?"

"About what?"

Despite the fire raging in his gut, he chuckled. Although he wanted nothing more than to taste her again, he settled for a touch. Fingering a golden curl, he tucked the cool silk behind her ear. "Right answer. Any more stipulations I need to know about?"

She dropped her forehead to his chest. When she straightened a moment later, he let her go, and she stepped back.

Residual heat softened her eyes. "Can I get back to you on that? I can't seem to recall any at the moment."

He fought a grin and crossed his arms to keep from reaching for her again. He might be making the biggest mistake of his life, but her candid honesty charmed him almost as much as her honey sweet body. "You've got yourself a deal, sunshine, *if* you agree to *my* conditions."

Some of the languidness cooled in her eyes. "You have conditions?"

He nodded.

"How many?"

He held up three fingers.

"What's number one?"

"Three dates won't do. I leave for Syracuse and training camp in three weeks. Give me until then or no deal."

Several heartbeats passed before she nodded. "What's the second?"

"I decide what we do on these dates."

She shook her head. "I'm serious about overcoming the attacks, Tuck. That won't happen if I don't push myself. To do that, the dates need to be in public places."

"Oh, I can guarantee you'll be pushed." He planned to do plenty of pushing. She wasn't the only one with a theory to test. "We'll deal with your fear of crowds, but from the sound of things, you don't have a lot of experience just having fun. Stick with me." He tapped a fingertip to her nose. "I'll give you three weeks you'll never forget."

He smiled when she swallowed. Hard.

"And three?"

"I've agreed to your demands. I expect you to agree to mine. Unlike you, I know the pleasure a man and woman can find together when the attraction is mutual, and don't bother trying to claim that isn't the case here. You practically melted in my arms."

She lifted her chin.

He grinned and held up a hand. "I'd never force a woman, but that doesn't mean I won't do my damndest to get you into my bed." He wasn't sure which of them was more surprised by his warning. A virgin. Damn, what was he thinking? The inner cautioning didn't stop him from jumping in with both feet. "Knowing that up front, if you insist on finding yourself a test stud, I'm your man."

Chapter 7

Crossing the street beside Tuck, CC stifled a groan. A man, a test stud, was the last thing she wanted, especially an irresistibly sexy flirt like Tuck. She scrunched her nose in a cringe. Okay, that was a big fat lie. She definitely wanted. Holy crap, did she ever. New to the experience, she nonetheless recognized the irresistible pull plucking at her girly nerve endings like teasing fingers for what it was. Longing. Hot, hungry and... completely unacceptable.

Who knew a firm pair of lips and a satiny tongue could cause a woman's normally logical thinking to misfire? By the time they'd finished brokering their deal, she'd been panting worse than Walter after a run.

Three weeks. Good Lord. His timeline coincided perfectly with her birthday promise, but she couldn't believe she'd agreed to spend the next three weeks with Kevin Tucker. Agreed? Ha! She'd practically baited him into agreeing, even after he'd warned he didn't plan to follow her rules. Had she lost her mind? Of course she had, but who could blame her when just the thought of kissing him again made her go all mushy and hot with anticipation?

A surreptitious glance to her side caught him watching her. Eyes full of teasing humor, he winked. The devil. She tore her gaze away. What was it about the guy? It wasn't as if he were movie star handsome. His male appeal had definite rough edges, but the slight imperfections didn't seem to matter compared to the twinkling humor found more often than not in his cobalt blue eyes. Gifted with more charm than any one man should be allowed, his type had brought about the downfall of women far more experienced than her. What chance did she have against all that grinning magnetism?

God, what was wrong with her? Hadn't she witnessed her mother's pain and misery, thanks to her father's womanizing? She should be immune to Tuck's dark and mysterious allure. Yet, here she was, fighting a giddy, consuming excitement every bit as powerful as the trepidation clawing at her mind like desperate fingers. Which only proved what she'd suspected all her life. Men like Tuck were sensual demons, devilishly smooth dealers in the powerful drug of unadulterated lust.

Perhaps she was suffering from a case of massive rationalization, but still… She had less than three weeks to fulfill her birthday promise, and freedom from her neuroses far outweighed the potential risk of falling under Tuck's spell. She'd made her deal with the devil and would stick to their bargain, but she had no intention of ending up like her mother by following through on the tempting promises of unspeakable pleasures in his enthralling eyes.

The trick was to keep her eye on the prize, which should be as easy as pie, considering how often reminders of Tuck's gigolo status came up. For crying out loud, in the three blocks from her condo to the park where Walter's lessons would be held, she'd spied six women shooting Tuck blatantly inviting smiles.

Six! Not that she was counting.

She shuffled to a stop as he paused at the top of a small rise overlooking the grassy lawn. At the bottom of the hill, a half dozen dogs and their owners formed a half circle. Among the group were five women and one man, along with a German shepherd, a boxer, two beagles, a sleek greyhound, and a white furball of an unrecognizable breed. Walter fidgeted at her side, anxious to join the pack.

The Barbie doll brunette holding the greyhound's leash turned and spotted Tuck. She lifted her hand and greeted him with a fingertip wave and a syrupy sweet smile.

Make that seven.

Tuck waved back and CC pressed her lips together. What the hell? Was he about to introduce her to one of his cast-off lovers? The possibility made her jittery with the need to announce an addendum to her rules. An exclusivity clause was in order. No way in hell would she be spending the next twenty-one days with Tuck and his exes. Unfortunately, having that discussion would have to wait. The park was full of strangers, six of whom were currently watching them with marked interest.

She bit back a snarky comment, sucked in a nervous breath, and sliced a condemning glance his way. "Friend of yours?"

The flirt didn't even have the grace to look uncomfortable. "Not exactly."

"Not exactly? As in just someone you've seen naked?"

He met her gaze and smirked. "Hey, what can I say? We gigolos have a reputation to maintain."

Ha! Keeping her eye on the prize was going to be a breeze.

His smirk slid into a sensual smile. "Jealous?"

"Not on your life."

He chuckled and tugged on her hand, leading her down the hill. "As it happens, I haven't had the pleasure of seeing Bridgette naked. She's the class instructor. We've never met."

CC rolled her lips flat into an embarrassed line. Guilt might have sunk its claws deep if not for the predatory gleam in the tall instructor's eyes latched onto Tuck as they approached.

"Hey, aren't you Tuck?" The lone male in the group, a barrel-chested man in jeans and a T-shirt, spoke before they'd come to a stop.

Tuck smiled congenially. "That's me."

"Well, I'll be damned." The big man performed an odd dance in his attempt to stay clear of the fluffy white dog running in nervous circles around his feet. A pink bow flopped in her top knot. He finally scooped the animal up, patting her head as he cradled her in his thick arms. He grinned in Walter's direction. "Now that's a dog. Never thought I'd ever be walking a Cockapoo, but the wife...well." He shrugged his wide shoulders and shot Tuck a what's-a-guy-to-do smile. "Women."

Bridgette opened her mouth, but before she could speak, one of the other class attendees, a forty-something blonde, carrying a few extra pounds, graced Tuck with a dimpled smile. Excitement twinkled in her blue eyes. "Wow. You're in our class?"

"Actually—"

"My husband is never going to believe this." The blonde rested a hand on the boxer's head. "He's your biggest fan."

Tuck grinned. "That's nice to hear."

"Fan?" A petite Asian woman held a phone in one hand and the German Shepherd's leash in the other.

Poodle guy answered her question. "Tuck plays for the Marauders."

A bland expression settled on the woman's brow.

"The Manhattan Marauders. They won the Super Bowl earlier this year."

"Oh. Football." She pointed the phone at Tuck and snapped a picture.

The last two attendees, stunningly sleek, redheaded twins, moved closer with their matching beagles to join the conversation. "Hi, Tuck. Remember us? We met at a players' meet and greet last year."

CC rotated her head slowly to shoot him a raised brow.

A grimacing smile crooked his lips. He looked away, cocking his head to glance between the twins. "Lilly and Lorna, right?"

The twin on the right pouted. "Linda and Lara."

He cleared his throat. "How could I have forgotten?"

Poodle guy cupped a hand over his mouth to cover his smile.

CC snorted disdainfully. How could he forget? More like how could he remember a mere two out of the thousands of woman he'd obviously seen naked?

The smile Bridgette offered Tuck was more than a few degrees cooler than the one she'd worn only moments ago. "We're honored you've joined us today, Mr. Tucker, but only dog owners are allowed to join in the class." She tossed her head toward a row of benches several dozen yards away. "If you wouldn't mind watching your"—she lifted a brow at CC—"lady friend and Walter, is it, from there?"

All eyes turned CC's way. Heat bloomed in her cheeks, and a tightening band around her chest threatened to steal her breath. Oh, crud. This was a bad idea.

Tuck slipped his fingers around her upper arm before she could spin around and run. His puckered brow indicated he noted her blooming distress. He dipped his head, bringing his lips to hers to speak quietly. "Breathe, sunshine. I'll be close by if you need me."

The breath he suggested sawed raggedly from her compressing lungs as he brushed his lips over hers in a gentle kiss. He straightened, eyeing her intently. Despite the deepening heat of her cheeks at his public display, she clung to the confident encouragement in his deep blue orbs.

If she needed him? She couldn't allow that to happen, ever, but if she was going to cave at the first sign of trouble, she might as well call a halt to her test right now and admit defeat. Not going to happen.

She nodded and dragged in a calming breath. He smiled and winked, then turned to wander off to the line of benches. She cast her gaze about. Several pairs of feminine eyes followed his departure, and she straightened her spine. She'd be demanding that exclusivity clause the moment class ended.

Chapter 8

"He did it again."

On the machine next to CC's, Kris turned her head. "Who did what?"

CC's feet thudded a quick pace on the treadmill's rolling belt. She shot her cousin a guilty grimace. "Tuck. He kissed me and killed a panic attack about to strike."

"What? When was this?" Kris jammed a fingertip to her control panel. The belt slowed to a stop. Eyes wide, she stared. "You sneaky dog. Why didn't you tell me you saw him again?"

"I thought I just did." Which was the reason she'd agreed to meet Kris at the busy private gym instead of working out at the much quieter Y around the corner from their condo. Since Walter's lesson in the park, CC had been swamped with doubts, and her cousin was the only person she could talk to about her arrangement with Tuck.

Kris swiped the small towel from the handrail and dabbed at her throat. "And *I* thought you'd decided to ask Ronald to help you out with your theory."

Funny, she hadn't given her agent a thought in days. Odd, considering how embarrassed she'd been over his rejection, but then, from the moment Tuck made his irresistible offer, she hadn't exactly been thinking clearly. God, the man scrambled her brain almost as much as he heated her insides.

Kris cleared her throat.

CC blinked. What were they talking about? Oh, right. Ronald's refusal. Her cousin already had a low opinion of her agent. His humiliating rejection was something she'd rather keep to herself. She shrugged. "I changed my mind."

A sly grin tipped the corners of Kris's lips. "You go, girl!" She flipped the top on her water bottle. "So, Tuck agreed to your little experiment? Details. I need details."

She glanced away from her cousin's intent regard. "There's not much to tell."

Kris leaned a hip against the rail and crossed her arms. A laugh sparkled in her eyes beneath arched brows. "You're a terrible liar, Cees, and worse at keeping secrets. At least from me. Spill it."

She scowled and punched the stop button on her panel. "Fine. I didn't change my mind. I approached Ronald with the idea of the two of us dating."

"And?"

She squirmed beneath Kris's watchful stare. Squatting on the belt, she snagged her duffle bag. "He declined."

Kris straightened away from the bar with a hiss. "The dweeb turned you down?"

"Shh!" CC glanced around. Thankfully, none of the several dozen patrons working out in the busy gym paid them any attention. After rising, she hopped from her treadmill and headed for the free weights.

Kris hurried after her. "Cees?"

She dropped her bag to the floor, selected two ten-pound hand weights, and straightened in front of the floor-to-ceiling mirror. Her biceps contracted with the first curl of her arms. "It was a nightmare. I thought he was going to swallow his tongue. He looked at me like I'd grown a second head and couldn't get out of there fast enough."

A low growl rumbled in her cousin's throat. "Bastard."

Guilt simmered in her belly. "Though I'd like to agree with you on that, I can't. Turns out he's seeing someone."

The towel hung from Kris's fingers as she folded her arms. "He's an uptight nerd. You got lucky, as far as I'm concerned."

"And stepped into the path of a runaway train. Guess who was standing outside the condo's open door and heard every humiliating word?" She nodded wryly as Kris's mouth formed a silent *O*, then explained how Tuck had shown up the day before and about his gift of the dog obedience classes for Walter. "The minute Ronald left, Tuck offered his services as test stud."

Having lifted her water bottle to her lips, Kris coughed. She dragged the back of her hand across her mouth. "Stud as in *stud*?"

"Is there another kind?" CC squeezed her eyes shut and dropped her arms to her sides. "God. I'm as bad as Mom."

"What do you mean?"

"Apparently she passed her inability-to-resist-a-bad-boy flirt gene down to me." She opened her eyes and turned her head. "I was scot-free, Kris. By the time I'd finished laying out my rules for the test, Tuck had changed *his* mind. He said no thanks, but instead of counting my blessings and sending him on his way, I practically badgered him into reconsidering."

Disappointment puckered the redhead's brow. "Why would he say no?"

"Why would he say *yes*? I'd just explained about the panic attacks. Talk about baggage."

Kris rolled her eyes. "Have you looked in the mirror lately?"

She scowled and purposefully turned her back on her reflection. Kris rolled her eyes, but CC didn't need to follow her cousin's gaze to know what she'd see. She'd never be considered a great beauty. Clearly, the knockout gene had skipped a generation. Unlike her mother, who stood at a statuesque five-foot-ten, CC took after her paternal grandmother. Not that she was a dog. Her five-four frame was well proportioned, with healthy breasts and slim hips, and her curly blond hair and pale skin complemented her large green eyes. With a little time and effort, she could be presentable, but at the moment, free of makeup, with sweat dampening her curls and the front of her T-shirt, she fell somewhere just short of average.

She smirked. "You're biased, Kris. Or blind."

"Of course I'm biased, and I'm not blind. Think about it. You've worked damn hard to remain anonymous. In an age where anyone can be found with a few clicks of the mouse, you've managed to avoid the grid. For all intents and purposes, you don't exist. You don't even have a Facebook account, for heaven's sake and yet, one of the hottest bachelors in the country took the time and effort to track you down. A man who goes to that kind of trouble has *got* to be interested."

She cursed her fair skin and the blush that heated her cheeks. "Oh, he's interested."

"Well then?"

Frustration filled her sigh. "You know how I am. I started babbling. He deserved to understand the full scope of the situation, but apparently, he's got a brain beneath all that brawn. The minute he realized how little experience I have had with guys, he slammed on the brakes. I should have done the same, especially when he warned if he consented to help me prove my theory, he'd be doing his damndest to get me into bed."

Kris's eyes went owl wide. "He said that?"

"Almost verbatim."

"Wow." Kris dropped to a weight bench with a faraway stare, then her brows snapped together. She slapped her towel to the padded leather seat at her side. "Man. Why doesn't stuff like that ever happen to me?"

CC spun to face her. "I'm serious."

With one long leg crossed over the other, Kris leaned back on her hands. "So am I. He's single, sexy as hell, and, if the rumors are true, knows his stuff in the bedroom."

No arguing there. If his kisses were any indication… She huffed. "Well, I don't. What's more, I'm not interested in learning."

Kris rolled her eyes. "Oh, you are so full of it."

She coughed a laugh, and they shared a grin.

Kris held out one hand to study her nails, then brought it close and frowned. "Oh, man. I've got a chip." She bent at the waist and rummaged through her bag. Sitting up, she sawed a nail file back and forth over the jagged edge. "Face it, Cees, you may live like a nun, but you're as attracted to a broad chest and a pair of muscled arms as I am. Besides, aren't you the one who said you're sick of being a twenty-six-year-old weirdo who's never had sex?"

CC jerked her gaze around the room. Relieved to find no one had heard, she lowered her voice. "No. I said I'm sick of being the weirdo who's never had a *date*."

"Semantics." Kris shoved the file into her bag and pushed from the bench to pick up a pair of weights. She joined CC at the mirror. "Girlfriend, there are millions of women around the world who would *kill* for the opportunity to study sex education under the tutelage of Professor Kevin Tucker."

She blew a derisive snort and resumed her reps. "Yeah, well, I'm not one of them." Her shoulder received a teasing bump and Kris grinned.

"Says the girl who practically *badgered* him into dating her."

Okay, there was that. She sighed. "He's a gigolo."

A dimple winked in Kris's grin. "A freaking gorgeous gigolo."

True. "He's pushy."

"He's a guy."

"And arrogant."

"He's a pro athlete. Comes with the territory. From what I've heard, he's also charming."

She couldn't argue with that. Still… "He's famous, Kris. He insisted on going along with us to Walter's first lesson. It was chaos. By the time class had ended, a mob had formed. You should have seen the way people thronged around him. He nearly caused a riot."

"Sounds like a good test for your theory."

She scowled. "I had something a little more anonymous in mind."

"You survived the riot without having an attack, right?

Damn it. She hated when Kris played the logic card. "Yeah."

"Well, there you go."

She dropped her arms to her sides and shook her head. "He's with a new woman every other week."

"Perfect. You didn't want to keep him." Kris waggled her brows. "Or did you?"

"No!" *Keeping* a man like Tuck was out of the question. She did *want* him, however, and that was the problem. Still, Kris was right. The whole point of her theory was to break the tethers that held her captive. Sex with Tuck would be one, big, honking, pleasant first in what she hoped would be a long line of firsts, but...

A long sigh escaped. "I'm scared, Kris. When it comes to sex, he's an all pro. I don't even rate rookie status."

"Who better to teach you the playbook than a pro?" She grinned at CC's groan. "Don't overanalyze this, Cees. You say you're sick of the status quo. Here's your chance to make some changes. Men like Tuck are a rare opportunity, meant to be enjoyed. I say go for it."

She squeezed her eyes shut. There was no doubt in her mind sex with Tuck would be enjoyable, but was she the kind of woman who could have a fling with one of the most sought-after men on the East Coast and walk away unscathed?

"Uh, Cees? I hope your silence means you've decided to play school with Tuck."

Yanked from her musings, her eyes blinked open. "Why?"

Kris tilted her head toward the front of the gym. "Because, unless I'm wrong, class is about to begin."

She whirled her head around. A confusing mix of horror, disbelief, and bemused pleasure lifted the hair on her arms as her shocked gaze collided with a pair of intent, cobalt blue eyes.

* * * *

"Well, I'll be damned. What's she doing here?" Tuck's gaze flicked to the grinning redhead before swinging back to CC where she stood on the other side of the gym. She stared at him, blinking. Pleasure coursed through him as her lips formed another of those light profanities she looked too sweet to know, much less use.

Beside him, the gym's owner, Max Grayson, turned from greeting Vern, the gym's time battered manager, and followed Tuck's gaze. "You know Kris?"

He shot him a brief, sidelong glance. "If you mean the redhead, then no. I was talking about the blonde."

Max shook his head. "I should have known. You and your blondes. Man, you need to broaden your horizons."

He laughed. "Haven't you read the papers? My horizons are broad and legendary, my friend."

Max grinned. "Who is she? I've never seen her in here before."

He spoke without looking at his friend. "She's not a member?"

"Not unless she signed up this morning, and you didn't answer my question."

"CC Calhoun."

CC began shoving a towel into a small duffel while the redhead frowned.

"We met a few days ago."

"She's hot."

Tuck jerked his head around to stab Max with a withering glare. Though he'd only met the man a few months earlier, it was impossible not to like Gracie's best friend from childhood. Bold, bawdy, and bulky with muscle, the cage fighting champion and gym owner was quick to laugh and unfailingly loyal to those he considered friends. He counted Tuck in that group, and the feeling was mutual. That didn't mean Tuck trusted Max when it came to women.

Before Jake Malone retired from the dating field by marrying Gracie, he and Tuck enjoyed a friendly competition, doing their best to steal the other's current lady love out from under each other's noses. With Jake out of the picture, Max had stepped smoothly into the game. By Tuck's estimation, the score between them was dead even.

Max chuckled and his gray eyes twinkled with challenge. A shiver of apprehension tap danced down Tuck's spine.

His friend ran long fingers over the short, black bristle covering his jaw. "Are you seeing her?"

Oh, hell. "Yes, I am. Stay the hell away from her."

"Oh, ho!" Max thumped him across the shoulders on a hardy laugh. "You've been holding out on me, buddy."

Damn straight he had. He'd often marveled at Max's ability to draw women. A product of the New York foster care system, the years of tough living showed on his battered face but hadn't touched his optimistic spirit.

Women flocked to his easy laugh and generous personality, despite his hoodlum looks. The same had been said of Tuck over the years, much to his amusement, but at the moment, he had no desire to laugh.

He bristled under Max's gleeful humor. "I mean it, Max. She's not available."

Max dropped his arm and shook his head. "Hot damn. First Jake, now you. Shit, it's an epidemic."

The fist of panic he'd come to recognize since meeting CC clenched Tuck's gut.

Max chuckled. "Damn, man. There's going to be a stampede of heartbroken women when the word gets out you're off the market." He rubbed his hands together and grinned. "But don't worry, I'll take up the slack."

Tuck scowled and turned. CC stormed in their direction.

"I'm not off the market, just on hold for a while."

"Whatever you say, but have you told *her* that?" Max's grin slipped to a polite smile as CC and her friend approached.

Lips pulled tight in a mulish line, CC came to a stop before them. She jutted out her chin like a prize fighter preparing to take a punch. "What are you doing here?"

Max snickered at his side. Tuck's clenched muscles loosened at her grumbled tone, and he couldn't help poking her a little. He crossed his arms. "I was about to ask you the same thing. Are you following me, sunshine?"

He nearly laughed when her mouth dropped open. She snapped it shut and spoke through gritted teeth. "I had no idea you'd be here."

"Are you sure? It wouldn't be the first time a woman tracked me down, then pretended ignorance."

Her back snapped straight, and her lips flattened out. Emerald fire spit from her eyes. "Why you arrogant... Don't flatter yourself. Stalking is your style, not mine."

He grinned. "I know."

Yanking on the strap of the bag hanging over one shoulder, she lifted her chin. "There are thousands of gyms in the city. How the heck was I supposed to know—" She blinked and that sexy little wrinkle creased her brow. "You do?"

He nodded and smiled. "Yeah, I do, but admit it. You're happy to see me."

An adorable blush bloomed on her cheeks, even as she narrowed her eyes. Still, the shadow of a smile haunted her lips. "You're an ass."

He laughed.

Max chuckled. "True that. We haven't been introduced. I'm Max Grayson. This is my place." He stuck out his hand.

"CC." After a slight hesitation, she placed her hand in his, shook it, and pulled her hand back quickly.

Tuck turned to her redheaded friend. "Nice to meet you. You're Kris, right?" Surprise widened her eyes and he smiled. "Max gave me your name."

CC's brows popped together while Kris accepted his hand with a grin. "And you're Tuck. I'm CC's cousin and roommate. She told me you've consented to help her test her theory."

CC shot her cousin a fulminating glare.

"Theory?" Max eyed him with a lifted brow.

Tuck's soft groan was echoed by CC's much louder one.

With a negligent toss of a shoulder, he dismissed Max's challenging grin. "Long story." He turned back to CC. Because he wanted to, and because it would fluster her, he brushed a fingertip over her cheek. "I thought you were working in your studio this morning."

A dimple scored Kris's cheek as she smiled. "I dragged her along. She spends too much time locked up with her sculptures and needs to get out more."

CC sent her a seething stare. Her cousin bared her teeth in a smile.

"I agree, and plan to change that." Tuck winked at Kris before pinning CC with his most charming smile. "Beginning now. Have lunch with me."

"Oh, I…" Refusal flashed in her eyes. She glanced at Kris, but if she was looking for support, she found none.

Kris dug in her bag and pulled out her phone. "Perfect. I have an appointment uptown."

The sexy wrinkle returned. "What appointment?"

The redhead held up a finger, brandishing the flaw in her otherwise perfect manicure in CC's face. "Paws and claws, babe, and there's a sweet pair of three-inch heels in a shop on Park just waiting for me to give them a good home."

CC pushed her hand aside to glare at the dark, skin-tight leggings and soft white, off-the-shoulder T-shirt covering Kris's long, slim body. "You just worked out. Since when do you go shopping in a sweaty leotard?"

Kris tossed her head. "This is New York. No one will even notice."

Max hummed low in his throat. His appreciative gaze slid down the curves displayed by the leotard in question. "I would."

Tuck nodded his agreement. "Me, too."

CC rolled her eyes.

Delighted laughter floated through the air as Kris patted Max's cheek. "Why do you think I wore it, handsome?" She laughed and dropped her hand, swinging her gaze to Tuck. "I've decided I like you."

Tuck offered her a generous smile, but as she turned to face him fully, all hint of humor disappeared from her face. Militant intensity gleamed in her eyes.

She stabbed the chipped nail into the center of his chest. "But if you hurt her, you die." With that, she sashayed toward the front of the gym, waiving her hand as she disappeared out the doorway.

Chapter 9

Tuck curled his fingers around Walter's collar and opened the door. Ronald, the stiff, stood on the stoop, dressed in the same type of conservative attire he'd worn the other day. Against the backdrop of the gentle summer day, the black suit hung on his shoulders like a sinister cape.

Surprise lit the agent's dark eyes. "Oh. I was expecting CC or Kris."

A low rumble sounded in the dog's throat, and Ronald puckered up like a teenage boy facing an angry father on prom night.

Tuck fought back a smile and tightened his hold. "Makes sense, since they live here."

"Is CC home?"

He pointed a finger at the ceiling. "She's upstairs."

"I'm Ronald Bartolini, her agent."

He shook the offered hand. "Kevin Tucker."

"I know." The slick car salesman smile didn't come close to reaching the man's eyes. "Congratulations on your Super Bowl win. That was one hell of a game."

"Thanks. Was CC expecting you?"

"No. I needed to talk to her about something and hoped to catch her working."

Tuck grunted, and instead of slamming the door in the asshole's face the way he wanted, he opened it wider. He didn't do relationships and wasn't in this for the long term. Jealousy was a foreign emotion. Nonetheless, he recognized the slow burn in his gut for what it was. CC saw the stiff as a friend, but he was still a man. A man she'd thought of first as a candidate to test a theory she never would have considered but for *his* kiss. That made Ronald Bartolini an adversary. One he'd need to eliminate. Starting now.

He shut the door and curled his lips in a sensual smile. "She's in the shower at the moment. Shall I tell her you're here?"

Ronald's eyes bugged out. "Oh. Oh, no, that's not necessary. I can wait." A phone jangled on a nearby desk and drew his gaze momentarily. He turned back and cleared his throat. "I didn't realize you and CC were…friends."

The comment came out more like a question, as if he were on a fishing expedition. Tuck was more than happy to chum the waters. "I'm not sure *friends* is the right term."

The phone rang a second time, and her answering machine clicked on.

"You're dating her?" Skepticism sharpened Ronald's tone.

Beep.

"Yeah. Why? Is there something between the two of you besides business?"

"CC, it's your father. I was hoping you'd be free to meet me for dinner."

Ronald shifted his briefcase from one hand to the other. "Not in the way you're suggesting, but I consider her a friend, as well as a client."

Tuck crossed his arms. "Is that so?"

"As a matter of fact…"

"Are you there, CC? Bobby Oakley and I are in town, working out some tour details. He'd like to see you, too. You know you always were his favorite."

Whatever Ronald had been about to say trailed away as his stunned gaze whipped to the phone. Tuck's brows shot to his hairline. He was as surprised as the agent at the mention of the rock 'n' roll legend.

A sigh floated through the machine. *"I guess you're not home. I left a message last week, but I guess you didn't get it. The band and I will be back in town at the end of the month for the kickoff concert for my new tour. I'd love for you to be there."*

Tuck's gaze crawled to the ceiling, above which CC was showering in preparation for their lunch date. Holy fuck. He'd sensed from the beginning there was more to her panic attacks than she was saying but… Ho-ly fuck! *His* new tour? If Bobby Oakley was part of the band, her father was Curt Jensen, lead singer of one of the biggest rock bands of all time.

Unease slithered down Tuck's spine as vague memories of old headlines flashed in his head. He'd been just a teen at the time but remembered how the kidnapping had captured the nation's attention. He recalled his mother's horror as she followed the story on the evening news. Three long summer nights while the famous singer pleaded for his daughter's life. The blond head of a little girl hiding her face and clinging to her father's arm at the press conference once she'd been recovered.

Jesus.

Ronald jerked out his arm and checked his watch. "I'll have to speak to CC later. If I don't leave now, I'll be late for an appointment. Let her know I stopped by, will you?" Without waiting for a reply, he turned and left.

Tuck paid him no mind. He scrubbed a hand over his mouth and chin. Shit. The panic attacks suddenly made sickening sense. She'd spent three days with strange, criminally-minded men, intent on getting rich off the terror of a nine-year-old girl and her family.

Walter rubbed against his leg, and Tuck bent to scratch his neck. "Christ. That explains a lot."

"A lot of what?"

He turned his head. Fresh from her shower, CC crossed the floor to pick up the purse she'd left on the long work table in the center of the room. Despite the freshly applied makeup and slim woman's body beneath tight jeans and a T-shirt, she appeared younger somehow, as if his mind superimposed the image of the frightened child she'd been in the old photos onto the woman before him.

He straightened. She'd refused to explain the source of the attacks or speak of her past. Mention of her father could put him on shaky ground, but he'd never believed in keeping secrets from a woman he was seeing. He wouldn't start now.

"You had a phone call while you were in the shower."

"And?"

"I believe the caller was Curt Jensen."

If he'd had any doubt she was the little girl whose terror was splashed across the airways and publications two decades earlier, it was put to rest. She blanched. Her gaze flew to the phone. A red light flashed on the small, black console beside it. Her eyes slid shut.

"CC?"

She held up a hand, palm out, and opened her eyes. Twin flags of color rode her cheekbones. "My family is none of your business."

The blatant evidence that she continued to hold him at arm's length stung even as the remoteness in her eyes tore at his heart.

"You're right. Nothing beyond what happens on our dates is my business. Unless you decide to share it with me."

Suspicion deepened the emerald of her eyes. Stubbornness flattened her lips.

"I wasn't eavesdropping. I simply overheard the message." He sighed when she remained silent. "You're the little girl who was kidnapped. That's what I meant by it explains a lot."

Her chin notched up a full inch. "I don't talk about that."

He nodded. "Understandable."

Like adversaries on a dusty western street, they faced each other as the silence stretched. They'd crossed a line he hadn't known was there, and although he wanted nothing more than to take her in his arms and ease the shadows from her eyes, he remained where he was. He hoped like hell she wouldn't decide to call a halt to their arrangement, but the next move was hers.

Finally, she dipped her head to stare at the floor. "It happened a long time ago."

Relief weekend his knees. She hadn't told him to go. "Some things are difficult to forget."

When she looked up, the ghosts in her eyes shredded his heart like clawing fingers.

"Others are impossible." Her chest heaved on a deep breath, and the strength that had carried her beyond her own personal hell was evident in her conscious effort to banish the memories.

He sighed. "If you'd rather a rain check on lunch, I understand."

Her body went stiff and hurt replaced the shadows. She turned and picked up a small pair of pliers from her workbench. "If that's what you want."

He crossed the room in a flash. Cupping her cheek in his palm, he turned her until she was forced to meet his gaze. "Don't do that."

She blinked. "I don't understand."

"Don't shut me out. I don't deserve it."

"I wasn't."

When she twisted her head, he let her go and dropped his hand.

"Weren't you?"

"No."

The sharp arch of his brow indicated his doubt.

Her sigh was a ragged expulsion of breath. "Okay, maybe I was, but I'm a mess, Tuck. No one could blame you for wanting to back out of our bargain."

He narrowed his eyes, and she held up a hand.

"I'm not belittling myself. Really, I'm not. I've worked hard, damn hard, to overcome the events of that summer, but I know my limitations. I see shadows in every corner. I can't go out in public without fearing some poor innocent person will speak to me and I'll freak out."

She laughed, harsh and derisive, and swept her hand in an arching swath to indicate his body. "Look at you. You're perfect. Nothing scares you. Nothing even *shakes* you. I have no idea why you'd want to spend time with me."

He leaned close. She backed away.

He followed until her ass bumped up against the workbench. "Then let me refresh your memory."

* * * *

CC expected him to take her mouth in the rough claiming his burning eyes proclaimed he desired. Instead, his lips brushed hers with a gentleness that spoke to her soul. Soft and sweet, his mouth caressed hers. Her eyes slid shut, and she savored his heated breath on her lips. The oddly pleasant combination of cinnamon and sawdust bathed her senses as he nibbled and licked and led her on a sensual journey of pure, simple pleasure.

Time stood still, free of the past and its evils. She reveled in his taste until urgency claimed them both. A muscled arm drew her body flush with his. Devouring, joyous, hot, his tongue dove deep. A violent shiver ripped through her at the brand of his hands roaming her back to cup her bottom, at the absolute rightness of his chiseled body pressed to hers.

She hadn't known. How could she understand the crazy compulsion to reach and grab for more when, before him, she'd never experienced what is was to be held in a man's solid embrace? His erection strained against the juncture of her thighs and birthed a need in the depths of her soul.

When he broke the kiss, she mourned the loss. Her head, heavy with lethargy, dropped to his chest. Subtle vibrations caressed her forehead when he spoke.

"I don't know what it is about you, but from the moment I turned around in that coffee shop, I haven't been able to get you out of my mind. You haunt me, CC."

Oh, God.

She pulled back to look at his face. No sign of his usual humor showed in his eyes. Intense and watchful, they burned.

"You feel it, too. Don't deny it."

She couldn't, not with her legs quivering and her heart thundering.

He dipped his chin in a brief nod as if she'd spoken. "I meant what I said that day I agreed to help you. I'm not the man for you. You're right. I don't do permanent, but until I put a name to this maddening hold you have on me, you're stuck with me."

She swallowed and nodded.

The intensity in his eyes softened, and his chest heaved on a cleansing breath. "Your past is your own, CC, to share or not, but I'm a good listener."

God, the man melts my circuits. Does he have to be a nice guy, too?

A slow smile curved his lips, and for a moment, she was afraid she'd spoken aloud.

"You think I'm perfect, huh?"

* * * *

CC tightened her grip on the bat, her lips flat with determination. "Like this?"

Tuck grinned and stepped around her to ease his body against her back. Pleased when she didn't object, he wrapped his arms around her shoulders. "Come on, relax. This is supposed to be fun."

"Easy for you to say. You've done this before, and that ball comes out fast." She craned her neck to eye the colorful machines at the far end of the two-story gallery.

After lunch, he'd suggested they visit the arcade on the next block. She'd cheered him on as he took his turn in the single batting cage and connected with every ball except two, but when he invited her inside so she could hit a few, she suggested the pinball machines might be more her style.

He wrapped his hands around hers and adjusted her grip. "I reset the speed. You'll do fine. Widen your stance." With an anticipatory smile, he dropped one hand to her lower thigh and pressed gently. As expected, she jolted slightly but then shifted her leg and foot. The move brought her ass into closer contact with his crotch. He stifled an appreciative groan.

Fringe benefits were a beautiful thing.

Although he regretted her discomfort over his learning her true identity, he couldn't fault the results. She hadn't exactly opened up about her family or the kidnapping, but since their conversation in her studio, something had changed. As if the prickly cloak of privacy she kept wrapped around her had slipped, she was more visibly relaxed than he'd ever seen her. His ego, along with his libido, strutted at the possibility the mind-blowing kiss they'd shared was the cause, but in truth, her new easiness most likely had to do with the fact she no longer had a secret to guard. Regardless, something fundamental had shifted between them, and he meant to make the most of it.

He curled his fingers around hers. "That's it. Relax your knees. You don't want to crouch, but a little bend will give you balance."

Beneath the fingers he slid down her arms, her skin was warm silk. Momentarily distracted, his mind conjured up erotic images of several other patches of skin in even softer locations, which sent blood surging to his cock. The low grade hard-on he'd been sporting since the day they'd met swelled and jammed up against the curves of her fine ass, displayed to perfection in another pair of softly faded jeans.

She straightened with a jerk. "Is that necessary?"

"That's unavoidable."

A blush stained her cheeks, completely at odds with her pointed stare when she glanced over her shoulder. He flashed an innocent smile and kept his arms around her. Right where he wanted them.

"My old man always said if you're going to take the time to do something, do it right."

Her eyelashes fluttered above lips twisted in a smirk. "A philosopher, huh? Is he a gigolo, too?"

He coughed out a laugh. For a woman who'd suffered such darkness in her childhood, she had plenty of spunk. With a grin, he swatted her ass and stepped back. She jumped at the unexpected tap, shot him a warning glare, and turned away. The bat wobbled next to her ear as she shifted her shoulders and wiggled into place.

He sucked air through his teeth and enjoyed the impromptu shimmy show. "Dad is a one-woman man. He claims that's a natural state of affairs for a man who's found the love of his life." Staring at her slim back, he rolled his shoulders against an odd tingle of disquiet and shoved aside the dangerous train of thought. He cleared his throat. "Mom says it's because no other woman would have him." He cocked his head when she said nothing. "I guess your father never took you to the cages or taught you to hit a ball."

There it was again, a tightening of her back.

She shrugged and spoke without turning around. "Curt isn't exactly the sports type." She waggled the bat, but tension pulled her shoulders taught. "I thought we were here to hit baseballs. Are we going to do this or what?"

"Loosen up, sunshine. You're going to strangle that bat. Here, like this." He covered her hands with his once more and massaged her fingers until they relaxed. "Okay. Now, keep your eye on the ball arm. You'll hear a small click as the ball settles into the cup before it's released. Ready?"

"Uh-huh."

He stepped back and his gaze dropped to her ass as she settled into position like a triple-A wannabe. A groan rumbled low in his throat. The woman had the sexiest batter's stance he'd ever seen.

Grinning, he fed coins into the machine beside the door, then exited the cage. "Okay, here it comes. Keep your elbows up. Don't lean too far forward. You'll get hit."

She yelped and stumbled backward. The ball whizzed by, thudded against the leather backdrop, and dropped to the ground.

She lowered the bat to look his way. "Are you sure this is safe? I could be killed if one of these balls hits me."

"Not if you stay clear of the batter's box."

The white box painted on the cement floor received a distrustful glare before she hopped back another step.

"Here comes another! You're too far back."

Another ball whipped by. She screamed and dropped the bat.

He shoved his hands into his pockets and tried not to laugh. "You've got to watch the ball, CC."

"Watch it?" She swept up the bat. "I can't even see it. Can't you turn it down or something?"

"I set it to slow pitch. Here comes another. Concentrate!"

Thud.

The business end of the wooden bat clanked to the ground. She spun on him, and that adorable wrinkle bisected her brow. Hip cocked, she held his gaze. "How can I concentrate when you keep tossing out instructions?"

He held out his hands. "I'm trying to help."

"Well, you're not. Be quiet and let me do this myself."

She spun away and hefted the bat into position.

"Spread your feet a little more. You need to balance—"

She stepped back and let another ball pass. *Thud.* "Are you finished, Mr. Bossy? I *can* do this, you know. I've watched the Sports Network."

He grinned and crossed his arms. "Oh yeah? Then show me what you've got, Ace."

A delicate huff flared her nostrils, and she shuffled her feet until they were spread properly. Wiggling into position, she lifted the bat to hover near one ear. On a click from the machine, the arm snapped up. The ball flew forward, and his brows rose in amazement as she stepped into the pitch like a pro. The crack of the bat echoed her solid connection, and the ball rocketed toward the netting at the far top corner of the cage.

She tossed a smirk over her shoulder, then ruined the effect by squealing and dancing from foot to foot. "I hit it! Did you see?"

Hands propped on his hips, he grinned. "You didn't just hit it, you crushed it."

"I did, didn't I? How many more balls do I get?"

She caught a piece of the next one, sending it foul to the right. The next three were clean strikes, and he had to laugh at the grim determination of her compressed lips. Six fouls followed, but she finally found her rhythm and connected for two singles and a double. Her bright smile, as the last ball sailed to the far net, was worthy of a home run.

He shook his head as she exited the cage. "I think I've been had. Are you sure you've never done this before?"

She shrugged. "It's physics. Trajectory and angles combined with timing."

"An artist with an understanding of physics?"

"You'd be surprised how much an understanding of physics helps when dealing with shapes and metals."

"Huh. The way the Red Sox are hitting this season, you could give them some tips."

Her laughter, carefree and easy, called to his libido like a red-tipped fingernail crooking in a come-hither invitation. Because he could, he dipped his head to brush his lips over hers and savored the slight catch of her breath. When he forced himself to step back, the languid softness of her eyes and breathiness of her voice nearly made him groan.

"You're a baseball fan I take it?"

He took her hand and led her toward the door on a quickened pace. So far, the hat and dark glasses had proven a great disguise, but that was bound to change if he kissed her senseless in the middle of the crowded arcade.

He led her outside and struggled to remember her question. "I'm a *sports* fan. If it's played with a ball, I'm in, and I come by my interest honestly. Dad's a lifelong Sox fan."

"Didn't he want you to play?"

He tucked her hand into the crook of his arm as they joined the throng of pedestrians on the busy sidewalk. "Sure he did. He took my brother and me to our first T-ball lessons. My sister played, too. I rose through the ranks of little league and played on my high school team. Understanding if I wanted college, I'd get there through athletics, I played every sport I could, but the day I picked up a football, my fate was sealed. Baseball and basketball gained me the offer of partial scholarships. Football bought me a free ride."

"Wow. Scholarships in three sports programs. That takes skills."

"Oh, I have skills, sunshine." He shot her a lecherous grin.

She rolled her eyes. "Sports, Tucker. Try to stay on subject."

He chuckled at her prim tone and guided her around the stalled crowd enjoying a juggling street performer.

"You went to Florida State?"

"Yep. Football, sunshine, and bikinis on the beach." His chest lifted on an exaggerated sigh. "I didn't think life could get any better."

She snorted. "Did you ever open a book?"

He arched a brow. "Of course. In fact, I know all the words to *Green Eggs and Ham*."

Instant color flagged her cheeks. "I'm serious."

"So am I. Want me to recite them?"

She looked away. "I wasn't commenting on the course loads of collegiate athletes. I'm just curious."

He laughed and pulled her out of the way of a woman barreling down the sidewalk with her eyes on the screen of her phone. He rested his free hand over the one on his arm and squeezed. "Relax. I was kidding. I maintained a three point eight grade point average and have a degree in business tucked away for the day I hang up my cleats." He'd also gotten a jump on retirement by dabbling in a few lucrative concerns in the meantime.

A wrinkle creased her brow, and she cocked her head to study him as if she wasn't sure how to take him. "Hmm."

"What?"

"A gigolo with a business degree who knows the words to *Green Eggs and Ham*. I guess you *do* have skills."

Curious stares shot their way at his hearty laugh. Tempted to pull her to a stop and kiss her sweet lips, he settled for draping his arm over her shoulders and tucking her close to his side. "Smartass."

"Look who's talking."

He caught her pleased smile out of the corner of his eye. They traveled in silence for several minutes until her condo came into view.

"Has it?"

He twisted his head to look down at her. "Has it what?"

"Has life gotten better? I mean, a pro career is something millions of people dream of." Beneath his arm, her shoulders jerked in a slight shrug, and she eyed the ball cap pulled low on his forehead. A brief shadow flitted in her eyes, there and gone, and took the light of laughter with it. "But fame and fortune come with a price."

She ducked from beneath his arm, and he followed her up the path to her stoop. Digging the key from her pocket, she turned and met his gaze. He didn't have a fucking clue what to say. She, better than most, understood the cost of fame.

He tucked a curl behind her ear. "I love what I do, so, yes. In a lot of ways, life couldn't be better. In others, not so much."

"Like?"

"Like the constant interest of the fans. It gets old." He tugged the hat from his head and shoved a hand through his hair. "There are times I'd give anything just to be left alone."

The moment the words left his mouth, he wished he could take them back. The stark understanding in her eyes squeezed his chest.

"You handle the attention so much better than I ever have."

Shit.

"Damn, sunshine. Don't." He rubbed a hand down her arm. "Don't cut yourself short. You survived what would have crushed a lot of people."

"Survived." She spoke the word softly, derisively. "Surviving is exactly what I've been doing instead of living, and I'm sick of it." As she had several times before, she shook off the mantel of gloom weighing down her shoulders and straightened. "Speaking of surviving, I had fun today, but I think it's time to ramp our dates up to something a little more challenging. Something a little less anonymous."

Afternoon bristle rasped against the palm he rubbed over his jaw as he considered his options. An evening with his friends didn't quite qualify for what she was suggesting, but what the hell. Max and Gracie already knew about her, which meant Jake did as well. The ribbing he'd no doubt take would be worth keeping their dating status from the general public for a little while longer. Their agreement was only for three weeks, and while he fully intended to help her overcome her fears, he wasn't quite ready to share her with the masses yet. He had his own agenda. One keeping him up, literally, and not just at night.

"How about a barbeque? Nothing huge but I guarantee, with this crowd, you'll definitely be challenged."

Her chest rose on a shaky breath. "Sounds perfect. When?"

"Tomorrow. Six o'clock."

She nodded. "I'll be ready. Thanks for today."

"My pleasure."

She rose onto her tiptoes and pressed her lips to his. As victories went, the chaste kiss was a disappointment, but as this was the first time she'd initiated any kind of intimacy, he'd take it. She pressed her key in the lock, swung open the door, and slipped inside.

Chapter 10

The next evening, CC sat at a table beneath a tall oak in the sprawling backyard of Jake and Gracie Malone's rural Long Island farmhouse. According to the articles she'd read about the family's convoluted relationships, Jake had met and fallen in love with Gracie while competing with her for custody of his six-year-old twin half-sisters, who also happened to be her nieces. Tales of the couple's very public battle and subsequent romance had filled the airwaves and tabloids several months back, trumped only by the scandalous revelations of Gracie's parentage.

CC eyed Gracie's father, where he stood with his wife, Sharon, and Jake at the long, built-in grill. Tom Walden appeared no worse for wear after having his life and sterling career sullied by sly innuendo and off-color jokes simply because he'd fathered a child he didn't know existed while little more than a teenager. Contrary to the speculation still popping up in the press occasionally, Tom and Sharon Walden's relationship appeared solid and loving, and the love between Tom and his daughter, Gracie, unmistakable.

Sizzling meat scented the air while the shrieks of little girls and barking dogs competed with deep male voices and the rock 'n' roll music flowing from outdoor speakers. Laughter drew her gaze to the back door. Tuck, his arm draped over Gracie's shoulders, stepped through the doorway. They stopped at the edge of the patio, and he grinned at Max Grayson. Two of Tuck's teammates, Mario Davis and Jamal Knight, along with their dates, laughed at whatever Max was saying.

CC rubbed a damp palm along the hem of her shorts. How the heck had she come to be here, included in an impromptu gathering of strangers representing close to forty years of pro football talent? Less than a week ago her reclusive life had been simple, if a bit boring, and, for the most part, predictable. However, predictability had flown out the window the moment Kevin Tucker turned around and flashed his killer smile.

Walter, followed by Murphy, the Malone's rangy Border collie, burst into the circle of close friends and nearly toppled the tall blonde on Max's arm. He pulled his date close as the Malone twins followed in a game of chase.

CC lowered her lashes and pretended not to study Tuck and Gracie. According to him, they were simply friends, but their body language spoke of something deeper. Despite the Malones' recent marriage, from what CC had seen so far, the claim of simple friendship between Tuck and his best friend's bride strained the bounds of believability. Through her research, CC had read the snarky stories alluding to the competition between Tuck and Jake as they competed for the same women over the years. Had Gracie been one of them?

Tuck dipped his head to speak into Gracie's ear, and her low laugh danced across the distance. The tensing muscles of CC's stomach announced the addition of yet another new emotion to the healthy dose of lust she'd been suffering since meeting Tuck. Linguists around the world had screwed up when they assigned the color green to jealousy. In her opinion, *red* was more accurate.

Don't even go there. You're not jealous. You're only using him to cure your neuroses, remember?

At that moment, Tuck turned his head, and his laughing gaze tangled with hers. He bumped up his chin, winked, and graced her with a dimpled smile. Her heartbeat took off in a manic gallop, and the red haze of jealousy fizzled beneath the liquid heat that flooded her body. A helpless shiver pebbled her skin. God, she was so screwed. With each passing encounter with her *test stud*, it became increasingly difficult to cling to her crumbling aversion to his stated agenda.

Gracie slipped from under his arm to cross the patio. She dipped into the chair across from CC. "I'm so glad Tuck convinced you to come along today. I've been dying to meet you."

She blinked. "You have?"

An open and friendly smile curved Gracie's lips and she nodded.

"Why?" Fire bloomed on CC's cheeks at her own bluntness.

Gracie laughed. "Are you kidding? Tuck looked like he'd been hit over the head with a hammer after meeting you the other day. Any woman who can pull that off is someone I just had to meet."

"Oh." Her gaze jumped in Tuck's direction and landed on Walter, fleeing from Murphy and the twins with a floppy stuffed animal clenched in his jaws. She started to rise to go save the toy.

Gracie waved her off. "Relax, they're fine."

She settled back into her chair. "He…uh, told you how we met?"

"Yes, he did."

She was going to kill him, right after she convinced Walter to bite him.

The pretty blonde arched a brow above an easy smile. "From the darting looks you've been shooting at us since you arrived, you may not believe this, but Tuck is just a friend. A good friend, I admit, but nothing more. He tells me pretty much everything." She shook her head in bemusement. "I can't seem to get him to stop."

CC flattened her lips in an embarrassed line.

"I am, however, among that choice group of women who have seen him naked."

CC's spine straightened away from the chair as she stiffened. Obviously, his *friend's* claim that he told her everything was true. The jerk. How dare he discuss their private conversations.

Gracie chuckled and leaned her elbows on the table between them. "It's a long story, but an innocent one. He played babysitter one night shortly before Jake and I married. After the girls were asleep, he wandered out to the pool. We arrived home earlier than expected. Apparently, swim trunks are optional in his mind but, for the record, we've never kissed, much less slept together. Like Max, I see Tuck as a brother I never had."

CC shrugged to cover her embarrassment. "Who he sleeps with is none of my concern."

Gracie's teeth flashed with her delighted laugh. "Oh, sweetie. You're a terrible liar. A definite disadvantage around a guy like Tuck. We're going to have to work on that." She folded her hands under her chin, turning her head to smile at her husband when he called out to announce the steaks would be done in ten minutes.

"We?" Resisting the urge to squirm in her seat, CC swallowed.

Gracie glanced over at Tuck and his friends. "We'll discuss it later, I'm sure. Hello, Walter." She bent to scratch beneath the dog's chin as he and Murphy trotted up to the table. Gently removing the tattered bunny from his mouth, she cooed. "You're a sweet boy, aren't you?" Murphy shoved his long nose beneath her palm and she laughed. "And so are you, Mr. Jealous."

Walter rounded the table to lean against CC's side. She dropped her hand to his head.

With a last pat to Murphy's side, Gracie rose. "I have a few things to do in the kitchen."

CC stood to follow. "Can I help?"

"No need."

On the other side of the patio, Tuck looked up and excused himself from the group to cross the flagstone.

Gracie smiled and bumped her chin toward the deep woods beyond the barn. "Tuck, why don't you take CC for a stroll while we wait for Jake to finish the steaks?"

His lips curled in a lazy smile. "Sounds like a great idea."

CC's gaze skittered to the dense line of foliage fencing the lawn. Unbidden, murky memories of dim light and thick and twisted old-growth trees crept into her mind. She fought off a shiver. The sinister reflections from three hellish days so long ago had kept her from venturing into the woods ever since. She wasn't interested in doing so now. "Oh, no. That's okay."

Gracie cocked her head. "Are you sure? There's a very pretty spring along the path. It's not far. Only about a three minute walk." She shot Tuck a teasing grin. "Even you should be able to stay out of trouble for that short a time."

His lips quirked in a smirk.

The breath backed up in CC's throat. Three minutes might as well be three days. The idea of entering a place where nightmares lived had bony fingers of dread closing around her windpipe. She met Tuck's laughing gaze. If she leaped into his arms and demanded he kiss her and restore her breath, she'd only look like a lunatic. She was on her own.

Sucking in a ragged breath, she clung to his calming presence and spoke as evenly as possible. "If you believe that, you don't know him as well as you think."

Gracie's delighted bark of laughter did the job of knocking back the looming attack, as did her feminine arm flung around CC's shoulders.

"Oh, CC. You and I are going to be great friends."

Her shoulder received a gentle squeeze, and then Gracie spun toward the house with Murphy at her heels. CC frowned as she disappeared inside. Great friends? Obviously Tuck hadn't told her everything about their…hmmm. What did one call a short-term deal that might or might not include sex? Relationship wasn't quite right. Neither was dating, really.

Though tempted, she didn't bother following to explain. What was the point? In three weeks, she'd see neither Gracie *nor* Tuck again. CC blamed her sudden sadness on the knowledge Gracie Malone was the type of woman she'd like for a friend.

"What's wrong?"

She turned. Tuck watched her with a focused intensity that heated her cheeks. Walter bumped against her thigh, and she grabbed at the distraction.

She bent to scrub at his neck. "Nothing."

"You're a sucky liar, sunshine. Something spooked you. Something to do with walking in the woods. What's going on?"

Well, crap. So much for believing him knowing her secret would make things simpler. Nothing was simple when it came to Tuck. Sure, he was a rascal, but he was a kind rascal who cared deeply about the people around him. He was also generous and naturally intuitive. Hadn't he recognized the onset of her attack that first day and stepped in to fix it? Of course he'd notice something was wrong, but their deal to test her dating theory was never meant to include a peek into her nightmares. Damn Curt and his phone messages.

"CC?"

She lied through her teeth. "I have no idea what you're talking about."

His sigh was full of disappointment. "Okay, if that's the way you want it, but I can't help if I don't know what's wrong." He shook his head when she didn't reply. "You and Gracie were huddled together like thieves. What were you talking about?"

Relief loosened her tensed muscles, and she dredged up a smile. "None of your business."

He arched a brow, but the beginnings of a smile tweaked his lips.

"She's…something else."

His chuckle held wry affection. "You have no idea."

"I'm not sure why, but I think I like her."

"Is that a bad thing?"

She shrugged. "Not bad, just disappointing."

"Disappointing how?"

"I suffer from panic attacks, remember? That type of thing tends to make a person keep to herself." At his questioning look, she sighed. "I don't make friends easily."

"You seemed to be doing well enough a minute ago. Besides, isn't that one of the objectives of your dating theory test? To allow you to be more socially active?"

"Yes, but…"

"But what?"

"Our bargain is for three weeks. Breakups normally cause people to choose sides, and she's your friend." She flicked her head, indicating his friends and their dates gathered around Jake and the Waldens. "These people are *your* friends."

He laughed, making her frown. "When you've gotten to know them better, you'll understand the word *normal* doesn't apply with this crowd." He wrapped his arm around her shoulders. "Anyway, we won't be breaking up when the three weeks are done. We'll be bringing our friendly bargain to an end. You have a tendency to overthink things, don't you?"

"I'm a realist." She shoved her hands into the pockets of her shorts.

Another squeeze. Tighter this time. "You're a worrier, but I promised to introduce you to the concept of fun. I plan to do just that, starting tomorrow, if you're free."

Her heartbeat accelerated as she visualized several decidedly naughty scenarios. Sultry images of what *he'd* consider fun. Heat flamed in her chest, then climbed upward to spread across her cheeks. His bark of laughter made things worse.

Mischief twinkled in his eyes as he cocked his head to study her. "For a virgin, you sure do have a dirty mind."

"Shh!" A quick glance proved no one but she was aware of his teasing. She turned back with a scowl, then crossed her arms in an effort to cover the tingling pucker of her nipples. Oh, yeah. Kevin Tucker was a lust-dealing demon.

His hearty laugh slowed to a chuckle, and he brushed a thumb over her cheek. "You can relax. I have something completely innocent in mind." Dimples popped in his wicked grin. "For now."

Chapter 11

Bent over her workbench, CC struggled to shove aside the pair of smiling blue eyes that kept popping into her mind. Tuck had promised to introduce her to the concept of fun, and if she'd learned anything over the last five days, it was that he kept his word.

Decked out in his usual disguise of hat and dark glasses, he'd arrived at her condo the evening after the Malones' barbeque and made good on his promise. With her hand in his, CC followed along as they worked their way through the crowd to stake out a spot on the lawn to enjoy the night's offering at Bryant Park's Film Festival. Sprawled on a soft blanket, she curled to his side as they nibbled popcorn and watched Bogey and Hepburn outwit the bad guys to find unlikely love on a tangled East African river.

Early the following morning, Tuck had tugged her up the famous steps of The Metropolitan Museum two minutes before the doors opened. He'd insisted they begin their tour with the Egyptian exhibit, his favorite he claimed. His hand rode the small of her back as they explored the many rooms. In the low light of the Tomb Chapel of Raemkai, he had pulled her into a dark alcove and snuck a kiss.

Two days later, at the rail of the East River Ferry, he stood at her back with his arms encircling her waist on the ten-minute ride to Long Island City. The afternoon drifted by as they strolled the center path of the waterfront flea market, stopping at booths and gobbling down sweets. She laughed, utterly charmed when he presented her with matching sun visors covered in gaudy flowers. One for her, the other for Walter.

That wasn't to say Tuck had backed off from his sensual agenda. Like the player he was, he was a pro at smoldering looks and sexy innuendos.

He kept after her constantly, and his campaign was showing signs of success. A tempting brush of his fingers along the sensitive skin at the back of her neck or a friendly arm tossed over her shoulders, it didn't matter. Her traitorous body clamored for more, no matter how strenuously her mind objected.

On Friday, he'd arrived at her condo with a loaded pizza and a six-pack of beer to help her celebrate the end of Walter's obedience lessons. She'd laughed as he'd presented her dog with a battered pair of his athletic shoes as a reward for a job well done. Although Walter hadn't come anywhere near graduating at the top of his class, he'd shown some marked improvement. With a little bit of patience and some consistency, Bridgette, the perky dog trainer, proclaimed he could be the model pet.

CC wasn't holding her breath. In fact, it came out in a snarl as he tore through her studio, his back feet slipping out from beneath him on the hardwood floor. He slammed into the wall but didn't seem deterred in his goal. Whatever that was. He was up and running like a shot, a trail of unraveled toilet paper flapping behind him.

"Geez, Walter. What the hell?" He took off, bolting for the hallway and the upstairs landing as if Animal Control was on his scent. After rising from her workbench, she gathered up the wasted paper and shoved it into the trash. She didn't have a clue how he'd managed to dig the roll out from under the bathroom sink and didn't want to know.

Flexing her fingers, she returned to her stool and the piece she was working on. It had been days since she'd had the opportunity to sculpt, and she was quickly absorbed. Afternoon sunlight had reached the high windows to dance on the hardwood floor when she finally blinked her way out of her creative fog.

She stretched her back, and her gaze skittered past the finished sculpture to fall on her cell phone. Her mother had called twice over the past couple of days, but with Tuck present both times, she'd been reluctant to answer. Inevitably, the conversation would turn to Curt, and while Tuck hadn't brought up her father since that one time in the batting cage, it was obvious he was curious.

Walter's nails clicked on the hardwood as he trotted over to present her with a peace offering. She plucked the slimy cardboard tube from his mouth and held it gingerly between her fingertip and thumb. "Thank you, Walter. That's disgusting."

The nub of his tale jerked back and forth like a metronome on crack.

She stretched to the side to drop his drool-soaked offering in the trash can and almost tumbled off the stool when her mother's ringtone made her jump. Righting herself, she stared at the phone. A shiver raced down her spine. Typical of her mother to call at the exact moment CC was thinking of her.

She frowned at Walter. "How does she *do* that?" He danced from foot to foot and barked, making her smile. She thumbed the phone's screen. "Hi, Mom."

"CC, baby!" Her mother's smile came through in her chipper greeting. "I just had to call and find out what's happened."

Uh-oh. "I'm...not sure what you mean."

"I dreamed about you last night."

The fission of apprehension expanded to a healthy dose of alarm. Her mother took her dreams seriously, despite the fact they never made a lick of sense to anyone else.

"Mom. I'm in the middle of a project. Can we—"

"You were dancing at your wedding. On a sawdust covered floor."

Oh, shit. If she says my bridesmaids wore cinnamon, I'm going to throw up.

"Sawdust! Isn't that peculiar?"

"Mom, I'm working."

"Anyway, I've consulted the charts."

Oh, goodie. She sagged on her stool.

"There are two potential possibilities. Oh, it gives me goose bumps even now." Excitement vibrated in her mother's thoughtful hum. "Listen to this. According to most of the experts, sawdust in a dream signifies the need to heal an emotional wound that's recently been opened."

She popped straight on her chair. Okay, yeah. That *was* peculiar, considering what she'd been up to all week.

"It's a sign," her mother insisted.

She dropped her head to her bench....

"I spoke to your father this morning. He said he left you a second message."

...and thumped her forehead against the surface.

"You have to speak to him, baby. It's fate."

She rolled upward and straightened. "No. It was a dream, Mom, and your interpretation. What was the other possibility, by the way?"

Her mother hesitated several seconds before giving her answer. "It said something about a fatal mistake looming."

Bingo. "That sounds like the more likely scenario when it comes to Curt, don't you think?"

A sigh blew through the phone's speaker. "CC."

"I'm fine. Kris is fine. Walter's fine. I'm hanging up now, Mom."

"I love you, baby."

"I love you, too."

She tossed the phone to the bench and squeezed the bridge of her nose, then yelped when the phone immediately rang again. Dropping her hand to her lap, she glared at the screen. The glare fizzled as surely as the nervous excitement in her stomach as Tuck's picture appeared. Though she'd given him her number when he asked, this was the first time he'd actually called.

She hesitated. A second ring taunted her, and she mumbled under her breath. "Don't answer, CC. Don't do it. A Tuck-free afternoon will do your willpower a world of good." Curling her fingers into her palm, she scrunched her eyes shut. A third chime sounded, and she squinted with one eye. "Damn it." She snatched up the phone. "Hello?"

"Hi-ya, sunshine. Whatcha doing?"

"I *was* working, but the phone keeps ringing."

His chuckle caressed her ear like stroking fingers. "Don't you hate when that happens?"

She grinned but offered him a snort. "Some people have no respect for work hours."

"Bastards."

The laugh gurgled up and out before she could stop it.

"How long have you been at it?"

She slumped until her elbows were propped on her bench. "About four hours."

He clucked his tongue. "Poor baby. Want me to talk to your boss? She sounds like a slave driver."

"She *can* be."

"She probably wouldn't let you take a few hours off to help out a friend then."

She smiled at his wheedling tone. "Probably not."

"Sounds mean."

"Oh, she can be a real bitch."

"A bitch, huh?" He was silent for several seconds, and then he dropped his tone to a croon. "What's she wearing?"

She didn't bother fighting the laugh this time. "Pervert."

"Hey, I'm a guy. We're wired that way."

She shook her head and smiled. "What do you want, Tuck?"

"You asked me that once before." No trace of teasing humor remained in his voice. "Are you ready to hear the answer?"

She swallowed. Well, she'd walked right into that one, hadn't she? "Uh. Not really."

A deep sigh. "Are you up for a ride?"

"Maybe." She blew out a relieved breath. "Where to?"

"Max asked me to stop by and check out a building he's thinking of buying. Then I thought maybe we could have a late lunch."

The clock on the wall said one. "How long do I have before you get here?"

"About a minute. I'm out front."

She slid from the stool and walked to the door. The red Jeep at the curb was comically distorted through the peephole lens. "Thanks for the advance warning."

He laughed. "I was in the—"

"Neighborhood." She spun and hurried for the stairs. "Yeah, I've heard that before."

"Well, this time it's the truth. You coming out or do I have to come in there and get you?"

"Give me five minutes."

"Geez, women."

She laughed as he disconnected the call, and she took the stairs two at a time.

* * * *

"This place is a dump, Max."

CC stepped over a pile of broken cement blocks and had to agree with Tuck. The stench was so bad her eyes watered. God knew where and what kind of creature had drawn its last breath beneath one of the various piles of discarded rubble.

Max stood in the center of the chaos, his hands on his hips and an easy smile on his face. "You should have seen the building on fifth when I bought it. Made this look like a five star."

"What'd this place used to be, a morgue?" Tuck's nose wrinkled. "Damn, it's rank in here."

"Pussy." Max grimaced and offered her an apologetic smile. "Sorry, CC."

She batted her lashes and waved him off.

"That stink is knocking fifteen percent off my lowball offer."

Tuck smirked and crossed his arms. "You really thinking of buying this rat trap?"

"I signed the papers this morning." Max shoved his fingers into the back pockets of his jeans and dropped his head back to study the high ceiling.

Surprise lit Tuck's eyes. "Well, damn. Congratulations." He looked around with a grimace. "I think."

"What are you planning to do with it?" CC shook her head and attempted to breathe through her mouth.

Arms spread wide, Max grinned. "Welcome to my new fight center and home."

Tuck's mocking laugh echoed off the filthy brick walls. "What are you, some kind of masochist?"

She rolled her eyes. "There's lots of potential here. I think it'll make a fine home. Don't listen to him, Max."

He crossed his arms and winked. "I never do."

A smirk twisted Tuck's lips as if he considered both of them nuts. She moved toward the nearest wall, and he laughed as she tripped on a rotted floorboard.

Max stepped up beside her and rubbed long fingers over the exposed brick, then wiped the black smudge on his jeans. "It'll need to be insulated, but I'm planning to keep as much of the natural brick as possible."

"A little sandblasting would get rid of the..." She leaned closer until her nose was almost pressed to the wall. "Industrial waste?"

Laughing, Tuck hopped over the twisted floorboard to join them. "You've got your work cut out for you, buddy."

"That's why I called you."

Tuck held up both hands. "Don't look at me. I no longer do manual labor unless it's on the field. I *hire* people to do it. Besides, I leave for training camp in a few weeks."

The breath stalled in CC's throat, and she turned away as Max grinned. "I'm more interested in your connections. I've got some major renovations in mind."

CC left them to their discussion of custom shelving and load-bearing walls, and wandered to the other side of the cavernous room. Pretending interest in an empty cavity cut into the brick that looked as if it might have housed a dumbwaiter at some point, she berated her pounding heart. Why should she care if Tuck left town in a couple of weeks? By that point, he'd be out of her life anyway. They had a deal. Plain and simple. So far, he'd lived up to his side of the bargain. She needed to live up to hers.

"You ready, sunshine?"

She turned. Both men watched her, but it was the carefree smile in Tuck's eyes that swelled the pang of loneliness in her heart. In two weeks, he'd be gone. Best she remembered that.

Chapter 12

"Why aren't we going in the front door?"

CC dipped her head to peer out the town car's open door. No windows shed light on the narrow track between the two towering buildings. Dark and gloomy after the lights of Broadway only a few short blocks away, the seedy back alley gave her the creeps. Murky memories threatened. Kris's hand holding hers backstage with rock 'n' roll thumping so loud CC wanted to cover her ears. Cameras flashing as they dashed through similar alleys into the relative safety of an awaiting limo.

Tuck held out his hand, and she shook off the strangling fingers from the past.

"Max and his date are meeting us inside, but I want to say hello to someone before we join them."

She placed her palm in his and stepped onto the curb. A single unmarked door was the only break in the aged brick wall. An ancient lamp struggled to illuminate the blocked letters, announcing the stage entrance to the downtown theater.

Several yards to their right, a small shadow scurried behind a row of wooden crates. She suppressed a shiver. "Does that someone have four legs and a tail?"

He chuckled and rapped his knuckles on the metal door. "Not the last time I looked."

Hinges creaked and light flooded the sidewalk. A wide smile creased the ebony face of the burly man filling the doorway. "Tuck! Hey, man. How the fu—er, sorry ma'am." Ruddy color stained his cheeks as he shot CC a shy smile before turning back to Tuck. "How the hell you doin', man?"

Tuck stuck out his hand for a vigorous shaking. "I'm doing great, Pit. I was hoping you'd be manning the back gate. How's Channelle?"

Laughter danced in the big man's dark chocolate eyes. Deep southern roots echoed in his baritone voice. "Mean as a rattler that's been poked with a stick. She took off a few minutes ago with the kids."

"Damn. You make sure to tell her I said hi."

"Will do, but she's gonna be pissed she missed you."

Tuck grinned. "How many years you been married now?"

"Been ten blissful, terrifyin' years." Pit heaved a pained sigh, but his shoulders shook with mirth.

Tuck turned to CC. "Pit and I crashed helmets before he retired to go into show business. He's the toughest left tackle I ever faced and Channelle is a sweetheart." He indicated the building with a sweep of a flat palm. "They own this place. Pit, this is CC."

"A pleasure, ma'am."

She nodded her greeting as he stepped back and opened the door wide. "You need an escort to Jessi's dressin' room?"

Tuck placed a hand on her lower back and guided her inside the busy staging area. "No. The show starts in a few minutes. We'll see her afterward."

"Jessi?" She spun on him. "As in Jessi and Spence?" When he'd suggested a concert for their next date, he hadn't mentioned country music's Grammy award winning duo or that he knew the superstars personally.

His shoulders rose in an easy shrug. "Jessi's my cousin."

She stared at him. Geez. Talk about a family of overachievers. Obviously, he had more experience with the spotlight of fame than she'd previously thought. "Of course she is."

He grinned at her grumbled tone, grabbed her hand, and clapped the theater owner on the back. "Good to see you, Pit."

"Same here. Don't be a stranger, man."

He shot his friend a two-fingered salute and led her through the backstage maze. They passed only a handful of people as they headed toward the front of the house. After climbing a long set of metal stairs, they left the utilitarian walls and piping of the backstage behind. A hush hung over the plush hallway running nearly the length of the building.

A tuxedoed usher manned his post several feet away and directed them toward a set of double doors. Nerves bubbled in her belly. With the exception of their trips to the park for Walter's lessons, which hadn't proven as bad as she'd expected, their *dates* had been relatively anonymous. The barbeque at the Malones' didn't count. Everyone there was a friend.

Tonight was the first real test of her theory. She was about to step into the lion's den with several thousand strangers, and the knowledge made her knees knock beneath the hem of her silk dress. Would Tuck's comforting presence keep her grounded, or would she lose her nerve, embarrassing herself, and him, in the process?

Maybe they should find a quiet corner and get to the kissing right now.

A hysterical giggle begged for release, and she flicked him a sidelong glance. Without his ball cap and dark glasses, his shaggy, sun-streaked hair and famous face were on display for all to see. Cool, confident, and freaking gorgeous, his dark suit fit his muscular body with mouth-watering precision bound to draw eyes.

He turned his head, caught her studying him, and pulled her to a stop. His fingers squeezed hers. "You okay?"

She slapped her free hand to her belly. "What the hell was I thinking? I can't do this. I think I'm going to throw up."

A soft smile curved his lips.

"Oh sure. Laugh. It's all fun and games until someone blows chunks."

He did laugh then, but he also wrapped her in his arms. She pressed her cheek against the cool material of his lapel and held on. His warm hand rode the slope of her back.

"Breathe, sunshine. You're doing great."

"You wouldn't say that if you knew how badly my legs are shaking."

His chuckle vibrated beneath her cheek. "I can feel them."

"Ohhhh," she groaned.

He contracted his arms in a gentle squeeze. "They're very sexy, even when they're shaking."

A tortured laugh gurgled up and out.

Another squeeze. "You're overthinking things again. Relax."

"How? There are thousands of people in there."

"Yeah." He dropped his chin to rest on the top of her head. "Thousands of people who paid good money to hear my cousin and her partner sing. They'll be looking at the stage. No one will even notice us."

She pulled back enough to look him in the eye. "Says the guy who's been on the cover of six magazines since the beginning of the year."

His teeth flashed in a wicked grin, and his voice dropped to a sly murmur. "Have you been counting?"

She would not blush. She wouldn't, but just in case… She tucked her head back into his chest.

Warm fingers spread over her back and drew lazy circles at her waist. "I'm flattered."

She cleared her throat. Embarrassed, she went on the offense. "Don't be. It was research."

The light swat to her ass made her squeak and jump back. He caught her chin with a crooked forefinger and lifted her face. "You're a beautiful woman. People are always going to look. I say, fuck 'em."

She squeezed her eyes shut against a wave of nausea. "I know this whole stupid idea was mine, Tuck, and I appreciate you stepping up the game by bringing me here, but I don't think I can do this."

He slid his hands up to cup her upper arms. Dipping his head until they were nose to nose, he shook her slightly. "You're stronger than you think, CC Calhoun. A survivor. Those people in there don't know you, and they don't give a damn about you. Why should you care what they think? Are you going to let fear steal the full life that should be yours?"

A harsh laugh escaped and tears stung her eyes and nose. How was he able to peek into her soul? Deep down to where the shadows reigned? Belief gleamed in his eyes. Belief in her. The strength of it, the strength of him, fanned a simmering flame. For him and for the full life he saw in her future.

She shook her head. "No. No, I'm not."

He dropped his forehead to rest against hers. "That's my girl." Straightening, he slid his hands down her arms to link his fingers with hers. "Remember, you're not alone. I'm right here. Just a kiss away."

His grin was so tempting she almost rose on her toes for a taste. She rolled her eyes instead.

Grinning, he squeezed her fingers. "Ready?"

She heaved a long breath and nodded. He released one hand and opened the door.

The excited din of thousands of concertgoers made her stomach muscles contract, but instead of entering the fray on the mezzanine floor as expected, he tugged her into a private balcony suite. She gripped the rail with shaking fingers and gawked at the mob of well-dressed strangers twenty feet below.

Turning her head, she cast him an accusing glare. "You might have mentioned we'd be in the penthouse suite."

His teeth flashed in an innocent smile.

Max and his slim redheaded date were already seated. He stood to greet CC with a warm hug, then introduced them to Amy. The lights began to dim, signaling the show was about to start, and the murmur of voices from below faded. Tuck guided her into a seat and sat beside her.

She leaned close, and he dipped his head toward her to hear her whisper. "How am I supposed to 'fuck 'em', like you suggested, if I never get within an arm's reach?"

His deep bark of laughter drew the attention of the couple in the next suite, along with a handful of people seated in the rows below them. He slid an arm around her shoulders and pressed his lips to her ear. "Baby steps, sunshine. Tonight's about foreplay. We'll get to the fucking…soon."

Holy double entendre. Jerking straight in her seat, she stared at the rising curtain and refused to acknowledge both the compelling tingles of heat causing a near riot in her lower body and the laughing devil at her side.

Along with her gifted singing partner, Jessi Tucker's undeniable talent quickly eclipsed CC's jittery nerves. At the tender age of twenty, Tuck's petite cousin owned the stage with a powerful voice and easy presence even seasoned entertainers would envy. Within minutes, CC found herself clapping along to the country pair's upbeat songs and sighing at the heart-wrenching lyrics. She grinned and decided charm must be a Tucker family trait when his cousin invited one of their young fans on stage for a sing along, then complained good-naturedly at how she was in danger of being replaced. The fine hair on CC's arms stood on end, and she clutched at Tuck's hand when Jessi closed the show by hitting and holding a note CC didn't think was humanly possible.

If she hadn't been a fan before, she was now. The theater began to clear, and she wore a happy smile as their group made their way backstage.

Tuck knocked on Jessi's dressing room door, and they filed inside. Jessi looked over, grinned, and raced across the room to throw herself into Tuck's arms. "You came!"

He laughed and kissed her cheek. "I told you I would."

She dipped her head to the side to peek around his shoulder. "Who'd you bring with you?"

New England roots were evident in her soft voice, so different from the powerhouse pipes and larger-than-life personality she presented on stage. He loosened his arms, and she slid to her booted feet.

"A couple of friends." He tossed an arm over her shoulders and turned. "CC Calhoun, meet my squirt cousin, Jessi Tucker." He pinched a long, dark auburn curl between his fingers and tugged.

Jessi slapped his hand away, but her deep blue eyes twinkled with happiness. "A pleasure."

"The pleasure's mine. The show was incredible."

Twin dimples dented the flawless skin of her piquant smile. "Oh, aren't you good for the ego."

"And this is Amy...." A wince twisted Tuck's lips. "I'm sorry. Max didn't mention your last name."

"It's Dunn." The tall redhead smiled. "CC's right. You and Spence put on quite a show."

Jessi's tinkling laugh was self-depreciating, and she dipped her head conspiratorially. "Spence was great, as usual. Don't tell anyone, but I'm a complete weenie. I suffer from horrible stage fright."

"Could've fooled me."

All eyes shot to Max. Typically, an easy smile rode his tough guy features.

Tuck bumped his chin in his friend's direction. "Uncle Ryan would tear me a new one if he knew I was introducing you to thugs, but this one's name is Max Grayson."

Max bared his teeth in a feral smile. Tuck returned one of his own. Jessi flicked Tuck a disapproving scowl, then turned back to Max. CC followed her gaze, eyeing Max's cropped hair and the dark curve of the tribal tattoo climbing out from beneath the collar of his dress shirt to twine around the back of his neck.

"Don't be mean, Tuck." Jessi's wide-eyed gaze roamed over Max in a bold survey. "Why, I'm sure your friend is a big ol' teddy bear."

Tuck choked on a short laugh. "You got the bear part right."

She waved him off with an airy swing of her hand and fluttered her lashes at Max. "Did I really?"

Confusion crinkled Max's brow. "Did you what?"

"Fool you?" She grinned and cocked her head. "You don't look like the kind of man who'd be easily duped."

Tuck turned on her with an arched brow. "You know a lot about men, do you, little girl?"

Jessi blushed and dropped her gaze to the floor. CC stifled a groan. Men could be such idiots. Clearly he hadn't noticed the fresh light of feminine interest in Jessi's young eyes as she stared at Max. From the indulgent curve of her lips, Amy had.

Max rubbed a palm over the dark stubble shadowing his chin and bent his knees until he could catch Jessi's gaze. "You're right. Not much gets past me. That's why I'm having a hard time buying the stage fright story."

She jerked up straight, and the wounded look in her eyes squeezed CC's heart. Obviously, pride was another family trait. Jessi poked out her chin at a stubborn angle, and the hurt gave way to a pointed glare.

Before she could blast him, he held up a hand. "Hold on. That wasn't an accusation." He shook his head, and his smile softened. "What I should have said is, anyone who can wow a crowd the way you just did has nothing to be afraid of."

Tuck smirked. "Spoken like a true teddy bear."

"Fuck you." A grin stretched Max's lips. "Didn't you say something about a late dinner? I'm starving."

"Max!" Amy's censorious gaze darted to Jessi, then back.

"It's okay, sweetheart." Tuck squeezed his cousin's shoulders. "The squirt grew up in the Tucker clan. She's heard much worse."

Jessi stared at Tuck's friend without blinking, and her melting smile spoke volumes. A twinge of embarrassed guilt made CC bite her lip. Like an unseen voyeur, she watched in helpless fascination as the young starlet lost a little piece of her heart.

Dismay weighed heavily on CC's shoulders as her gaze sliced to Tuck. She knew just how little Jessi Tucker felt.

Chapter 13

"CC? You're awfully quiet. You okay in there?"

She chewed her lower lip and her forehead wrinkled as she peered over her shoulder into the trio of mirrors. Hell no, she wasn't okay. She tugged at the red lace thong bisecting her ass cheeks like crimson dental floss. How did strippers stand these things? And how had Tuck ever persuaded her to agree to this embarrassing exercise? She spun around and popped her head through the slit in the dressing room curtain.

"I'm not stepping one foot out there in this thing."

Like a pasha taking his ease in his private harem, Tuck was sprawled on a soft leather couch surrounded by a half dozen, iridescent silk pillows. Fingers laced on his flat belly, his thickly muscled chest tested the seams of the black, short-sleeved T-shirt molded over his upper body. Beneath khaki shorts, one tanned calf was propped over the other knee.

He shot her an innocent smile. "Aw. Come on. You showed me the others."

True, and the private fashion show had proven a costly mistake. Wasn't her willpower already shaky enough? Self-sabotage wasn't only stupid, it was dangerous. Holy crap, she was playing with fire. But geez, how was she supposed to stay focused on holding him off when everything within her cried out to step into his arms and discover what all those sensual promises in his eyes and kisses were about?

Still, who knew standing before a man in a tiny bikini would be so…titillating? Or that the blatant desire in his eyes would deliver an irresistible sense of feminine power? Uh-huh, and that feminine power had nothing on the tempting fantasies his heated gaze produced.

She winced and tugged the curtain tight around her face. "Yeah, well, the others had actual material. This thing is nothing more than a couple of strings and three quarter-sized scraps of lace. I'm practically naked."

The smile slid from his face. Ruddy color bloomed on his cheekbones, and his eyes blazed with wicked intent. He dropped his foot to the floor, and his palms went to his knees as he sat forward. "Then I'll join you in there."

She nearly ripped the curtain down as she jerked an arm through the panels and held out her hand, palm forward. "Don't you dare!"

His lips turned down in a pout worthy of a five-year-old, but to her immense relief, he remained seated. "That's not fair. I want to see."

"I mean it, Tucker. Don't get off that couch."

He shook his head. "That's just mean, sunshine."

Mean or not, she meant what she said. If he thought she'd let him, or anyone else, get a peek at her in this obscene excuse for swimwear, he was off in the head. He sprawled back on the couch, but she didn't trust his acquiescence for a second and hesitated closing the curtain to rid herself of the stripper suit. Thankfully, the boutique owner provided a timely diversion. She entered the private salon and bent to slip a napkin and a glass of sparkling wine on the low table in front of him.

"Is there anything else I can get you, Mr. Tucker?"

His trademark dimples flashed and boyish anticipation sparkled in his eyes. "Well, Alison, now that you mention it. Got any pizza in that back room?"

The stylishly dressed merchant didn't blink an eye at his ridiculous request. No doubt the dollar signs spinning in her eyes had caused her lids to malfunction.

"Pizza can be arranged. What toppings do you prefer?"

"Oh, for heaven's sake." CC yanked the curtains closed and tore at the strings of the miniscule top barely encasing her nipples. She stripped the thong from her hips and tossed the offending garment onto the tufted couch. Grabbing her panties, and shoving her legs into them, she grumbled beneath her breath. "You're an idiot, CC, and he's the devil."

Shorts pulled on and buttoned, she snatched up her blouse. The couch held half of the two dozen colorful bikinis she'd voluntarily donned and modeled over the last hour and a half. Her gaze fell on a silky, teal number, and she shivered, recalling the male appreciation in Tuck's eyes as she modeled it.

She frowned. *There's nothing wrong with your old suit. Lots of women wear a one piece.*

Her shoulders sagged on a weighty sigh. She was in trouble. Big trouble. Tossing the strap of her purse over one shoulder, she exited the changing room and stalked by him without glancing his way. He leaped to his feet and, laughing like a loon, trailed after her as she headed for the nearest exit. Before she could reach the front door, he wrapped his fingers around her arm and tugged her to a stop.

The boutique owner spoke behind them. "Oh, dear. Is there a problem?"

He turned and brought CC with him. "No problem, but you can cancel that pizza."

With precise bearing, the shop owner clasped her hands at her waist. She didn't even glance CC's way. "Have you made your choices?"

He turned to CC and cocked his head. "Have we?"

"I don't need—"

"Admit it. You liked the pink one." He dipped his head, bringing his face closer, and dropped his voice to an intimate croon. "And the sexy teal one. So did I."

Heat fired in her chest and raced to her cheeks. The devil had the audacity to grin, and without waiting for a response, instructed Alison to ring up the two suits.

* * * *

An hour later, Tuck wheeled the Jeep into a private, gated community. Waved through by the smiling guard manning the booth, they passed the sculpted lawns of spectacular homes, each one grander than the next.

"Where *exactly* are we going?" When they'd swung by her place to pick up Walter and she asked where they were headed, he'd answered simply, "the beach." She'd assumed they were headed for one of New Jersey's many public beaches, but homes like these didn't occupy the coastline where the throngs spent their days sunning and surfing. The moneyed set had their own exclusive real estate and guarded it well.

"A friend of mine has a place on the water. It's beautiful. You'll love it."

Before she could comment, he turned the Jeep onto a cobbled drive and stopped before a ten-foot-tall curved iron gate. He punched a code into a panel inset in a brick wall, and the gate swung open. Her jaw nearly dropped when the sprawling mansion, looking more like a five-star resort than a private home, came into view.

At least two dozen chimneys rose from a series of pitched roofs, above what she estimated was close to one hundred windows. A second, smaller version of the grand structure sat in the distance. She'd been raised by a rock star, at least until she was nine, and had experienced the creature comforts that came with the kind of wealth most people only dreamed of, but this was ridiculous.

"Who *is* this friend?" She dipped her head for a better view through the windshield as he brought the vehicle to a stop. "A Kennedy?"

He laughed and twisted his upper body to tug a pair of red swim trunks from beneath Walter, where he perched on the backseat. "Nothing so glamorous. He spends his time on Wall Street, not Pennsylvania Avenue. Come on."

Walter leaped out of the Jeep after him and loped off to investigate a row of crisply sculpted shrubs. Tuck rounded the hood as she slid out the passenger door. The blue of the Atlantic sparkled beyond the canopy of lush trees. He guided her down a brick path, and they left the buildings behind.

"Aren't you going to stop in to say hi and at least let your friend know we're here?"

"I would if he was in residence, but he's not. We have the place to ourselves." He slowed his steps. "Did you want a tour before we hit the beach?"

She shot a quick glance over her shoulder and shook her head. "The sun would be down before we finished."

He grinned and grabbed her hand.

They passed through a second gate at the back of the property, and like a postcard, a half mile cove of pristine sand and surf greeted them. A flock of gulls skittered back and forth at the edge of the water. Walter spotted them and raced off to give chase. Far off in the distance, a lone figure cast a line into the churning surf, but otherwise, the beach was empty.

She glanced around with a frown. "There's nobody here."

"Yeah." A satisfied sigh lifted his chest. "Ain't it great?"

To their left, a glass-fronted bungalow edged the sand. Several lounge chairs occupied the charming wraparound deck. He produced a key from the pocket of his shorts and tugged her up the steps, then paused. His shrill whistle pierced the air. Walter pivoted in a wide arc and raced back.

The open floor plan included a comfortable seating area, a small kitchen, and a full bar.

"There's a bathroom through there where you can change." He bumped his chin toward a set of double doors at the back of the room and moved behind the granite island to the bar. He bent to open a mini-fridge. "Do you want something to drink?"

"I'll take a bottled water if they have it."

He straightened with a beer bottle in hand. One sandy blond brow arched over his laughing eyes. "Water?"

She shrugged. "It's important to stay hydrated."

He shook his head and pulled a water from the fridge. "Puritan."

She snatched the bottle from his hand and ignored his chuckle to stalk toward the double doors. Inside the full bathroom, decorated in a beach theme of pale blue and yellow tiles, she blew out a heavy breath and sagged against the closed doors. An afternoon spent alone on a private beach with Tuck wasn't what she'd had in mind when she proposed her dating theory and, after that bikini fashion show, was far too intimate a prospect for her shaky equilibrium.

They needed to have another conversation on the fundamentals of her dating theory, but after his whispered comment the other night, she was reluctant to bring up the subject.

We'll get to the fucking...soon. That was what she was afraid of or, more precisely, not afraid enough.

She bumped the back of her head against the wooden door and welcomed the dull lash of pain. With his smiling eyes and broad shoulders, the man was a walking temptation. And, damn it, the irresistible pull of his larger-than-life persona wasn't just physical. He was also a nice guy.

The trouble was, he didn't fit into the self-centered, player's mold where her experience insisted he belonged. Unlike her father, who demanded every ounce of attention from those who had the misfortune of spending time in his presence, Tuck didn't seem to have a selfish bone in his body. With each moment they spent together, her lifelong distrust of men battered against those moments of gentleness, caring, and loyalty he displayed.

She'd willingly waded into uncharted waters. If she didn't watch out, she was going to drown.

Nerves danced in her belly as she pushed off the door. She shoved aside the disturbing musing and dug through her bag. Her fingers hesitated on the silky material of the teal bikini.

Hmm. You think this is sexy, huh?

Self-preservation reared its head, and she tossed the suit aside. She bypassed the pink one as well and held up her own navy blue one-piece. As armor went, the two-year-old suit was beyond ridiculous, but in an emergency, one used whatever was at hand.

Five minutes later, false bravado firmly in place, she stalked through the opened doorway. All thought of armor and self-preservation flew from her mind as her feet stumbled to a stop. Across the room at the wall of windows, Tuck faced the panoramic view of the Atlantic. The bright red trunks rode low on his hips, but otherwise, his muscular body was bared to her view. A healthy tan deepened his skin to a light bronze, highlighted by the serrated, barbed wire tattoos wrapped around his thick biceps. The artist in her sighed in appreciation. The woman fought a sensual shiver.

His wasn't the first bare, male back she'd ever seen. The billboards of Time's Square flashed advertisements featuring the sculpted bodies of bare-chested men on a regular basis, and she'd been to art school. Granted, she'd been the class freak, slipping in at the last moment to take a seat in the back of the room and leaving long before class ended, but thanks to numerous anatomy lessons with live models, she'd documented the muscle and sinew of the naked male form in numerous mediums. However, none of those gym-sculpted bodies came close to the picture of male perfection that was Tuck.

A hot fluttering churned low in her belly as she slid her sketchbook and charcoals from her bag. Some temptations weren't meant to be resisted, after all.

On bare feet, she crossed the distance to toss her bag on the long couch. "Don't move."

Of course, he didn't listen. He turned to face her as Walter rose from the rug near the door to pad toward her. She twirled her finger in a turnaround motion, flipped open her pad to a blank page, and sat. "This won't take long. Turn around and look out at the water for a few minutes."

He propped his hands on his hips. "Why would I do that when there's a much better view right in front of me?" His gaze dropped to the square cut neckline of her suit, then roamed over her breasts and belly to skim down her legs. A crooked smile tweaked his lips when he looked up again. "Very nice."

She refused to acknowledge the fingers of pleasure dancing over her skin at his appreciative inspection and rolled her eyes. "Turn around, Tuck."

Silent laughter twinkled in his eyes, but he complied.

She selected a pencil, and without taking her eyes off the line of his shoulder blades, drew the charcoal across the page in swift strokes. Shadows and lines quickly gave form to well-defined deltoids and the deep crevice of his spine.

"Do you always carry a sketchbook with you?"

She smudged at the curve of one shoulder joint with the pad of her thumb. "I'm an artist. It's required." His shoulders shifted on a soft chuckle, and her pencil paused. "What?"

"Looks like I'm going to get to see your etchings after all."

A smile tugged at her lips. "Who says I'm going to show you?"

He glanced over his shoulder and blasted her with a boyish grin. "I'll show you mine if you show me yours."

Her gaze slid down his mostly bare form, and she swallowed. If he showed her any *more* of his, she'd go under for sure. She pointed a stiff finger at the window, and with a laugh, he turned back to the view.

Typically, he didn't remain silent. "Have you always carried pencils and paper with you?"

She glanced up at the innocent question. Dark memories flooded her mind, and her fingers clenched around the pencil. She stared at his back, all sleek lines and muscled curves. He hadn't pushed her on the kidnapping or her family since overhearing Curt's message, and the lack of pressure had made his offer to listen if she wanted to talk oddly tempting.

Why the idea tugged at her so strongly, she wasn't sure. She'd never been comfortable speaking about the events of her childhood with anyone, including the countless therapists her mother dragged her to over the years. And yet, for reasons she didn't understand, she trusted him.

She chewed at her lip in indecision. Invisible scars shaped her life, but wasn't that the whole point of her dating theory? Her memories and the debilitating hold they had on her were the reason she was here with him. Would baring her soul to Tuck help heal the scars once and for all, or simply make the bleeding worse?

Are you going to let fear steal the full life that should be yours?

Damn it. No, she wasn't. She'd already stepped outside her self-imposed box with their dating agreement. Maybe it was time she took the next step.

A deep breath filled her lungs, and nerves tightened her voice. "Not until after the kidnapping."

He turned slowly to face her, and his penetrating gaze held her captive. No trace of humor showed on his sober face, and his lips were compressed into a flat line. Silence stretched between them, and she nearly lost her nerve. An embarrassing tremor shook her hands, and she set aside the sketchpad. She held on to the charcoal as if it were a lifeline.

"You were right the other night when you guessed I was spooked about going into the woods. I don't venture into the forest. Ever."

He dipped his chin in a brief nod. "You were held in the woods?"

She dropped her gaze to the pencil she held and drew her thumb over the tip, leaving a black smudge behind. "In an old cabin." A shudder rippled through her as she revisited the trauma of her childhood memories. Her voice rose several octaves, making her sound almost childlike, but she couldn't help it. "For years I had nightmares about creepy, gnarled trees grabbing at me as I ran through the dark."

His bare feet appeared in her field of vision, and he crouched in front of her. She lifted her gaze and locked on to the steady security in his blue eyes.

"Th-the m-men who took me kept me locked in a closet. It was very dark, but sometimes, light would creep beneath the crack under the door. Enough to see my surroundings. I found a broken crayon in the corner, and whenever I got really scared, I drew pictures on the back of the door."

"Sunshine." His tortured whisper pierced the menacing fog swirling through her mind like a malevolent wraith. He rested his palm over the top of her hand to still its slashing movements as if she marked the door of her prison even now.

A jagged whimper racked her body, and she struggled to return to the present. His hands came to her arms, but she reared back. When he would have dropped his hands to bracket her hips on the couch, she grabbed one and squeezed his fingers and hoped he understood. What she needed was a lifeline, not a rescue. If she was going to escape the past and its ghosts, she'd have to do so on her own.

She shuddered on a cleansing breath and shook her head. "I never saw their faces. They wore masks and left me alone for the most part, but whenever I heard one of them coming to check on me, I hid the crayon in my sock so they wouldn't take it."

She dropped her gaze to the pencil in her clenched fingers. "I don't remember a lot about the night the FBI found me. Mostly, it's just blurred images and fear, but the crayon was on the nightstand when I woke up in the hospital the next morning." She looked up. "It's blue."

The warm palm he cupped over her cheek heated her chilled skin. "It *is*, as in you kept it?"

"Yeah." She nodded and scalding tears stung her eyes. Her laugh came out as a wry cough. "Weird, huh? But the thing is, more than the thousands of people who were searching for me, more than the FBI agent who discovered the cabin, and the men who got me out"—she squeezed her eyes shut as the tears welled and overflowed—"that crayon saved my life."

The pad of his thumb brushed through the salty trail on her cheek in a gentle caress, and he dipped his head until only their mingled breath separated their lips. "Not weird. Brave."

Chapter 14

A pleasured sigh shivered through CC as Tuck covered her mouth with his. The slide of his lips over hers wasn't gentle. Need and urgency accompanied the deep plunge of his tongue. A blast of fire heated her from the inside, and she answered the call, tangling her tongue with his in a desperate plea for more.

The world tipped as he surged up and forward. A strong arm bracketed her waist, and she thrilled to the friction of his hard chest against her peaked nipples. Warm fingers spread over the skin of her back, left bare by the low dip of her suit, and guided her down until she lay sprawled on the couch. He joined her, all tangled arms and legs, and the weight of him, solid and delicious and covering her from chest to knees, dragged forth a moan.

He ended the kiss, lifting his head, and the breath caught in her throat. Shaggy, sun-dipped hair fell forward to frame the tight lines of his face. Dark and stormy, his eyes gleamed with sensual intent, but there was a question in them as well.

Did he think she wasn't with him? Completely and without reserve?

Like the mist after a summer storm, her doubts evaporated beneath the heat of his study. The question of whether or not she was making a colossal mistake by opening herself to him, emotionally or physically, no longer mattered. Nothing this strong could be wrong.

She answered his silent question by tangling her fingers in his hair and dragging his mouth back to hers. His low groan shimmered through his chest to hers and awoke a hunger she'd never known. Her nipples, already tight with need, prickled with a painful urgency as they rasped against the hard plains of his chest. Her body surged upward in a feline arch as if it had a mind of its own. The move shifted his weight and ground his erection against her mound.

Her senses went flying.

She gasped into his mouth and swiveled her hips. The contact sent shards of unbearable pleasure ricocheting outward from her clit. Adrenaline, thick and strangely numbing, oozed through her bloodstream and left a languid heaviness behind. Who knew the simple press of male flesh on her sensitive nerve endings would feel this good?

"Oh my God."

He lifted his head. A grin tweaked his lips. "Like that, do you?"

She swallowed but couldn't find the words to describe her surprise and pleasure. A nod was all she could manage.

"Me, too."

He dipped his head to cover her lips in a blazing kiss, nipping, sucking. His tongue sunk deep, and his fingers trailed a warm path from her lower thigh to her hip. Every part of her clamored for more. Beneath closed lids, her eyes rolled back in her head.

Oh dear Lord. The devil has magic hands and a freaking magical mouth.

He proved her silent claim true a moment later when his lips left hers and traveled in a sensual tour over her cheek. A gentle bite on her earlobe and her eyes flew open. Moist heat bathed the shell of her ear as he soothed the lobe with his tongue. She stared at the ceiling and welcomed her body's natural response. A much hotter moistness swelled the secret folds between her thighs.

Need, primal and instinctive, demanded she move, and she desperately wanted to touch. Since the moment she'd left the bathroom and her gaze had fallen on his beautiful back, her fingers had itched to explore the adorable twin dimples peaking just above the low cut of his suit.

She wrapped her arms around his shoulders and slid her palms down the smooth muscles of his back. He was so big. So solid. So warm. Frustration nearly made her growl as her fingertips encountered material where those dimples should be. She dipped her hand beneath his waistband but never reached her goal.

She froze and lost track of her thoughts. How was a woman supposed to think with a man's callused hand riding up her thigh, over her waist to the underside of her breast? Tiny shivers of excited anticipation raised bumps on her skin, and her nipples puckered painfully. A low moan vibrated in her chest as he shifted his upper body and cupped her mound with his wide palm. The moan became a tortured gasp at the press of his thumb on the hardened bud beneath her suit.

Piercing, white-hot lightning shot through her, and her hips jerked in reaction. Her breath came in pants. "Tuck!"

Eyes glittering, he smiled, though tension rode his features. "It's okay, sunshine. This is part of that petting you were curious about." The tip of one finger dipped beneath the silky material of her suit at her left breast. He tugged until the strap slipped down her arm and her breast was exposed. The cobalt blue of his irises deepened as he stared at the plump mound. He swept his thumb across the bottom curve, and a dark smile curved his lips. "You're beautiful."

Shifting on one muscled arm, he lowered his head until his lips hovered a breath away from her straining nipple. "So beautiful."

He stabbed at the tightened bud with the tip of his tongue. Balanced on a knife edge of pleasure and pain, she jerked convulsively. A rumble of encouragement vibrated in his throat as he laved the oversensitive tip with wet heat.

Tugging at the other strap, he dragged the suit farther down her body. His hand continued lower, slipping beneath the material, and his long fingers spread over the bare skin of her belly.

Hot! She was freaking hot, and watching what he was doing didn't help. She was an artist. Her work often manifested itself in sensual lines, but she'd never seen anything as erotic as the sight of his gilded head against her pale skin. His wide mouth and firm lips paying sweet homage to her breast. His large hand buried beneath her suit while his talented fingers slowly approached the junction of her thighs.

He turned his head, and his heated gaze locked with hers. She panted and anticipation tightened her stomach muscles. A wicked grin curved his mouth as he lowered his head and closed his lips around the fullness of her breast and sucked. Hard.

Sensations she'd never known, never knew existed, tumbled through her like crashing waves. She squirmed beneath him. "Please."

His throaty hum pulsed against her flesh as his fingers slid into the tight nest of curls between her thighs. A buzzing began in her ears. She might be a virgin, but she wasn't a stranger to the forerunners of orgasm. A woman had needs, after all, even one with a natural distrust of men, but nothing she'd ever experienced on her own could have prepared her for Tuck's touch.

Disappointment surged through her when her nipple popped free of his lips and his fingers stilled in their quest. He turned his head, and frustration burned hot in his eyes.

She pushed up on her elbows. Why had he stopped, and why was he glaring at her bag?

Confusion cooled the haze of lust, and as if a switch was flipped, the buzzing in her ears became a distinctive ringtone. Her eyes slid shut, and she flopped back to the couch.

Oh, Mom. Your timing is terrible. As usual.

His fingers dragged over her belly, and he pulled his hand out from beneath her suit. She opened her eyes and wanted to cry as he tugged the straps up over her arms, covering her.

"You should probably get that."

She stared into his sober gaze for a long moment, then rolled to her side. He shifted his weight enough for her to reach into her bag. Thumbing the phone's screen, she answered the call. "Hello, Mom."

"Where are you, baby? Are you all right?"

The muscles of his arms bulged as he pushed off her. He jammed the fingers of one hand into his hair and mouthed, "I'm going for a swim". Her gaze zoomed in on the impressively tented front of his trunks until he turned abruptly and stalked for the door with Walter following.

Her eyelids slid shut, but the enticing image stayed with her. "I'm fine, Mom. I'm at the beach." She jackknifed her legs and rolled to stand. Moving to the windows, she watched as Tuck's long legs carried him across the sand and into the surf where he dove clean and disappeared beneath the waves. Walter bounded after him with joyous abandon.

"Are you sure, baby? I sensed a strange vibration in your aura and got concerned."

Her gaze jerked to the couch she'd just vacated. Well, hell. Could hovering on the brink of orgasm vibrate one's aura? Thankfully, her slightly hysterical laugh sounded more like a cough. "Nope, no vibrating here." Well, except for the remnant weakness in her shaking legs.

"That's odd. Maybe I'm sensing a forerunner to something that hasn't happened yet."

If you'd called three minutes later....

"Oh, well. Time will tell. Do you have any idea what time you'll be home?"

The hair stood up on CC's neck. "Not really. Why? Where are *you*?"

A slight hesitation, then, "I decided to do a little shopping so I flew in this morning."

Great. Just what I need.

"Shopping? More like you flew in to try and convince me to see Curt."

"That's not true, I—"

"Mom." She slid her fingers through her tangled curls and shoved them back from her face.

"Okay, that's part of it, but I can't help it. The time has come for you and your father to put the bitterness behind you. Besides, I've missed you and Kris. Can't a mother spend some time with her girls?"

She heaved a sigh as Tuck rose from the waves with his back to the shore. He shook his head, and a spray of water shot out in all directions from his shaggy mane. "I'm not questioning your motives, Mom. I know what they are and don't want to spend the next few days arguing."

"Then we simply won't argue."

She dropped her chin to her chest. As usual, her mother's sunny promise masked the determination behind her true quest. "How long will you be in town?"

"Oh, no more than a couple of days, maybe three."

Her eyes slid shut. Three days? With Tuck leaving for training camp in less than two weeks, every day was precious.

"It'll be fun. We'll do lunch and visit a few museums, and I really do need to shop."

She sighed. "Where are you? Do you need to be picked up?"

"No, I'm fine. I'm at the Plaza. Will you be home in time for dinner? I thought we could meet at Carmine's. My treat."

On the beach, the roped muscles of Tuck's arm bunched as he chucked a rock into the surf. Walter dove in head first to retrieve it. "I'll be there. What time?"

"I made reservations for seven."

"Fine. I'll see you in a little while. I've got to go."

"Okay, baby. We're going to have fun. You'll see."

Right. Her mother pestering her to see Curt for two days…maybe three? Yeah, that sounded like a blast.

"Bye, Mom." She thumbed the phone and tossed it to the couch.

On the beach, Tuck bent to pick up another rock. He sent the stone flying, and she gnawed at her lip. He'd nearly brought her to orgasm only moments before—would have, if not for her mother's untimely interruption, and she had no idea what happened next. Had he fled so quickly because she'd made it clear discussing her family was off limits and wanted to give her privacy? Or was he upset she'd taken her mother's call at such a moment? The erection straining the seams of his suit proved tossing rocks to her dog on the beach wasn't how he saw the next few minutes going.

As bold as he was, she doubted he'd let her act as if that heavy duty petting session never happened. Not that she would. She'd made her bed—she huffed at the apropos expression—and wasn't at all disappointed at the thought of sleeping in it. No. Of her own freewill, she'd stepped over a line she never thought she could, both emotionally *and* physically, and the sky hadn't fallen. Quite the contrary. For the first time in her adult life, victory over the neuroses that kept her chained seemed possible, and a normal life dangled within her reach. She'd be damned if she'd crawl back into her self-induced cave of exile.

Perhaps the vibration her mother claimed she sensed was the brand new hope of freedom pulsing in her heart. Whether he knew it or not, Tuck's brash and bold assistance was largely responsible for her transformation from frightened rabbit to optimistic woman. She owed him a debt she couldn't ever repay, but she planned to try.

Her head flooded with possible scenarios of how she could show her appreciation, and she cleared her throat. He was right. For a virgin, she did have a dirty mind.

Her only concern was protecting her heart in the process. It would be so easy to fall for him. She was already halfway there. No, guarding her heart was essential, because she obviously had no willpower when it came to her sexy, freedom muse, and it was only a matter of time until they consummated what they'd left unfinished with the ringing of her phone.

Their agreement would end in less than two weeks, but she'd survived nearly two decades under debilitating panic attacks. Surely, she could keep her heart detached for so short a time. And if she failed? Well, she'd cross that bridge if and when she came to it. The demon lust dealer had done his work well. One taste, and her mouth, along with another hot and greedy body part, watered for more.

After plucking several towels from the cabinet near the door, she stepped outside and descended the steps to the sand. Uncertainty dragged at her feet. What, exactly, did one say to a man who had recently sucked your nipples while his fingers played your body like a master musician?

She eyed Tuck where he continued the game of fetch with Walter a dozen yards off to her right. He was a man who met life's battles head on. It made sense to tear a page from his playbook and do the same.

As if sensing her presence, he turned. He bumped up his chin in greeting, but his usual boyish smile was absent.

Oh, hell. The direct approach would have to wait, at least until her maniacally beating heart slowed enough to allow her to breathe.

Dropping the towels on the sand where they'd stay dry, she broke into a run. She hit the surf, and as she'd watched Tuck do minutes earlier, she arched into a dive.

* * * *

Tuck waded into the water as CC reemerged from her dive to bob in the chest high waves. Pushing through the surf toward her, he studied her face. A pink blush stained her high cheekbones, and her full lips were drawn tight in a flat line. Clearly she was rattled over the heavy petting they'd indulged in. Considering her lack of experience, he'd have been surprised if she weren't. But virginal embarrassment didn't account for the haunting shadows in her thickly lashed eyes, any more than guilt over touching her as he had was responsible for the cataclysmic shifting in his chest.

Jesus. Locked in a closet. Most nine-year-olds would have closed in on themselves in terror and, in a way, she had, but she'd also grabbed at survival, clutching it in her fingers in the form of a blue crayon.

She had no idea how strong she was, but he did.

He ignored the heavy pounding of his heart, knocking against his ribs as the urge to rip apart her kidnappers clashed with a longing to wrap her in his arms and promise her nothing would ever hurt her again. The former wasn't possible, but neither was it necessary. The men responsible for holding her in the woods would live out their lives in five by eight cells, suffering much worse than the pain from a few broken bones. As for the latter… She might have turned to fire in his arms, singeing both his mind and body with her heated response, but that was simple chemistry. Nothing had actually changed. They had a deal. A short-term one, and exposing his growing primal need to hold her close and protect her from the world's harms would only scare her off.

He floated close, holding her gaze. "You okay?"

She shoved dripping hair out of her face. "I, uh…well."

He smiled softly and scraped a fingertip over her cheek to pluck a clinging hank of hair away and tuck it behind her ear. "Take a breath, sunshine. We'll get to what happened on the couch, I promise, but, for now, I assume that was your mother on the phone. Is there a problem?"

Her harsh laugh was muffled by the palm she dragged over her face and mouth. "Not exactly." They rose on a swelling wave, and she curved her lips in a weak smile. "She's in town for a couple days."

He treaded water at her side. "That's a bad thing?"

She turned her head to stare out at the horizon. Like diamonds on an endless bed of blue, the sunlight sparkled on the water, but the sight paled against the sober intensity of her profile. "She wants me to see Curt."

"And you don't want to." It wasn't a question.

She turned and met his gaze with haunted eyes. "No, I don't." She dipped her head and looked away. "If that makes me sound like a selfish bitch, so be it. I don't owe him a damn thing."

The band around his heart squeezed tighter at the bitterness of her tone. He'd once asked about the root cause of her attacks and had a sneaking suspicion he'd just found the source. He drifted closer on a rising wave. "I was pretty young at the time, but I remember seeing a picture of you with your father after the kidnapping. The two of you looked pretty close. What happened?"

She jerked her head up to stare. "Pictures can be deceiving. Even when hundreds are taken. Especially then."

He shook his head. "I don't understand."

"I know. I'm sorry." She squeezed her eyes shut briefly and sighed. "As frightening as the kidnapping was, the months following were worse. Curt's sister, Kris's mother, was killed in a car accident two months before the kidnapping, and Kris had come to live with us. Instead of taking us away somewhere private where we could heal and feel safe, my father booked a year-long tour and took us along as props. He never missed an opportunity to toss me in front of the cameras."

Anger bulged the clenching muscles of Tuck's treading arms.

"I was nine and on the verge of a breakdown. I couldn't eat *or* sleep. The nightmares were..." She shuddered and a sudden sheen of tears shimmered in her eyes. "Nothing mattered but Curt's floundering career. For a rocker on the verge of invisibility, the sudden publicity was like winning the lottery."

"Jesus." Tuck swam closer, needing to touch her, to remind her the painful memories were all in the past and could no longer hurt her, but that wasn't true. The memories tortured her still. He rubbed a hand down her arm. "What about your mother? Didn't she see what was happening?"

CC sniffed and blinked away her tears. "She's always been blind when it comes to Curt, and she was busy with her modeling career at the time. It wasn't until six months later when she opened her eyes, after a mutual friend of her and my father's cornered her and threatened to kidnap me himself. I have no idea what was said or what kind of threat she used to wrest us away from Curt, but I was almost ten and weighed fifty-three pounds when she whisked me and Kris to a small villa in Italy. I haven't seen him since."

Dark and lethal, fury churned in the depths of Tuck's soul. His stomach muscles clenched, and his fingers curled with the need to clamp around her father's throat and squeeze in repayment of every hurt he'd caused his daughter. But killing Curt Jensen wouldn't release her from the terror she'd labored under all these years. Only facing her fears and putting them behind her could do that.

Tuck wanted nothing more than to stand by her side and help her do that—if she'd only let him. His gaze roamed over her face before locking on her eyes. "Then maybe it's time you did."

Chapter 15

Walter squeezed inside the moment CC opened the door to her condo. He padded straight to his toy box to retrieve one of Tuck's old shoes, then across the floor toward Kris and Ronald. They stood with their backs to CC at the shelves holding her finished works.

"The gallery owner practically begged me to convince her. It's the opportunity of a lifetime." Her agent ran a fingertip over *Yearning*.

Kris crossed her arms. "Obviously, CC doesn't see it that way."

A grunt of frustration rumbled in Ronald's throat. "She has the kind of talent that could make her famous, but does she listen?" He looked down at Walter when the dog bumped against his thigh as he wiggled between them to grin up at Kris.

CC gritted her teeth and shut the door with a thump. "Maybe I don't want to be famous."

Ronald jumped and spun around to face her. Guilt stretched his smile thin.

Kris yanked the tattered shoe from Walter's mouth and tossed it into the hallway. "Hey, Cees. Look who I found loitering on the stoop. Oh, and you'll never guess who's in town."

"I heard." She crossed the room to dump her bag on her workbench.

Her cousin zeroed in on her nose. "Then you'd better do something about that Rudolph beak. How many times has Natalie told us, 'sun damage isn't only dangerous, it leaves wrinkles'?"

She touched her nose and winced at the sunburn's heat. Great. One more thing for her mother to complain over. Her gaze met Ronald's. He struggled with a smile. It withered and died when she arched an accusing brow.

"I didn't expect you." Although she probably should have. He'd left several messages saying he needed to see her but, embarrassed over their last encounter, she'd been avoiding him.

Ever the gentleman, he didn't mention the calls or the encounter. "I'm sorry to barge in unannounced, but I was hoping to talk to you." He ran his gaze down her legs, bare under her shorts, and cleared his throat. "If this isn't a good time, I can come back later."

"I—"

"Don't worry about me." Kris gathered her laptop case and small Prada clutch from the couch. "I'll be upstairs freshening up for dinner." She flicked a glance at the clock on the wall. "Keep an eye on the time. You know how your mother hates to be late." She swept from the room without another word to Ronald.

CC shook her head, crossed her arms, and turned on her agent. "What were you talking to Kris about?"

"I—"

"Don't ever go behind my back, Ronald. I consider that type of thing a deal breaker."

He had the grace to wince. "I wasn't. Honestly." His gaze slid to the empty hallway leading to her and Kris's upstairs apartment. "All I did was mention the gallery's offer, and she started pounding me with questions."

Of course she had. Kris was nothing if not protective. For whatever reason, she disliked and distrusted Ronald. She probably considered grilling him her duty. "I know how pushy my cousin can be, which is why I haven't immediately tossed you out the door."

He shoved his hands into the pockets of his slacks. "I'm sorry. I shouldn't have shown up without letting you know I was coming."

Walter nosed his favorite toy into her palm. She tossed it over the couch. "Forget it. What did you need to talk to me about?"

He cleared his throat. "I've been thinking about what you asked me last week."

Oh, shit. Would this day ever end? Her proposition was the *last* subject she wanted to discuss with him. She turned her back to walk to the fridge and pulled out a bottle of water. "I told you to forget that. It was a stupid idea."

"I disagree."

Her fingers paused in the act of twisting off the bottle cap, and she turned slowly.

His dark gaze held hers, but he shuffled his feet as if the subject made him nervous as well. "I feel awful about the way I reacted to your request."

I've stepped into a nightmare.

She rolled her head back and stared at the ceiling. "Ronald, please. I told you—"

"Hear me out." His strained smile didn't reach his eyes when she dropped her head and met his gaze. "Your offer was honest and sweet, and I flung it back at you like an asshole."

True, but still…

"I'm sorry. If you can forgive me…" Change jingled in his pocket as he breathed deeply. "I'm hoping you'll give me a do-over."

She blinked. "Do-over?" Trepidation tensed her muscles as his smile turned hopeful.

"I'd like to change my answer."

Oh, geez. Talk about awkward. How was she supposed to explain her offer hadn't been sweet *or* honest? She'd simply needed a man, and he was the only one she knew. Well, except for Tuck, and… She frowned. "Wait. What about the new woman?"

His shoulders rolled in a careless shrug. "That didn't work out."

What am I, the consolation prize? She sipped from the bottle. "I'm sorry to hear that but, as it happens, I've started seeing someone."

"Kevin Tucker?"

Surprise widened her eyes. So much for worrying their dates so far had been too anonymous to properly test her theory. She rarely read the papers and hadn't had time to think since meeting Tuck, much less pay attention to headlines. Was it common knowledge the Marauders' lady killer wide receiver had found himself this month's woman? As far as she knew, they hadn't drawn the attention of anyone in the press, but that didn't mean some enterprising reporter hadn't snapped a picture from behind a tree somewhere.

The possibility had her suppressing a shiver. "Yes. How'd you know?"

His brows rose as if in surprise. "I stopped by the other day, and he was here. Didn't he tell you?"

"No, he didn't." And she'd be asking him why the hell not as soon as she saw him.

"Strange. I asked him to."

She shrugged off her disquiet to ask a question of her own. "If you've known I've been seeing Tuck for days, why ask for a do-over now?"

For a moment, an odd tension tightened Ronald's jaw. Disappointment? Or was anger the cause of his clenched teeth? She dismissed the possibility even as the thought formed. Although his personality tended toward serious, in all the time she'd known him, she'd never once seen Ronald angry.

Whatever emotion she had imagined was gone almost as quickly as it appeared. Concern darkened his eyes, and yet, his words held the sharp edge of condescension. "Because I'm worried about you, CC. He's got a reputation for using women and then walking away. I'd hate to see you get hurt."

So would she and, up until a few days ago, she might have agreed with his sentiment. Not anymore. After what she'd shared with Tuck about her father, his suggestion it was time she see Curt bristled, and she'd have to deal with that, but she no longer believed the worst of Tuck's press. Sure, he was a player, but he was also an honorable man. She couldn't speak for all the women he'd dated over the years but, with her, he'd laid his cards on the table straight from the start, including the fact he wouldn't be around long term.

An all-pro wide receiver didn't need anyone to fight his battles but, annoyed at Ronald's blatantly disdainful affront to her intelligence, she jutted her chin. "I appreciate your concern, but you needn't worry. I'm a big girl and, the truth is, if anyone's using the other in my relationship with Tuck, it's me."

His brows popped up in surprise, and his smile was strained. "I didn't mean any insult. I just hope you know what you're doing."

"I do." She flashed her teeth in a feral smile. "Now, what's this about convincing me? To do what?"

His strained smile went positively flat, and he held up a hand. "Don't shoot the messenger, but the Arts Council contacted Putnam Gallery. It seems they have an open slot in the Summer Show. A single slot. I sent Putnam several of the pictures I took last week. They'll enter another artist if you're not available, but they want you, and they want *Yearning*."

Walter shoved the shoe back into her palm, and she glanced down into his unblinking eyes.

Shooting him would be too messy. Let me bite him on the ass.

If only. With a half-growl, half-sigh, she slid onto her work stool and eyed the sculpture on the shelf. "No."

Ronald moved closer. "Do you realize how important this is? The Arts Council, CC. Their influence is worldwide."

"You know my feelings on this. No shows."

He stopped on the other side of her bench and rested his hands on the surface to lean toward her in earnest. "Technically, this wouldn't be your show. Yours would be one piece among dozens. There'll be twenty-six other artists featured, including Dugan McDonald."

Fingers of fear slashed at her like nettles. "I'd be expected to appear." She shook her head in denial.

"An hour, CC. You know McDonald. He's a prima donna. He'll suck up all of the oxygen." Ronald pushed off the bench and straightened. "We'll be lucky if anyone notices you're there, and you won't be alone. I'll be right beside you." His dark eyes pleaded. "Leave your name out of it if that's what you want. We'll insist the piece be listed as Anonymous. The Council requires the artists make an appearance, but all you'll have to do is show up, shake a few hands, and leave."

She squeezed her eyes shut.

"Please, CC."

Her eyes popped open at his quiet plea. A note of desperation she'd never heard before made his voice tight.

"You know I believe in you, and in *Yearning* specifically, but the boost to my agency wouldn't hurt."

Unease tingled up her spine. She sat up straighter. "What's going on? Is the agency in trouble?"

He dropped his gaze to the surface of the bench, and his lashes shuttered his eyes. "Not trouble, exactly. Things have just been a little slow." He looked up. "I'm in a bit of a financial bind. Please, CC. I've always respected your wishes and never demanded you to do something you weren't comfortable with, but I'm asking you now."

She stared at him and wondered if there was more to the agency's woes than slow sales. Her gaze flicked to *Yearning* and back. He stood there, watching her with wounded pride glittering in his eyes, and guilt slapped at her like a stinging hand. He was right; he'd never asked more of her than she was willing to do, but the thought of facing a bunch of elite strangers as they pressed her for commentary about her art clogged the breath in her lungs.

Before she fell into the depths of a full-blown attack, she slid her eyes shut. "When do I have to let you know?"

"By Tuesday at the latest."

"Okay."

The breath left him in a rush. "Thank you."

She opened her eyes to spear him with a no-nonsense stare. "I said I'll think about it, not that I've made a decision."

He nodded and his lips tilted in a relieved smile. "That's fair. Thanks, CC. I'll be in touch."

* * * *

Tuck straddled the poolside lounge chair next to Gracie's and sat. "Nice bathing suit."

She smiled and flexed her toes, her feet and legs bare below her slim business skirt and blouse. One high heel rested on its side at the foot of the lounge, the other on the ground. "I just got back from meeting a client in the city. God, how did I ever survive all those years in Manhattan? It's a zoo."

"Face it. You and Jake have become countrified."

A happy sigh eased from her lungs. "Yes, we have."

"Rednecks." He chuckled and brought his beer bottle to his lips. A dozen feet away, the Malone twins, soaked to the skin in their matching pink shorts sets, giggled and shrieked as Murphy gave a full body shake. Soapy water flew in every direction. The dog leaped from the plastic tub to bolt across the yard, and the twins gave chase, skidding on the soggy lawn and going down in a tangled heap.

He shot Gracie a grin. "That's gonna leave a mark."

Laughter twinkled in her eyes. "I know. They're a mess. They'll *all* need baths when they're done."

He toed off his flip-flops and made himself comfortable. "Just toss them in the pool. Bing, bang, done."

She shook her head and laughed. "God help your future children."

Tilting his head her way, he sneered. "My kids are going to love me. If nothing else, they'll be tough little buggers." The surprised arch of her brows made him frown. "What? They will."

"Of course they will. I've always believed you'd make a good father, but that's the first time I've ever heard you mention kids of your own." Her lips curved slyly. "Do you have CC to thank for your sudden enlightenment?"

"Thank or strangle," he grumbled, then brought the bottle back to his lips. "I haven't decided which yet."

Her back sprung straight from the chair, and she swung around to drop her feet to the patio and fully face him. "Holy crap. I was kidding. Holy *crap!*"

He aimed the beer bottle at her nose. "If Angel and Charlie hear you using that language, you're toast."

Her violet gaze slid to where the twins had recaptured Murphy and were attempting to drag him back to his bathtub. The dog wasn't having any of it. She turned back with a dismissive wave of her hand. "They can't hear us. What's going on?"

"Nothing." Shit. He should have kept his big mouth shut.

"Baloney. Your poker face sucks. You're easier to read than a book."

He sat forward and jerked a glance over his shoulder, but Jake was nowhere in sight.

She rolled her eyes. "He's on the phone. He'll be a few minutes. Now, talk. Are you in love with her?"

Slumping back in his chair, he shut his eyes. "I don't have a fucking clue."

They'd spent most of the last week together, and yet he'd found no explanation for his almost gut-wrenching need to be with her. The punch to his chest as she'd shared her memories had all but destroyed his hope that a good, old-fashioned bout of sex would exercise the unexplainable hold she had on his mind and body. He had a very real fear sex with CC would only make matters worse.

"Speaking of language."

He opened his eyes.

A happy smile tipped the corners of Gracie's mouth. "I like her, Tuck. A lot."

He blew out a harsh breath. "So do I."

"She obviously has feelings for you."

"Maybe, or maybe I'm just a means to an end."

"Why would you say that?" Disapproval wrinkled her nose. "You've dated too many groupies. They've made you cynical."

"True, but not in this case." He set the beer aside and jammed the fingers of both hands through his hair.

CC might have feelings for him. Damn, he hoped so, but less than two weeks ago she'd seen him as simply a way to attain her goals, and now that she'd begun to open up to him about her past, he understood her single-minded determination to change her reality.

The men who planned and executed her kidnapping would spend most of their lives in a cage, but the punishment didn't fit the crime, in his opinion. As for her father... What a fucking prick. What kind of animal did that to his kid?

All of them deserved to suffer the way she had. The way she still did. If he could get his hands on them, he'd tear them limb from limb, but that wasn't reality. Reality was the brave woman fighting to reclaim her life. Her strength of will humbled him as much as her sunny smiles, sassy personality, and beautiful body turned him on.

She'd compared him to her father that first day and, considering her justifiable feelings for the man, Tuck was fighting an uphill battle. In her mind, he was still the gigolo she'd called him. Unless he could somehow change her opinion, he'd be out on his ass in less than two weeks.

He dropped his hands to his thighs and turned his head to meet Gracie's gaze. "The thing is, this relationship between us? It started because she couldn't breathe."

"And now?"

"And now I'm the one who can't. She takes my breath away."

Her smile went dopey, and he sighed.

"I'm screwed, Gracie. I haven't even slept with her yet, but I can't shake her from my mind." He dragged a hand over his face in frustration. "She's like…a tick."

"Oh, my. That's flattering."

Her tinkling laughter made him smile. "Fine. A funny, irresistible, *sexy* tick."

"Much better." She leaned her elbows onto her knees. "So, what's the problem?"

He looked away, and his gaze landed on the thick line of tall pines that had spooked CC the other day. Her past, her identity, wasn't his to share. She'd known too much betrayal in her life. He wouldn't add to it, but Gracie wouldn't let him get away without some sort of explanation.

He turned his head. "I told you about the panic attack."

She nodded.

"It wasn't an isolated event. Apparently, she's suffered from them most of her life, with good reason. I can't share the details, but she went through some major shit when she was no more than a kid. I'm talking the kind of stuff that will give you nightmares."

Her smile fell and concern darkened her eyes. Picking up his beer, he shared a carefully edited version of CC's proposition and her reasons behind it.

When he'd finished, confusion creased Gracie's forehead. "I'm not sure I understand."

"Neither did I, at first. Long story short, she agreed to date me, temporarily, in order to test her theory."

"You're kidding?"

"I wish."

"How temporary?"

"Three weeks." At the mention of the fast approaching deadline, apprehension landed a solid blow to his gut. He shook off the vehement denial echoing through his head with a practiced shrug. "I jumped at the opportunity because you know me. That's about how long most of my relationships last, and with training camp coming up, I'll be leaving anyway."

"And?"

"And as screwy as it sounds, her theory's working. With each date, she's grown less skittish and more confident. Hell, she hasn't given me a reason to kiss the breath back into her in days." The beach didn't count. What happened between them this morning had nothing to do with panic attacks or the terrors of her past and, damn it, if not for the interruption, she'd know it, too.

She grinned at his frown.

He picked at the label on his beer with his thumbnail. "Whether she knows it or not, she's healing. The problem is, the more time we spend together, the more I want that for her, but although I've had some success dimming the shadows in her eyes, only she can banish them completely. I plan to be there when it happens."

"Why, Tuck, who knew you were a romantic at heart?"

He blew a scoffing laugh. Romantic, hell. He was a sap and most likely a fool. To heal completely, CC would need to conquer all her demons, including her father, but from the way she reacted when he suggested it might be time to face him, she hadn't appreciated his effort to help. If he pushed too hard, she'd be gone.

Gracie leaned forward to lay a hand on his arm. "Sounds a lot like love."

"Hello, asshole. I didn't hear you arrive."

Gracie glanced behind them to smile at her approaching husband.

Tuck dropped his head to the back of his chair with a thud. "Fuck."

Jake rounded their chairs, bent to drop a kiss on his wife's mouth, and straightened. He glanced over his shoulder at the twins. "Hey, girls. Uncle Tuck said the F word." He turned back with a sneering grin.

Angel paused in her chase of Murphy. "But he doesn't have a swear jar."

"That's okay." Gracie sat back and reclined on her chair once more. She crossed her bare feet. "Jake does, and they're each going to put five dollars in his jar. Aren't you, boys?" She smiled at her groom.

"That's ten dollars," Charlie added helpfully.

Tuck snickered at Jake's scowl. Family life had introduced his friend to a whole host of new experiences, including a curse-free vocabulary, backed up by financial penalties.

Jake crossed his arms. "Making time with another man's wife is dangerous for a man in your position, my friend. It's hard to catch a ball with a broken arm."

Gracie laughed and patted the lounge at her hip. "Sit down, you idiot. Your best friend is in the middle of a crisis."

Jake dropped to sit beside her. His fingers ran absently along the length of her bare leg as he flashed his teeth in a taunting grin. "Of his own making, I'm sure."

"Look who's talking." Tuck made his smile sly. "How's the checkbook? Things are slow in the league front office. It's only a matter of time before you give them another reason to fine you."

"Haven't you heard? I'm officially off Doug Costa's hit list." Jake squeezed Gracie's knee. "The league commissioner loves my wife *and* her baked ziti. I believe *you're* his new target."

She crossed her arms. "Are you two done swapping testosterone bombs?"

They traded grins. "Yeah," they said in tandem.

"Good, because Tuck's in love with CC."

Jake's head whipped around to stare at her before jerking back.

Tuck groaned. So much for hoping to keep that little gem a secret. He pinned her with a glare.

"What? You thought I wasn't going to tell him?"

He sat forward, ignoring Jake's intent gaze, to wrap his arms around his bent knees. "Since I'm not completely sure how I feel, I was hoping you'd keep your big mouth shut."

His insult didn't seem to register. She sent Jake a knowing smile. "Tuck's scared."

Jake laughed. "Tuck's a pussy."

"Fuck you."

Dual little girl voices called out from the other side of the pool. "Twenty dollars!"

Pride lit Gracie's features. "That's exactly right, girls. You're getting so good at adding."

"I'm outta here." Tuck rose from the chair to jam his bare feet into his flip-flops. "Talk about a zoo."

Gracie sat forward. "Do you want my help? I could talk to CC for you."

"No, thanks." He sliced a disgusted grimace her way. "I think you've helped enough already." He ground his molars at Jake's booming laughter and turned to cross the flagstones toward the back of the house. Mere feet separated him from escape when Jake suddenly stopped laughing.

"Wait. Why does he need help? What's going on?"

"I'll explain it to you later, Malone."

Tuck dropped his head to his chest as he grabbed the doorknob. "Shit."

"Twenty-five," all four Malones yelled at his back.

Chapter 16

"I'm sorry, Cees. I'm such an idiot. I should never have brought up the subject." Kris hovered at the center of the studio. Her restless fingers, mangling the strap of her purse, displayed her remorse.

CC flipped the lock on Walter's cage. He squeezed from between the bars before the door swung open and trotted over to his box of toys. She rounded her workbench and waved off her cousin's concern. "Don't worry about it. You know Mom. If not the Arts Council's offer, she'd have found some other topic to hassle me over."

Her cousin dipped her chin in a nod and tipped her head as if in contemplation. "Like Curt. What's that all about? I know she still loves him, despite everything he's done, but why the sudden push to get the two of you together?"

CC shrugged out of her light jacket, damp from the drizzling rain falling on the city, and tossed it onto the couch. "Beats me."

As expected, her mother had badgered her about Curt throughout dinner, switching subjects to the Art Council's offer when CC proved stubborn.

Kris eased a hip onto the corner of her workbench and crossed her legs. "What are you going to do?"

"I have no idea." She slipped onto her stool. "What aggravates me most is she made some good points. About the show, not about seeing Curt." She scowled. "He proved long ago fatherhood isn't his thing. I mean, it's been sixteen years. I've heard from him, what? Four times, including last week's two calls?"

"He must want *something*."

"Yeah, but what? Apparently, aged rockers and their classic tunes are all the rage in certain circles. By all accounts, his career is rock solid these days. Even if it weren't, dredging up the kidnapping to get press would be a waste of time. Two decades have passed, and I'm hardly the sympathetic figure I was when he paraded me around for profit. A reclusive daughter who spends her time twisting wire into shapes in her studio would bring nothing but yawns from the music industry news junkies."

A grimace wrinkled Kris's nose. "Except, you haven't been spending *all* your time in your studio. Not lately, anyway."

"Shit. Do you think he knows about Tuck?"

Walter bumped her knee as he slid between the stool and the bench leg to drop to the floor, where he proceeded to maul a rawhide bone.

Kris's shoulders jerked in a shrug. "There's been nothing about the two of you in the papers, that I've seen, but this is Manhattan and Curt knows a lot of people. Someone could have seen you together and mentioned it to him."

She dropped her forehead to the workbench and groaned.

"Or maybe he's had an epiphany and wants to beg your forgiveness for being a prick and a rotten father."

Turning her head, she met her cousin's gaze and sat up.

"No frigging way," they said in unison, then grinned.

Kris leaned her hands back on the desk. "Screw it. He can't play whatever hand he has up his sleeve unless you cooperate. Tell him to piss in his guitar case and forget about him."

For the first time since her mother's call saying she was in town, CC laughed.

Kris swung out her legs and slid to her feet. "In the meantime, I have the next few days off. I'll run interference with your mother until she leaves town."

"You don't have to do that."

"But I want to." She cocked a hip and tugged the strap of her purse over her shoulder. "Don't take this wrong, but she was right when she said you'll never truly be healed until you face the world like the strong woman you are."

CC swiveled on the stool to face her. "And like I told her, I'm working on it." Stepping outside of her safety zone hadn't been easy, but she'd done it, even before she'd made her deal with Tuck.

"I know." Kris's teeth flashed. "And it shows. Remind me to give Tuck a big fat kiss next time I see him."

Crossing her arms, she smirked. "Yeah, I'll be sure to do that. What do you mean it shows?"

She winced at the sting as Kris flicked a fingertip down her sunburned nose. "When was the last time you willingly went to the beach or to a barbeque?" She didn't wait for an answer. "But it's more than that.

Despite your mother being in town and your father's sudden calls, not to mention the dweeb pushing you to do a show, you look happy, Cees."

Did she? Was she? She scrunched her nose in a silent examination of her feelings. Was that happiness lightening her heart, and was the subtle easing of the terror that had held her in its grip for so long the reason or was a certain sexy wide receiver responsible for her growing sense of optimism? Ultimately, the answer didn't matter, since she never would have found the former without the latter. God knew she'd made little progress overcoming her ghosts on her own. Despite her efforts to fulfill her birthday promise, each consequent step outside her safety zone had been as frightening as the last. She hadn't been making the kind of progress she'd hoped for, but from the moment Tuck had barreled into her life that had changed. She wasn't cured. Not by a long shot, but for the first time, she believed she might actually have the chance at a somewhat normal life.

"Whatever Tuck is doing, it's working."

Tugged from her musings, she blinked at her cousin. The memory of his head, dipped to her breast as his tongue swirled around the tip, brought the heat of a blush to her cheeks.

A sly smile tipped the corners of her cousin's mouth. "I rest my case. He's good for you, cuz."

For her? That was debatable, but there was no doubt he was good. She spun away and began to straighten the tools littered about the bench top. "You have no idea."

"Shut. Up!"

CC turned to look at Kris.

Kris's arms dropped to her sides as if they had turned to lead. "Did you sleep with him? Tell me you slept with him and, for God's sake, don't leave out any of the details."

"I haven't slept with him, so there's nothing to tell." She glanced down at her lap. Okay, that wasn't technically true. There was plenty to tell. She'd come as close to having carnal knowledge of Tuck as a woman could, but no way could she give the details. They were too personal, too intimate, to share, even with Kris.

"But you plan to. All right, Cees!"

"I haven't decided yet."

"Ha." Kris pressed her fingers to the top of CC's head and forced her to look up. She studied her heated cheeks. "That blush says you have." She bared her teeth in a challenging grin, then turned toward the hallway and wiggled her fingers above her head. "My work here is done. Good night."

She smiled as her cousin flounced from the room, then leaned her arms on the workbench with a sigh. Had she truly decided to sleep with Tuck? Caught up in the swirl of raw emotion, there hadn't been a lot of thinking going on this afternoon. Not on her part, anyway. One moment she was sharing one of her darkest memories and the next she was in his arms. If she'd been thinking clearly, would she have ended up squirming beneath him on the verge of orgasm or would she have danced away from the dangerous flame he lit within her once again?

Whatever the answer, her lack of willpower when it came to Tuck proved it was only a matter of time before she ended up in exactly the same place she'd been when her mother's call interrupted them. The question was could she hold out until the end of their agreement? Sensual memories flooded her mind and her nipples peaked. She slid her hands over each breast as wet heat pooled between her thighs.

She groaned. Not a chance in hell.

Walter scrambled to his feet and rested his head onto her knee. She rubbed his silky ear between forefinger and thumb. The truth was, although an addiction to Tuck was the last thing she needed, experiencing the promises of untold pleasures in his eyes was a temptation she didn't want to resist. Not any longer.

Though the changes were subtle, her life had already been irreversibly altered. She was stronger than she'd been only days before. Stronger than she'd ever considered she could be. Tuck's influence was responsible for much of the progress she'd made, but she didn't discount her own contribution to her growing confidence.

He may have been the catalyst, but she'd been the one to face the fears. She'd taken steps she'd always thought were impossible. Baby steps, to be sure—she smiled at the memory of his intimate teasing—but with each inch forward, she found she wanted more. More of her fledgling freedom, more of a full life, and definitely more of Tuck.

Taking a chance and having her heart broken scared the crap out of her, and yet, hadn't that been what she'd been doing for the past ten days? Taking chances?

She wanted it all, and to get it, she was going to have to leave her safe and lonely existence behind. A great plan in theory. Did she have what it took to pull it off in practice?

Her purse lay on the couch beside her coat. She scooted from the stool and rounded the bench to rummage through it. Tuck had input his phone number and address in her phone. In case she needed to reach him, he'd said. She scrolled through her contacts until his information popped up on the screen.

Scooping up her coat, she stalked to the hallway and stopped at the foot of the stairs. Her dog climbed them in a loping run and disappeared beyond the landing. "Kris, I'm heading out for a little while. Keep an eye on Walter for me, will you?"

Her cousin's muffled voice called back, "Where are you going?"

"To Tuck's."

A moment of silence was broken by the pounding of bare feet. Kris slid to a stop on the landing. She tossed a small bag down the stairs. CC snagged it in a fumbling catch.

"What's this?" Plastic crinkled as she opened the bag to look inside.

"A three pack of super-duper, nothing's-getting-through-these-suckers condoms."

She crushed the bag shut with convulsing fingers and looked up.

"Never go on a booty call without them."

She swallowed and almost changed her mind right then and there, but the encouraging smile on Kris's face wouldn't let her.

"Be careful, Cees. And have a blast!"

Chapter 17

By the time CC stopped in front of Tuck's door, her palms were sweating so badly the plastic bag nearly slipped from her fingers. She stared at the golden 3C embossed on the glossy wooden door. What was she doing here? She didn't do booty calls. She wasn't even sure what one entailed... But she could guess.

The bag crinkled in her fingers and she gasped. Afraid he'd open the door and find her strangling a bag of condoms, she shoved it into her purse. A deep breath and she lifted her hand to rap her knuckles on the wooden panel. Silence greeted her. She swallowed back nerves and flicked a furtive glance up the empty hallway, then down. Rolling her shoulders, she knocked again.

More silence.

Why hadn't she thought to call first? Maybe he wasn't home or, oh, God. Oh, shit! What if he wasn't alone? She never had gotten around to requesting that exclusivity clause. The sunburn on her nose stung as she scrunched her face in a panicked grimace.

She'd taken three steps toward the elevator when the door clicked open at her back.

"CC?"

Skidding to a halt, she chanced a glance over her shoulder. Her pulse catapulted into the stroke zone. Unlike her bright red nose, the noonday sun had deepened the tan on his tough-guy face, highlighting the jagged, pale pink scar slashing one brow. His shaggy haircut stuck out on one side of his head, as if he'd thrashed the gold-tipped locks with the careless shove of his fingers. The sleeves of his battered Marauders T-shirt had been torn away and left his shoulders bare, and a pair of soft cotton athletic shorts clung to his muscled thighs above long legs and bare feet.

She pivoted to face him. "I—" *God, I should have thought about what I was going to say before I knocked.* "I'm sorry. I shouldn't have come."

She moved backward several steps.

"Wait." He held out one hand. Holding the door open with one foot, he leaned his upper body back inside as if reaching for something.

She whipped around, intent on the elevator doors ten feet away.

"Wait, CC."

She fled down the hall and jammed her finger to both call buttons. Eyes glued to the contrasting arrows above the double doors, she willed one of them to light. Up or down, it didn't matter, as long as she got out of there before he could follow. "Come on. Come on." Pressing the buttons multiple times did nothing to speed the car's arrival.

Her frantic gaze ping-ponged about the long hallway. An exit sign jeered at her from above the stairway door twenty yards away. She shot a glance over her shoulder and yelped as Tuck plunged into the hall and loped in her direction. The elevator dinged at the exact moment his muscled arm snaked around her waist from behind.

"Where are you going?" His warm breath bathed her ear.

She fought a shiver. "Home. This was a stupid idea."

"No. No, it's a great idea." He shifted but didn't lessen his hold on her. Arm draped over her shoulders, he turned her and led her back to his condo door. "I'm glad you're here. I was just thinking about you."

"You were?" She twisted her head to look at him, her brows jumping together in a suspicious frown. "Why?"

The corner of his mouth tweaked in a soft smile, and she jammed her eyes shut. Suspicion probably wasn't the right mood to set when one was on a booty call. Not that it mattered. As she'd said, coming here was a stupid idea.

He slashed a keycard through the slot beside the door. It opened with a quiet snick, and he wasted no time escorting her inside. As he slid his arm from her shoulders and turned to shut and lock the door, she glanced around.

The living area consisted of a large, sunken space. Built around the stunning view of Central Park through the far wall of glass, the room was sparsely furnished in what she imagined was stereotypical bachelor fashion. A huge, flat screen TV hung over a granite fireplace, but other than several black TV components, a long leather couch, low coffee table, and a single pole lamp, the room was empty. Off to the right, four stools fronted a breakfast bar wrapped around a galley kitchen. A pizza box and several Chinese takeout containers sat on the countertop.

She jumped when he grasped both her hands and dipped his head to meet and hold her gaze. Genuine regret darkened his eyes. "I don't like the way we left things this afternoon."

She looked away, dropping her focus to the center of his chest. "Neither do I."

He drew a deep breath, and the T-shirt stretched taught against his well-developed pecs. "How you decide to handle your father is your call. It's not my place to push you into doing something you're not ready to do."

If only her mother were of the same opinion. Why was it the one person she'd actually *asked* to help was the only one not insisting he knew the best way to go about pushing past her fears? But she didn't want to talk about Curt or her fears. She'd stepped way outside of her box coming here, and she had no idea how to go about asking for what she hoped came next. She was counting on Tuck to understand and take the lead.

"Not even if I want you to?" Embarrassed, despite being unsure if he'd catch the deeper meaning behind the question, she kept her eyes on the enticing bulge of muscle inches from her nose.

A fingertip beneath her chin lifted her face. If his blazing blue gaze was any indication, he was an expert at reading between the lines. "Are we still talking about your father?"

Her throat clicked on a heavy swallow. "Not exactly."

A hint of a smile teased his lips. "Good. He's a selfish prick. I'd much rather talk about what happened on the couch."

Oh, thank God. But talking about it wasn't exactly what she had in mind. If she was going to pull this off, they needed to get to it before she lost her nerve. "Do you mind if we sit down?"

"Not at all."

The warmth of his large hand radiated to her lower back through the thin material of the little black dress she'd worn to meet her mother for dinner. She dug in her heels as he started to lead her toward the couch. He stopped and arched a brow.

Nerves tangled her insides in a knot. "I was thinking...that is..." She jutted out her chin and jumped headlong into her own probable destruction. "Why don't you show me your bedroom?"

His pupils dilated until the blue of the irises was almost eclipsed. Tension tightened the skin covering his cheekbones. "Are you sure?"

Not in the least, and if you don't hurry it up, I'm going to hurl. "I'm sure."

She was pressed up against him before she could blink. The tight squeeze of his arms compressed her rib cage as his mouth claimed hers in a slow kiss that made her toes curl. Her legs weren't quite steady when he released her, grabbed one hand, and began tugging her toward a short hallway off the kitchen.

He snagged a bottle from the built-in wine rack at the end of the breakfast bar as they passed. Several steps later, he stopped short, then backtracked to the kitchen. "Here. Hold this." He handed her the bottle and turned to scrounge through a drawer. A few seconds later, he straightened and held up a corkscrew with a grin. Tucking it into his pocket, he snagged two glasses by the stems, grabbed her hand, and hurried for the door at the end of the hall.

He pounced on her the moment they stepped over the threshold of his private lair. Sweeping her into his arms, he stalked across the room. One of her shoes slipped from her foot and thumped to the floor as he bent to peel back the dark comforter. He lowered her onto the cool sheets of the king-sized bed, set aside the glasses on the bedside table, and lifted a knee to the mattress. With his spread hands propped on each side of her shoulders, he lowered his body over hers.

She squeezed her free hand between them and attempted to push at his chest. She was all for fast, but this was ridiculous. "Slow down, Tuck."

He dipped his head and began an exploration of her neck with warm lips. He spoke against her skin. "So you can change your mind? Not a chance."

Goose bumps broke out and chased the trail of his fingers as they whispered over her collarbone to dip beneath the neckline of her dress. His hand burrowed deeper and cupped her breast.

"Tuck."

His murmur of encouragement bathed her neck with damp heat and made her shiver. He rotated his hand, rasping his palm against her peaked nipple as he kneaded her flesh with magic fingers. Despite lying on her back, she grew lightheaded as answering shock waves shot straight to her clit. Good Lord. She'd be a puddle of goo before he'd removed a single strip of clothing.

Teetering on the edge of orgasm, she squeezed her thighs together to hold off the inevitable. "Tuck."

His heated mouth sipped its way over her chest.

"Tuck!" She pinched a lock of his hair and tugged gently to get his attention.

"Ouch." His fingers stilled, and he raised his head. "Why'd you do that?"

"Because this is my first time. I didn't want you to miss it."

His brows puckered. "How could I miss it when I'm right here with you?"

"Believe me, if I hadn't stopped you, in less than a minute, I would have left you in the orgasmic dust."

A slow smile curled one side of his mouth. "Really? Damn, that's sexy."

An embarrassed blush heated her chest and climbed to her cheeks. "It is not. It's pitiful. I may be a virgin, but I can read. I know what sex is supposed to be, and going off like a starting gun before the game even starts is not it."

His smile turned positively wicked. "Oh, sunshine. You couldn't be more wrong." He brushed his thumb over her nipple. "Do you trust me?"

She squeezed her eyes shut, and her answer came out as a low wail. "Nooo."

"Yes, you do." He chuckled and flexed his fingers in a lingering caress. A shudder ripped through her as he slid his hand free of her dress. "There's nothing wrong with a starting gun, as long as it's aimed properly."

Before she knew what he was about, he'd scooted his body toward the foot of the bed until the width of his shoulders forced her clenched legs apart. Her eyes popped open, and she lifted her head to look down her body. Cradled between her spread thighs, he tugged the hem of her dress up to rest against her belly. With his lips an inch from the silky black panties covering her, he slipped a fingertip under the material and peeled it to the side.

He looked up and winked. "Bang."

He dipped his head and sealed his hot mouth over her swollen flesh. Blinding colors exploded, and her own keening cry echoed in her ears as she went off like a roman candle on the fourth of July.

* * * *

Tuck pushed onto his elbows. For a moment, his hungry gaze lingered on the dew-glistened flower flaring his nostrils with its sweet scent. With regret, he shifted the material of her silky panties back into place and lifted his head. Eyes closed, ecstasy etched on every curve of her glowing face, CC lay sprawled in sensual abandon. The sexy black dress was bunched around her waist, her slim thighs pale in the low light. A black high heel dangled from the toes of one foot. Her fingers curled around the neck of the wine bottle in a lazy grip.

He smiled and rolled to his feet, rounding the bed to slide the bottle from her fingers. He bent to slip the shoe from her foot. His gaze slid over her sleek thighs to the scrap of black silk between them and he straightened, leaving the dress as it was.

With the corkscrew he pulled from his pocket, he scored the bottle's foil cover and peeled it back. He twisted the spiral worm into the cork. Her lashes fluttered open, and she blinked at the ceiling.

"Welcome back." The cork came free with an audible pop.

Her head sagged to the side. For several heartbeats she simply stared, and then her eyes widened comically as if she'd forgotten he was there. She slapped both hands over her face.

A laugh rumbled in his chest as he poured two glasses. Setting the bottle aside, he eased onto the bed at her hip.

The mattress dipped beneath his weight, and she spread her fingers slightly. Her green eyes peeked from between the digits, and the heels of her hands muffled her voice. "Have you ever had one of those moments when you don't have a clue what to say?"

"Nope." He held out a glass.

She groaned but dropped her hands and sat up, accepting his offering. "Of course you haven't."

He grinned at her grumbled tone and bit back a laugh as she glanced down at herself and nearly bobbled the wine in her rush to shove her dress down in a more modest covering. Tucked beneath her hips, the material refused to cooperate to her satisfaction. Finally, she darted a hand behind her, snagged one of his pillows, and plopped it into her lap.

He arched a brow, and she squinted her eyes as if daring him to comment. He didn't bother. She'd learn soon enough, modesty and sex didn't exactly mix. Rock hard and throbbing, his cock twitched beneath his shorts in an urgent demand he begin the lesson immediately, but she'd asked him to slow things down.

He'd give her three minutes.

The expensive vintage, sliding down his throat as he gulped at his glass, may as well have been three dollar plonk. His wine snob friend in city hall would be horrified. Gritting his teeth, he stretched out on his side and propped his head in his palm. "How'd things go with your mom?"

"My mom?" She froze with the wine glass suspended an inch from her lips, and her gaze skittered down his body to where his painful hard-on tented his shorts. She lowered the glass and shook her head. "I don't understand. Are we done?"

He choked and nearly spewed a mouthful of seventy-five dollar chardonnay across the sheets. "No. We've barely started."

"Then why are you asking about my mother?"

He dragged the back of his wrist across his mouth. "You asked me to slow down."

"Well, yeah. But that was before you..." She cast a furtive glance around the room, as if she might locate her mother hiding behind the curtains, and dropped her voice to a whisper. "You *licked* me."

A helpless laugh burst from his lips. Fuck. Her unique mix of sensual innocence and bold curiosity was going to kill him but, damn, what a way to go.

He stretched his arm over the side of the bed to set his glass on the floor, then rolled up on his elbow. He wrapped his fingers around the back of her smooth calf and rubbed his thumb over her kneecap. "I sipped at your pleasure, sunshine, and have never tasted anything as sweet."

Flaming color erupted on her cheekbones, but she didn't look away.

"Admit it. You liked it."

Her lashes swept down, and she dropped her gaze. "You know I did."

A low purr rumbled in his throat at the sweet stroke to his ego. He pushed up from his elbow, and she lifted her head. Embarrassment shimmered in her eyes, but she didn't cower as he crawled toward her, bracketing her feet, calves, thighs, and then hips with his hands and knees. Pride swelled in his chest. Little Miss Sunshine might be a novice when it came to sex, but as she had in her quest to overcome her past, she didn't back down from the unknown.

He paused with his mouth an inch from hers and plucked the still-full glass from her fingers and set it aside. She lifted her chin, cutting the distance between their lips by half. He smiled. Time was up.

"There's more, sunshine. So much more." He leaned in and covered her mouth with his.

Chapter 18

It was about time.

CC curled into Tuck's kiss, stabbing her fingers into his hair to keep his talented mouth where it could do the most good. Not that it hadn't done a whole lot of good earlier but, at the moment, she was eager to experience that "much more" he'd mentioned. The impressive bulge straining the cloth of his shorts said he was too.

The world tilted suddenly as he scooped an arm around her hips and, taking her with him, rolled to his back. With a gasp, she came to rest on a bed of solid muscle. Her lids fluttered open to find his eyes inches from hers. The sensual intent in the piercing blue orbs flamed the reignited fire between her thighs.

"I rushed you earlier and shouldn't have. But I won't apologize for wanting you."

Pressed against the firm plates of muscle that made up his chest and stomach, she marveled at the heavy thump-thump of his heartbeat against her breasts and the solid proof of his desire cradled between her thighs. "I don't need or want an apology." She slid her fingers from his hair to cup his jaw in her palms. "I came here of my own accord, Tuck. I want this. I want *you*."

A shudder rippled through him, and his arms contracted in an iron band about her. "I'm all yours. This is your show. You set the pace. Whatever you want, it's yours."

"Really?" Arching back several inches, she stared at him. "My pace. Whatever I want?"

He slid his warm palm down her back and over her ass to cup her bare thigh beneath the hem of her dress. The firm cut of his lips softened, and dimples popped in his smile. "Lady's choice."

A hum shimmered in her throat. She liked the sound of that. She braced her hands on his collarbone and sat up, straddling his thighs, and crossed her arms. "Okay, then. Lose the shirt."

His abdominal muscles contracted in a crunch as his upper body rose several inches from the bed. He reached one hand over his shoulder and tugged the T-shirt over his head. The flick of his hand sent it floating to the floor. He tucked his hands behind his head and let her look her fill.

This morning at the beach she'd been focused on the beauty of his back, but his front deserved similar accolades. Roped veins broke from beneath the swell of his pecs to travel over muscled biceps. Unlike the waxed presentation of so many of the male models her art classes produced, a light spray of hair started at his collarbone and shadowed his pectoral wall. Slightly thicker where it swirled around the twin discs of his nipples, the dark blond curls narrowed to a thin line bisecting the ridges of his abdomen to flare around the dip of his belly button. The treasure trail, as it was referred to in several of the women's magazines she'd read, disappeared beneath his waistband.

Her fingers itched to follow the tempting path, and because he'd said whatever she wanted, she did. His stomach muscles quivered beneath the light brush of her fingertips, and her gaze flew to his face. No smile, wicked or otherwise, rode his lips, and his eyes burned into hers.

She didn't look down when her fingers encountered his shorts. Encouraged by the heated passion tightening his features, she shimmied lower on his hips, twisted her hand, and burrowed her fingers beneath the waistband to find the treasure she sought.

Wonder filled her mind as she wrapped her hand around the heated column of his erection. The breath hissed through his teeth, and the veins vining his arms bulged in stark relief as if he clenched his hands beneath his head.

"Whatever I want," she reminded him.

He blew out a short breath. "Even if it kills me."

A laugh gurgled up her throat. No chance of that. She wanted him alive and hearty. A growing sense of power made her almost giddy. He might not feel like smiling, but she couldn't help herself. Despite not an ounce of experience in the game of sex, she had him right where she wanted him.

She cocked her head and gave him her most seductive smile, then squeezed gently. "Tell me if I do anything wrong."

A choked laugh shook his body. "Take my word for it. You're a natural."

Waves of pleasure won out over seduction. She giggled like a girl. "I'm having fun."

"Just as I promised," he gritted out from between clenched teeth.

He had a point. He'd fulfilled that particular promise, and it was time to repay the favor. She pursed her mouth in a pout. "You don't look like you're having much fun."

"I will if you'll slide your hand down a little."

She glided her closed fist over him to the base of his cock.

"Now up."

She complied.

"Down again."

She stilled her hand and arched a brow. "I think I get the picture."

"Thank God." His eyes slid shut.

"Maybe this will help." Grinning, she slipped her hand free of his briefs. His groan of disappointment was cut short as she curled the fingers of both hands beneath the elastic band of shorts and briefs, and tugged the cloth down to his knees. His erection sprang free, and the breath caught in her throat.

A virgin she might be, but she wasn't a green kid. She'd studied anatomy and, thanks to sex education classes supplemented with romance novels, she knew the fundamentals, but holy shit. He and Too Long Tucker had more in common than just a name. Okay, Tuck wouldn't match up to L.A.'s premier adult film star in a side-to-side comparison, but it was close. Her newfound sense of power fizzled like a deflating balloon.

The bed shifted as he rose onto his elbows, and she looked up and swallowed. "I'm sorry, but I don't see how that thing is going to fit."

His laughter grated against her embarrassment. She lifted onto her knees and climbed off him. He kicked the shorts free of his feet and jerked forward. Grasping her hips, he lifted her as if she weighed nothing and dragged her up the bed to deposit her by his side.

"It's not funny," she grumbled when he continued to chuckle.

"Yes, it is." He leaned over her and brushed a curl back from her forehead. "We'll fit perfectly. You'll see."

"I don't see how." With his engorged penis nudging insistently at her hip, it was impossible to relax, but neither did she want to call a halt. She sighed. "Obviously, I suck at lady's choice. Maybe you should take over."

"My pleasure." He dipped his lips to her neck, and shivers chased up and down her spine. "But I meant what I said. If I do anything you don't like, if I go too fast for you, let me know."

She murmured her agreement and arched her neck to give him better access. He took full advantage, depositing tiny love bites down the sensitive cord on one side. His lips reached the strap of her dress and paused.

He fingered the thin silk. "Why don't we get rid of this?"

She rolled her shoulders upward as his fingers went to the tab in back. The material loosened with the rasp of the zipper, and he peeled it away, dropping a kiss to her shoulder before rising up onto his elbow. She lifted her hips to aid him, and he drew the dress down over her hips and legs. He tossed the silk to the foot of the bed.

The heat of his gaze, starting at her feet and traveling to her face, brought goose bumps.

"Damn, you're beautiful."

He looked at her with a mix of admiration and desire simmering in his eyes, and she believed him. She shimmied an inch away, enough to leave a small gap between them, and dropped her gaze to his straining erection. Now that the initial shock had begun to fade, she could appreciate the perfection of his male form. All of it.

She looked up. "So are you."

His grin made her smile.

"Well, you are. I've never seen a fully erect penis in person before. Only relaxed ones. I guess I overreacted."

"There's my girl." He cocked his head suddenly. "Wait. How many penises have you *seen*?"

"Twelve." She jerked a shoulder in a defensive shrug. "I'm an artist, remember? Male models have them, but they don't usually have a hard-on when they're posing for a class. This one guy did, though." She scowled at the memory. "Sort of, but he was a weirdo. None of us were impressed."

He dropped his forehead to the crease of her neck. His shoulders shook with silent laughter.

God, I'm babbling. She squeezed her eyes shut and mentally cleared her throat. "I'm going to shut up now."

His shoulders shook harder.

Great, here she was, on a bed, wearing nothing but a bra and panties, and the naked sex god with her was laughing. At this rate, she wouldn't need Kris's super-duper condoms. Which might be a good thing. Considering the size of him, they probably wouldn't fit anyway.

She shook her head and refused to admit defeat. If the condoms didn't work, she'd march down the street to the drugstore and get the biggest ones they had, but after the stress of coming here in the first place, she wasn't going home to her empty bed without having carnal knowledge of one well-hung wide receiver.

It was her own fault her first foray into the world of sex had derailed so badly, but she knew a sure-fire way to start the train running again. She slid her hand over her belly to her thigh and dragged two fingertips from the base of his cock to the head. He stiffened and jerked up his head. Pleasure glimmered in his eyes.

She fluttered her lashes. "I think I'm ready now."

He didn't give her a second to reconsider. His mouth crashed down onto hers, and his hand came to rest on her belly. Anticipation skirmished with excitement as he expertly popped the front snap of her bra. Cool air washed over her puckered nipples and tightened them further. He released her mouth and, as he had at the beach, danced his lips down to one straining peak. His tongue stabbed and his lips nibbled, and she arched helplessly into his mouth.

The sweep of his large palm carried her panties down her thighs to her knees. She scissor kicked them the rest of the way off. His warm hand made the return trip to her mound, and she whimpered at the exquisite plucking of his fingers.

Apparently, once her body was primed, it took little to light the fuse. Hot and primal, need coursed through her blood. As his thick thigh slid between hers, she once again found herself hurtling toward the abyss. Her head lashed back and forth in denial, and she cried out on a wail. "Tuuuck."

"Stay with me." Hovering over her, his features, pulled tight with tension, swam into focus. "Stay with me, baby."

"I'm trying. I don't think I can."

She panted as his hand shot out, knocking the lamp from the bed stand. The bottle of wine wobbled as he yanked open the drawer.

"They're in my purse."

Wrist deep in the drawer, his hand jerked about in rapid search. "What is?"

"Condoms."

He froze and disbelief widened his eyes. "You brought condoms?"

"Kris."

"What about her?"

She squeezed her eyes shut and growled.

"Fuck it." His hand dug deeper into the drawer. "We'll talk about her later." Relief flooded his face, and he held up a foil disc. The wrapper disintegrated in his teeth, and he rolled to his back to cover himself in three fast strokes, before rising up over her once again. Supporting his weight on one forearm, he grasped his cock in the other hand and lowered his hips between her thighs.

Paused at her entrance, he watched her with eyes full of hunger and heat. "Breathe, sunshine."

One pump of his hips was all it took. Her breath caught at the delicious stretch of her inner muscles as he slid home, and though tempting shock waves fired in a haphazard pattern, orgasm hovered just out of reach.

Dazed by the shear wonder of being joined with him, she stared at his still face. He settled down onto both elbows, and she gasped at the delicious rasp of his chest hair scoring her nipples.

"Okay?"

"Better than."

Some of the tension left his face with his smile, but not all of it. Sweat glistened on his brow. "You're a greedy little thing, aren't you?"

When he had a point, he had a point. She smiled and nodded.

His chest jumped on a pained chuckle. "I love that about you. You ready for more?"

Her chin bobbed in anticipation.

"Then hold on, baby, because we're about to fly."

He began to move, slowly at first. A sweet pump of his hips. An answering pull inside. His lips met hers and his tongue joined the dance, in, out, stab, retreat. Every fantasy she'd ever had of what it was like to be with a man was eclipsed by the reality of coming together with him. Gentle, yet strong. Giving, yet greedy, he moved over her, in her, with her. Together, they left the world behind for a magical place one soul could never reach on their own, and when ecstasy found her again, she wasn't alone.

Chapter 19

Feet propped on the coffee table, her legs bare beneath the T-shirt she'd pilfered from Tuck's closet, CC dipped her spoon into her bowl.

"What's your stance on baseball?"

She turned her head. "Other than kicking your butt in the batting cage the other day, I don't have one." She bared her teeth in a cheeky grin.

Tuck's eyes gleamed with silent laughter. "I cleaned your clock, little girl." Bowl balanced in his palm, he scooped up a heaping spoonful of sugary sweet cereal and popped it into his mouth.

"Ha! Your word against mine."

"Care for a rematch?" His mouth worked the oversized bite, crunching audibly before he swallowed. "I'll make sure there are witnesses this time."

She snickered. "Anytime, big guy."

He grunted and dove in for another bite. Two hours in his bed had left them both ravenous. He'd offered to call for takeout, but she'd dismissed the offer. Tonight was theirs. She didn't want anyone else to intrude, including the delivery boy from the Chinese restaurant around the corner. She'd almost changed her mind, however, when inspecting his cabinets proved his taste in food ran toward that of a twelve-year-old boy.

After licking the spoon clean, he tipped the bowl to his lips and drained the remaining chocolate flavored milk. He sat up to set them on the coffee table, then flopped back with a satisfied sigh. "Some friends of mine are playing tomorrow. I thought you might enjoy a game."

She eyed him suspiciously. "Will there be people there?"

He flashed a grin. "A few."

"I'm serious about taking the challenge to the next level. How can I judge my progress if I never put myself out there? How few?"

"Enough, and I promise they'll be within arm's reach."

Mackenzie Crowne

The reminder of their agreement, and of the clock ticking down to its conclusion, dimmed her pleasure in the moment and she looked away. Regrets were for another day. Her gaze fell on the double doors at the far end of the living room. She pointed her spoon. "Where does that go?"

He bumped up his chin. "If you're done with that, I'll show you."

She slipped one last spoonful of the sugar coated Os into her mouth and set aside the bowl.

He stood and held out his hand. She put her palm in his, and he pulled her to her feet. Light flooded the large studio when he flipped a switch. She'd expected a gym. Maybe some free weights and a treadmill. The woodworking shop was a complete surprise.

He wandered over to a high table and ran a hand over a partially built box of some sort.

"You build furniture? Here?"

He shrugged and dusted his hand on the drawstring pajama pants riding low on his hips. "The shop is soundproofed, and it has its own ventilation system, but it's not technically necessary. I do everything by hand. No power tools. Working with my hands relaxes me, and it's a good workout. You'd be surprised at the muscles used by swinging a hammer or sliding a plane."

She stepped to the far end of the table and swept a fingertip over the surface, leaving behind a squiggly line in the film of fine dust. "That explains the sawdust."

He leaned a hip against the table and crossed his arms.

She curved her lips in a smile. "The day I met you. You smelled like cinnamon and sawdust. I thought you were a carpenter."

Straightening away from the table, he dropped his arms and stalked toward her. A familiar twinkle lit his eyes. "You smelled me?"

He kept coming forward, but she held her ground. The bare expanse of his chest fanned the simmering coals of desire, and she lifted her chin. What the hell. It was only one AM. By Manhattan standards, the evening had just gotten started, and she could think of several delicious ways to spend the next few hours.

She tugged the tiger's tail. "And *tasted* you. It would have been difficult not to, what with your tongue in my mouth."

He stalked closer, wicked promises glittering in his eyes. "The tongue has a lot of interesting uses."

She gulped. Oh, hell yeah, it did. She melted into his arms as they wrapped around her, and she spoke against the lips that brushed hers. "Oh, yeah. Like what?"

His dark smile said he meant to show her, and over the remainder of the night, he did.

* * * *

"You seem a little tense. What's wrong?"

CC shot Tuck a glance where he sat on the other side of the limo's backseat. Dropping her at her condo this morning, he'd warned her to be ready by three. The car service limo pulled up to her curb two minutes early, and when she asked why he wasn't driving, he'd introduced her to Edward, who apparently drove him occasionally, then made an offhand comment about afternoon traffic.

"You mean, other than my mother coming to town to pester me into seeing my father and Ronald insisting I enter a piece into a show the Art Council is running? Not a thing."

"You forgot to add being exhausted after a horny wide receiver kept you awake most of the night."

There *was* that but, surprisingly, she didn't feel tired in the least. Sated, energized, and greedy for more, but not tired. And if he thought she was going to stroke his ego by telling him so, he'd have to be disappointed.

He chuckled when she turned away.

"Why would an art show be a problem? Isn't that how you artists make a living? By selling it?"

She pursed her lips and turned her head slowly, but before she could comment on how art shows usually meant meeting a bunch of strangers, she blinked at the familiar spirals of the Robert F. Kennedy Bridge flashing by the window beyond his shoulders. "Where are we going?"

"The Stadium."

She gaped at him. "*Yankee* Stadium?"

"You agreed we'd go to a game."

"Well, yeah, but I thought you meant a little league or sandlot game. I pictured a smattering of locals on metal bleachers, not a stadium full of Yankee fans."

"What do you have against Yankee fans?"

"What do I have...?" She squinted at his innocent smile. "Don't be obtuse. You know what I'm talking about."

"Yeah, I do, but you're the one who said it's time to ramp up your test, and you won't get over your fear of crowds without facing them. The way to best a beast is head on."

"Thanks for the psychological pep talk, Dr. Freud."

He laughed and she groaned, doing her best to ignore her racing heart.

"Relax. Like at the concert, the crowd will be watching the field, not you." Mischief sparkled in his eyes. "Unless we end up on the Jumbotron somehow. But don't worry. If that happens, I promise to give you mouth to mouth."

Instant panic tripled her racing heartbeat.

"That's not funny," she grumbled.

His secret weapon dimples made an appearance. Okay, maybe it was a little funny, and she appreciated his attempt to make her laugh, but his humor didn't lessen the familiar contracting of her trachea.

Her gaze snagged on the hulking form of the stadium in the distance. "I'd prefer testing it somewhere less crowded, if you don't mind." She swallowed a whimper. "Like Times Square."

Without warning, he slid across the car's bench seat. His mouth was on hers before she could object. Instantly, his cinnamon and sawdust scent assaulted her, filling her nostrils and expanding her lungs. A low hum of pleasure sounded in his throat just before he lifted his head.

He smiled at her. "Better?"

She nodded silently.

"Breathe, CC."

She sucked in air tasting of him, sniffing strongly to prove the point. "I *am* breathing. How else would I know you've been working in your woodshop?" He dipped in for another kiss and she stiff-armed him. "But I'll be able to do a better job of it if you back off a little."

He chuckled and complied. She scooted closer to the car door and clamped her fingers around the armrest. God, she'd be naked and on her back in no time if he kept up those magical kisses. After last night's marathon of indulgence, one would think she'd be too sated to get worked up. He was right. She *was* greedy.

The car exited the highway toward the stadium, and her fingernails made indentations in the sleek leather armrest. He turned to look at her, and she knew she was pale. Couldn't be helped, not with the looming prospect of facing down fifty thousand people front and center in her mind. "This is a bad idea."

"You said you were ready."

She met his steady gaze. "I know, but—"

"Relax, sunshine. I've got your back." His gaze slid over her chest before popping up to twinkle at her. "And your front."

She scowled as the demon drug heated her insides. "I haven't jumped out of the car to escape, have I?"

He eyed her hand on the door. "You look like you might be considering it."

She yanked her hand back, tucking it into her lap. The fact that she hadn't jumped from the car was evidence of the incredible progress she'd made in facing her fears, and the knowledge lit a fire of excitement in her belly. While her heart thundered in her chest, she was still here, and not because of an abstract promise she'd made on her last birthday. She was here because she'd somehow begun to believe in herself. She had Tuck to thank for the transition, at least partially, but after her complete caving to his agenda last night, she wasn't about to hand him another victory by admitting it.

"Fine. Have it your way. But if you end up having to schlep me out of the stadium over your shoulder after I've fainted, you'll have no one to blame but yourself."

Blue heat sprang to life in his eyes. "I think I can handle you, and since I can't imagine anything sweeter than getting my hands on your hot little body again, I can't say I'd mind doing a little schlepping." He winked and tugged on his ball cap disguise.

When she bit her lip, he sighed.

"I'll take it off later, if you want, once you've settled down a little, but first we have to run the gauntlet to our seats."

Edward pulled the car to the curb, and Tuck turned away. She craned her neck to peer out the window and nearly chickened out at the mass of bodies streaming toward the entrance. The gauntlet? God help her.

Thanking Edward, Tuck accepted his card for the return trip, then held out his hand. The palm she placed in his was clammy. He lifted a brow, assisting her from the car, then tucked her fingers in the crook of his arm. She slipped on her sunglasses, and almost immediately they were swallowed up by the teaming rush of fans entering the stadium.

She made use of her breathing technique. In and out, slow and easy, but no one gawked. No one stopped short, then rushed forward to ask for Tuck's autograph, or even seemed to note his presence. The tight band of anxiety loosened around her chest, and she began to think she might just survive the afternoon.

At the gate, he presented their tickets and led her through the swarming halls to their seating section. Bright sunlight hit her face as they exited the tunnel. She blinked behind her sunglasses. The salty scent of popcorn mixed with the tang of hot dogs and made her nostrils flare. At the bottom of the steep flight of stairs, the cardboard brown of the pitcher's mound and baselines was stark against the verdant green carpet of grass. She descended the steps beside him until he stopped at the second row from the bottom, twenty feet from first base. She slid past him, stepping by the row of strangers to the seat he indicated.

"Wow," she said as he slid into his seat beside her. "We're practically on the field."

He grinned. "Yeah, great seats, aren't they? The guy who owned them ran into some financial difficulties or he never would have parted with them."

"People are allowed to own seats?"

To her left, a bald, beefy stranger with an impressive beer belly snickered. She stiffened, pressing her back into the chair as he leaned around her to grin at Tuck. "She's cute, but she doesn't know shit about baseball."

Tuck grinned, and she shot him a raised brow. "Fuck you, Mike. Season ticket holders, sunshine. With the Yankees, available seats are pretty much impossible to come by unless you strike a deal with a current holder."

"And second row, first base line is the golden ticket of season tickets." Mike belched.

She grimaced and he blushed.

"Sorry. There was a mob ten thick rushing Parker for those seats. I'm not sure how he did it, but your boy here beat them all out for the prize."

"I have superior negotiation skills," Tuck said lazily. He winked at her, his smile full of sultry suggestion. The memory of how his negotiating skills had paid off just a handful of hours ago heated her cheeks in a blush.

"More like a superior bank account." Mike shoved half a hot dog in his mouth and chewed.

Tuck chuckled. "CC, this loudmouth is Mike O'Toole."

Mike shifted in his seat, his wide shoulder brushing hers, to hold out a hand.

She tried not to stare at the glob of mustard clogging the corner of his mouth. "Uh, hi, Mike." She placed her hand in his large paw, happy to find it uncrushed when he released it after a hardy pump.

"Pleased to meet you, CC."

"Mike considers himself the resident expert on all things baseball," Tuck explained.

"I *am* the resident expert, around here anyway." The big man winked. "Anything you want to know about the game, honey, you just ask."

"I'll keep that in mind."

Tuck signaled a passing vendor, procuring two plastic cups of cold beer and held up two fingers to another vendor hawking hot dogs. She flinched when the man tossed two foil wrapped missiles from the aisle. Tuck caught them with practiced ease, and she watched his twenty dollar bill make its way down the row of fans to the waiting man.

Like a palpable force, excitement for the coming competition vibrated through the stadium. The rumble of shifting bodies was surprisingly loud as she, along with the crowd, rose to her feet for the national anthem. Disconcerted, she examined the odd sense of camaraderie that came from singing along with fifty thousand strangers. She snuck a peek at Tuck. He sang unapologetically, his deep voice added to the thousands of others. Contentment softened his tough-guy features.

An answering softness turned her insides to mush, and she looked away. Last night, as he'd been about to change her body irreversibly, if not her life, he'd made a comment that had kept her awake long after he'd drifted off beside her. Sure, "I love that about you" wasn't the same as I love you, but the word, coming from his lips and directed at her, made her heart skitter with a hope she had no business feeling.

She blinked as the anthem came to an end. There was nothing she could do about her foolish heart at the moment and, in the end, she didn't regret her decision to spend the night with him, or the three weeks of their agreement. She might be playing with fire, but oh, what a lovely way to burn. He was right. She'd allowed her dysfunctional past to cheat her of a normal future. Well, that was done. Today she'd taken a wide step toward emotional freedom, and so far, at least, the results were promising.

The next few hours passed in a flurry of wild euphoria and nail-biting anxiety. The lead changed hands six times in the first eight innings, much to the home fans' dismay. Finally, with one inning to go, the Bronx Bombers were out front, but just barely. Despite Mike's announced prowess of baseball facts, Tuck made a point of explaining the game in process.

The courtesy was unnecessary. Thanks to Kris, CC knew more about most of the major sports, including baseball, than she cared to. Though her cousin lived for football, the large screen TV upstairs in their living room was forever tuned to whatever sport the season offered, once the gridiron boys hit the golf courses, of course.

She didn't bother correcting Tuck's misconception of her knowledge. In fact, she was as charmed by his gentle tutoring as she was his obvious enjoyment of the game. With boyish enthusiasm, he celebrated each success along with the fans and players, and added his voice of displeasure to the crowd's when things didn't go the Yankees' way.

In the bottom of the ninth, she groaned along with everyone else when the tying run advanced to third. Thanks to the left fielder's bobbled catch, the visiting player slid into third with an inch to spare. The stadium erupted in catcalls and boos as the runner was judged safe. Like jack-in-the-box bookends, Tuck and Mike leaped to their feet to join the melee.

"That's bullshit." Mike tossed his third hot dog wrapper to the ground in disgust. "He didn't tag up. Hey, Ump, are you blind? He didn't tag up. He was running before the ball was caught!"

On the field, the third base coach made his argument to the umpire with waving arms and bulging neck veins, to no avail. The on-deck batter moved to the batter's box.

Mike dropped back into his seat and turned to Tuck. "Do you believe this shit? He didn't tag up."

"They must be asleep in the dugout." Tuck sat down with a frown. "Why the hell aren't they challenging the play?"

"Maybe because there's nothing to challenge." Both men turned to stare at her. Tuck's lips turned down in a slight frown, but Mike looked as if he'd swallowed a bug.

"You don't know what you're talking about, CC." He flung out an arm toward the Jumbotron. The crowd booed as the replay cued up. He turned to her with a smirk. "He left the bag before the ball was caught."

"Cut her some slack. It's her first game." Tuck swung an arm around the back of her seat.

She shrugged. "The sacrifice fly rule states the runner can leave the moment the ball touches the glove, not when the ball is caught. If the fielder hadn't bobbled the ball, he'd have caught him."

Twin looks of disbelief met her assertion. She burst out laughing.

Before either man could comment, the crack of the bat drew their attention. The popup went high and sailed foul, skimming the first base line. CC followed the progress of the first baseman. With the game winning catch within his reach, he raced straight toward their seating section, head thrown back in the sunlight.

Time seemed to slow as she followed his steps. Arm extended, he stretched out like a ballet dancer in the midst of a graceful leap, and with a quiet poof, the ball tucked into the pocket of his glove. Unfortunately, momentum wasn't his friend. One leg clipped the rail, and he sailed straight for the fan sitting directly in front of her.

She had no time to cringe as the man ducked. To his credit, the player twisted his body at the last moment, in an effort to avoid a head-on collision. He didn't quite manage the maneuver. Pain exploded in her right cheekbone, and a solid thud to her chest burst the air from her lungs on a whoosh.

Mayhem ensued. The euphoric roar of the crowd pulsed in her ears as two hundred pounds of hard athlete pinned her in her seat. Her face throbbed, and pain radiated from her sternum, lessening instantly when the player rolled from her lap to lift his glove triumphantly.

"Jesus, CC."

Tuck's frantic voice reached her above the chaos of tangled bodies and the roaring crowd. His worried face swam into view. He squatted down in front of her. Over his shoulder, the first baseman's eyes were full of concern. He ignored the celebratory pats to his back to lean close.

"Are you okay, ma'am?"

"I'm fine." She lifted shaky fingers to her cheekbone. How could something so numb hurt so bad? She attempted to straighten in her seat.

"Don't move." Tuck glanced over his shoulder. "Get a medic down here."

Panic reared its ugly head. "I don't need a medic. I just need to get up."

"You took quite a hit, ma'am. The stadium medics are going to want to check you out."

"No!" She clawed against Tuck's hands on her shoulders, giving up when he held her firm. "I mean, I'm fine. I don't need anyone to see me. Please. You, ah, you should get back to the field." Her attempt at a smile only increased the throbbing. "I promise you I'm fine. I just need some room."

"Give her some room," Tuck growled. "Mike, get these people out of here."

Mike turned. "You heard her, folks. Get lost."

A shaky sigh escaped her as the player took her at her word and began making his way back to the rail. The handful of people crowding around quickly lost interest in her, understandably distracted by the celebrity first baseman in their midst, and she thanked God no one but Mike seemed to recognize Tuck. With two sports giants hovering over her....

"Damn, sunshine. I'm sorry." He touched a finger to her cheek. She flinched and his eyes blazed. "You are hurt! Where are those medics?" he demanded of no one in particular.

Mike settled into the seat next to her and indicated the stairs. "They're on their way."

She jerked straight in her chair and slapped a hand over her throbbing cheekbone. Unfortunately, her new position allowed her a clear view of the field and the far wall beyond it. Her breathing hitched, and she watched her own eyes widen in sixty-foot tall, high definition.

"Oh…" Her moan throbbed against her sternum. "Oh, shit."

Tuck's head whipped around. When he met her gaze once more, his eyes were as wide as hers. "Fuck, I was only kidding about appearing on the Jumbotron."

She began to pant. The Jumbotron—at Yankee Stadium! With her luck, she'd make ESPN's play of the day.

"Breathe, CC. Oh, hell."

"I—" She gulped. "Can't!" Spots danced in her vision, and if she could have managed it, she'd have given Kevin Tucker a black eye. The world was closing in around her, and it was *his* fault.

"Yes, you can, baby." He leaned in until his eyes were all she saw. "Yes, you can."

"Give us some room, folks." The strange male voice sounded far away. Tuck looked to his left suddenly, and she figured the paramedics had arrived. The knowledge didn't help.

"CC, look at me."

She blinked and focused on Tuck's steady blue eyes.

"I'm not going to let anything happen to you." He jerked his head toward the aisle and offered her a constrained smile. "I'm not sure these guys will let me schlep you out of here without a fight. Instead, let's test that theory, shall we?"

He dipped his head and closed his mouth over hers. She jolted. Beyond panicked, she forced herself to focus on the firm lips touching hers. He sipped and nipped, rubbing the tip of his tongue over her bottom lip. Sound retreated, darkness threatened. She fought against oblivion, clinging to the knowledge she wasn't alone. Tuck was here. She was going to kill him when she got the chance, but he was here.

"Sir. If you'd step back, we need to take a look at the lady."

Snickers of laughter competed with Tuck's low growl. He shifted his head, and his mouth owned hers. His familiar scent registered; cinnamon salvation expanded her struggling lungs. Relief came in a rush. She gasped and gulped at his mouth, desperately drawing in his attack-stopping gift. With frantic fingers, she clutched at his T-shirt. Arms, strong and sure, surrounded her, tucking her closer and pinning her arms between them. She gloried in the feeling of safety as a brush fire of heat burned away the last vestiges of the looming attack.

She purred low in her throat, struggling to free her arms. Her need to pull him closer was overwhelming. She shoved at his chest, yanking her arms up and around his neck as he shifted to give her arms room. Her fingers banged against something hard, then slid into his hair. She opened her mouth and thrilled to the immediate thrust of his tongue. Sucking at the silky marauder, she tugged him close on a needy moan.

The sharp pain in her chest turned the moan to a groan. The hot wave of pleasure receded, leaving recollection in its wake. Laughter and the roll of cheering throughout the stadium didn't quite drown out the loud clearing of a throat.

"She doesn't look hurt to me." Mike's voice held a grin.

Her eyes popped open, inches from Tuck's. He pulled back and grimaced, an apology in his worried eyes. Her gaze flew to the top of his head. His ball cap had disappeared, and without the disguise to shade it, his gold-tipped hair gleamed in the bright sunlight.

"We still need to check her out," a deep voice replied. "If you wouldn't mind, Mr. Tucker."

Chapter 20

CC frowned as the car rumbled over the gravel drive toward the historic farmhouse. "I don't think this is a good idea."

Tuck pinned her with a stubborn stare. "You're not checking into a hotel, and my place is out. I'm sure they have it staked out, too."

She'd balked when he suggested she spend a few days at the Malones' farm, but Kris's excited phone call, saying ESPN was parked at their curb, made going home out of the question. The mystery of how they'd known where to find her was answered when Edward made a call to dispatch. Apparently, someone at the field had gotten the tags from the limo as they made their escape, and an enterprising intern at ESPN had called the car service for its pick-up location. Edward promised that wouldn't happen again.

"I don't want to impose. The couch in my mom's suite will be fine for a few nights." She cringed at the thought and he smiled.

"Jake and Gracie know all about being hounded by the press, and you heard Gracie yourself. They don't consider you an imposition. Quit overthinking things, CC. It'll be fine. You'll see."

Edward brought the car to a stop in front of the house. Tuck grabbed her hand and tugged her from the limo's backseat. With hesitant steps, she let him lead her past the sunny-faced daisies lining the walkway. Hanging planters, overflowing with summer colors, hung from the railings. A pair of hummingbirds buzzed like miniature bell ringers as they flitted from bloom to bloom. The almost musical squeak of the screen door added to the sense of serenity as Gracie appeared on the porch.

She greeted them with a wide smile. "Welcome to the Malone anti-press bunker."

At CC's side, Tuck chuckled. "Thanks for letting us hide out for a while."

Gracie grinned. "No problem. You're not the first couple to take shelter here."

Guilt poked at CC. "I appreciate this, Gracie. It won't be for long."

An airy wave dismissed her concern. "Stay as long as you need. We have plenty of room, and with Mary gone to Ireland for a month—she's more of a friend than housekeeper—it'll be nice to have another woman around."

Linking her arm through CC's, she led them inside. After showing them both to the suite upstairs where they'd be sleeping, together apparently, she dragged CC down to the huge family kitchen with Tuck following.

"Where are Jake and the rugrats?" He straddled a chair at the oversized table and sat. CC set her cell phone on the table and slid into the chair next to his.

Gracie crossed to the refrigerator and pulled out a beer. She handed it to Tuck, then ducked her head back into the industrial sized appliance. "When the girls heard you were coming, they insisted he pick up a couple of pizzas for dinner." She emerged with a bottle of wine and a bag of frozen peas. A pair of wine glasses were plucked from a rack above the counter, and she turned. "Come on, CC. My office is more comfortable."

CC darted a gaze at Tuck but rose to follow as Gracie strode from the room.

"Hey, what about me?" The chair legs scraped as he called to their backs.

"No men." Gracie didn't pause or even turn her head. "CC needs some girl time."

"Gracie." A warning rang in his tone.

She waived a hand over her head and kept walking. "Entertain yourself. Jake will be back in a few minutes."

"I need girl time?" CC trailed Tuck's friend like a baby duck after its momma.

"Yes, and I do, too."

They stepped into a cozy den, and Gracie shut the door behind them. A cold fireplace took up most of one wall. A second was covered with shelves of books. Another held a poster-sized print that had graced the cover of *Sports Illustrated* earlier this spring a week after Jake had broken the touchdown record. The shot captured him, dressed in his Marauders uniform and stretched out in the air with a football an inch from his fingers. The large frame was surrounded by smaller pictures of Jake and Gracie, the twins, Tom Walden and his wife, and several other faces CC didn't recognize.

"Here." Gracie held out the peas. Her eyes widened when CC removed her melting ice pack to make the exchange. "Ouch! Do you need to see a doctor? The girls' pediatrician lives about a mile down the road, and he makes house calls."

"Oh, that's not necessary. I'm fine. It's just a bruise." She winced as she pressed the frozen vegetables to her cheek.

"That's one hell of a bruise." Gracie settled onto the couch and tugged a corkscrew from the drawer in the white pine coffee table. She patted the cushion at her side. "Have a seat. Would you like a glass?" She held up the bottle of chilled chardonnay.

"Please." Sliding onto the couch, she accepted the glass Gracie poured.

"You're going to have an impressive shiner." Gracie peeked sideways at her as she poured a second. "But I'd say that soul deep kiss Tuck laid on you at the stadium makes it worthwhile, don't you?"

She plunked the glass down with a ringing thud. "You *saw* that?

A smile curved Gracie's lips and she sat back. "Sweetie, about two *million* people saw that."

"Oh my God." Her eyes slid shut, and she swallowed against the nausea bubbling up her throat.

"I thought you knew. Isn't that why you're here?"

She opened her eyes to find confusion in Gracie's."

"I'm here because my condo is being watched." She tossed the peas to the table and swept up her glass. Swallowing a healthy gulp, she shook her head. "I knew the camera was on us when I saw my face on the big screen, but…" Another gulp drained the glass, and her breaths came in pants. She wiped her lips with her fingers. "I swear, my brain misfires when that man is around."

Gracie grinned and picked up the bottle. CC nodded and golden liquid splashed into her glass. A crystal chime rang when Tuck's friend tapped her glass to the rim.

Gracie sipped, sighed in appreciation, and lowered the glass to her lap. "It's been my experience that the right man can definitely scramble a woman's brain."

Panic pulsed through CC's heart. The *right* man? Oh, no. No. No. No! "That better not be true or I'm screwed."

Tinkling laughter escaped Gracie's lips. "I don't see why. He's single. Funny. Has a job that pays well. He's gorgeous." She ticked off her list of Tuck's attributes with raised fingers and a wry smile. "And charming. Sometimes a little too much for his own good, I admit, but he obviously cares for you."

CC wiped a damp palm on the thigh of her jeans, then shifted the glass to her other hand to repeat the process with the second. "You forgot to add he's the most eligible bachelor on the East Coast and goes through women like drag racers burn through tires."

"Both true, but that was before he met you."

The heat of her blush intensified the throbbing in her cheek. "It's not like that."

"Isn't it?" Gracie tipped the rim of her glass in CC's direction. "I don't know what that kiss looked like from your perspective, but from where I was sitting, I'd say his racing days are over."

She groaned.

"I'm serious, sweetie. I've watched R-rated movies that didn't contain that much heat."

Her dried palms went dewy. If what Gracie was saying was true....

Hope she hadn't dared allow before suddenly snuck in to steal her breath. Could Tuck's friend be right? Did the passion in his eyes transcend the bounds of simple lust? The possibility both tempted and frightened.

Don't be a fool, CC. He's Kevin Tucker. An expert player. A man who's left a trail of broken hearts in his wake.

What was she thinking? So they had passion between them. So did a pair of cats when the moment was right. And when the moment passed, they scratched and hissed and went on their way. Alone.

She shook her head. "He'll be leaving for training camp in a couple weeks."

"So is Jake, and they'll both be back when camp is over."

"Yeah, but Jake is..." She opened a flat hand and flicked it between them. "And you are..." A helpless sigh shuddered from her lungs. "Your situation is different."

Gracie swirled the wine in her glass. "Not so different. You're sort of preaching to the choir, CC. It wasn't long ago I was making the same type of arguments, all of which turned out to be wrong."

The hand dropped to her side. "I appreciate what you're saying but, honestly, this thing between Tuck and me is only temporary."

"Because of your agreement?"

She sat up straighter. Damn it. Their arrangement was a private affair, as were the many details she'd shared with him about her life. Her family. A chill raced over her. What else had he blabbed? "He told you about our arrangement?"

A nod was her only answer.

"Then you should understand." She brought the glass to her lips, but only sipped this time. Gulping the first glass had left her a little dizzy. Did concussions make you woozy? Maybe she *should* see a doctor. Cool fingers brushed her arm, and she blinked.

"What I understand is that Tuck has feelings for you, and if I'm reading you right, they're not one-sided."

Feelings, not cared for. How did she know that? Had he shared them with his friend, and what type of feelings exactly? The kind a man had for a woman he was sleeping with or something more? A knock interrupted them before she could ask.

The door creaked open, and Tuck popped his head in through the gap. "Pizza's here." He held up the phone she'd left on the table. "And your mother called. She's on her way."

CC bobbled her glass onto the table and leaped to her feet. "What? Why did you answer, and why in the world did you tell her where I was?"

He pushed the panel open completely and straightened in the doorway. His sheepish smile resembled more of a grimace. "Sorry. Your phone rang, and I saw it was your mom. You answered her call the other day, and I figured…" Apparently, he didn't enjoy sheepish. His brows drew together and his shoulders shot back. "Fine. I shouldn't have answered, but once I had, I was afraid not to tell her. She saw a tease on the local news channel for tonight's sports report, and she sounded hysterical. She kept babbling about emotional wounds and fatal mistakes and demanded to know where I'd stashed you."

"Oh, dear Lord."

Closing the distance between them, he held out the phone. "Call her back. Tell her you're okay."

She slapped a hand to the top of her head. "Like that would do any good." She turned to offer Gracie a sick smile. "I'm so sorry. My mother can be a little…intense. She'll insist on hovering. It would be best if I just checked into a hotel."

"Nonsense." Gracie rose to her feet and headed for the door. "We have plenty of room. Come have some pizza before Jake and the goblins devour it all."

"We'll be out in a minute." Gracie paused at Tuck's comment. He bumped out his chin. "Close the door behind you, will you?"

She nodded.

He cupped his fingers around CC's neck the second the door clicked shut. "I'm sorry."

She found it impossible to be angry with him when he was touching her. "No. I'm sorry. I shouldn't have snapped at you."

He slid his other arm around her waist and pulled her closer. "You've had a hell of an afternoon. You're entitled to a little...*snit*."

She snorted a laugh, and he tightened his arms around her. She dropped her forehead to his chest with a smile.

"That's better. Now, what was your mother talking about with wounds and fatal mistakes? She didn't seem to be making any sense."

A groan gurgled up from her belly and spilled from her lips. He reared back and tucked a finger under her chin, lifting her head until he could meet her gaze.

"My mother often doesn't make sense." She shot a glance at the closed door. "I shouldn't tell you this, wouldn't tell you normally, but since you'll be meeting her in a little while, I think you should know."

Apprehension crossed his brow. "Know what?"

She looked him dead in the eyes. "If you tell anyone what I'm about to say, I'll deny it. *After* I kill you."

He grinned, and shifting one arm to release her, he slashed his finger over his chest, crossing his heart.

"Okay, but I mean it. Not a word."

He nodded.

Her chest heaved on a deep, hesitant breath. "My mother thinks she's psychic." She jammed her eyes closed briefly on a wince.

"You're kidding?"

"I wish. She gets some pretty kooky ideas, and she's a bulldog about seeing them through."

He laughed. "I can't wait to meet her."

"Ha! You say that now, but you'll be singing a different tune when she pulls out her Tarot cards and starts in on you about your perfect mate."

"Okay. Now I'm scared." The twinkle in his eyes belied the sentiment.

"Don't say I didn't warn you."

He dropped a kiss on the tip of her nose, and a subtle whiff of sawdust flared her nostrils.

Oh, no.

He turned and pulled her to the door.

She sawed at her lower lip with her teeth and stopped him before he could open it. "Would you do me a favor?"

He turned to face her, and his laughing eyes were suddenly serious. "I'd do anything for you."

An internal whimper caught in her throat before it could escape. Well, shoot. She'd think about what he meant by that later.

She cleared her throat. "Would you take a shower before she arrives?"

Chapter 21

"Um. I need to tell you something before my mother gets here."

CC curled her restless fingers into fists on the tabletop and darted a nervous glance around at the curious faces. With her mother soon to arrive, the secret of her identity would be out in a few minutes anyway. Though Natalie Calhoun no longer walked the runways, her famous face, and her connection to Curt, were well known. A preemptive strike seemed the wisest course.

Gracie's gaze dropped to the hand Tuck laid over CC's, and she pushed back her chair. "Girls, how about you take your plates into the den?"

"Like a picnic?" Charlie's eyes lit with pleasure.

"I get to pick the movie." Plate in hand, Angel scooted off her chair and darted for the hall.

"You picked last time," her sister called, scrambling to follow. Murphy trotted after them.

"I'll be just a minute." Gracie gathered their glasses and a handful of napkins and disappeared through the kitchen door.

Tuck squeezed CC's hand. "What's up?"

She shook her head without meeting his gaze. Her identity would forever be tangled with the stories of her kidnapping. Other than with Tuck and a handful of doctors, she'd never willingly opened the topic up for discussion. If she had a choice, she wouldn't do so now, but if she was going to bare her soul to his friends, she'd rather have to say it only once.

Jake pushed his plate forward and propped his muscled forearms on the table. "Why is it I have a bad feeling in my gut?"

"Oh, hush, Jake." Gracie rushed back into the room and slid into the chair beside her husband. "They're all settled. What is it, CC? What's wrong?"

A familiar tightening banded her chest, and she blew out a ragged breath. "My mother is Natalie Calhoun."

"And her father is Curt Jensen," Tuck added quietly.

She turned to find his eyes on her. Sober, supportive, they bore into her, and the back of her throat stung with threatening tears. She swallowed them back and offered him a grateful smile.

"Fuck me." Jake eased back into his chair.

"Oh, CC." Understanding bloomed in Gracie's eyes. Her gaze shifted to Tuck and clung there momentarily before returning. "Oh, sweetie."

CC straightened her spine. "I only mentioned it because you're bound to recognize my mom. I didn't want you to think I was keeping secrets from you." And she wanted the inquisition on what had happened all those years ago done and over with before her mom was around to add to the conversation.

"Totally understandable."

"Fuck me," Jake repeated.

"That's ten bucks for the jar, pal." Gracie turned to him with a stern scowl.

He rolled his eyes, picked up his slice of pizza, and aimed it at Tuck. "You know the guys are going to rip you to shreds over that performance at the game today." His teeth cut through the slice of pizza in an enormous bite.

Tuck's hand relaxed on CC's and he laughed. "Don't I know it."

"I forgot the shredded cheese." Gracie rose to cross to the fridge. "Would anyone else like a beer?"

CC blinked, her gaze jerking from face to face. What the hell? Most people would have peppered her with questions about the kidnapping and, braced for the assault, she wasn't sure what to think as the conversation moved on to the pennant race standings, Max's new building, and a controversial multiple trade sure to shake up the world of pro football. Tuck had claimed normal didn't apply with the Malones. Apparently, he was right.

* * * *

Tuck hid a smile as Natalie yawned for the third time in a minute, and CC huffed out a frustrated sigh. The twins had been in bed for hours, and Gracie and Jake had gone upstairs ten minutes earlier, but Natalie Calhoun continued to hover, clucking her tongue at the shiner that had blossomed on her daughter's cheek as the evening progressed.

Tuck was anxious to hit the sheets as well, but not because he was tired. Yeah, the idea of slipping into CC's sweet little body again was a definite distraction, but it was more than that. The tension in her body and face as she revealed her parents' names to his friends tore at his heart. It was a testament to her strength that she hadn't flat out refused to stay once she learned of her mother's impending arrival and what that would mean, but how much could one, slight woman take?

He respected her desire to overcome her panic attacks and was proud of the progress she'd made. It couldn't be easy for her to relive the memories now she'd begun to share them with him, and after today's fiasco at the game, the pack of interested reporters was one more weight bearing down on her slim shoulders.

While she'd waved off his apologies over what had happened, insisting she'd been the one to demand they step up the dates, it tore at his gut that he'd inadvertently added to the stress she was already feeling. Hoping to minimize the fallout, he'd slipped away earlier and called his contact at ESPN. With a little luck, the press interest would fade with the exclusive interview he'd promised to give the man, but in the meantime, he wanted to sweep her into his arms and take her away to a place no one could find her, then make sweet love to her until the shadows faded from her eyes.

She scooped the remote control from the coffee table and turned off the TV. "It's late, Mom, and there's a perfectly good bed waiting upstairs for you."

"What if you have a concussion? I'm fine right here with you on the couch. Go to sleep. I'll wake you in an hour to make sure you're okay."

Slouched in the chair across from them, Tuck cleared his throat. "I'll keep an eye on her, Ms. Calhoun."

The smile that had graced countless magazine covers beamed his way. "I told you, it's Natalie."

"Right." He linked his fingers together on his belly. "Natalie, CC's right. You must be tired."

Indecision wrinkled her brow. "Well, if you're sure. Do you have an alarm on your phone? Concussions are nothing to be ignored."

CC rolled her eyes and stood. "I can set my own alarm, and I don't have a concussion. I'm going upstairs. Come on, I'll show you to your room."

Natalie rose from the couch, and Tuck pushed up from the chair to follow. Upstairs, CC stopped before one of the four bedroom doors and pushed it open.

Natalie peeked inside, then straightened and moved into the room. "Oh, isn't this lovely?"

"Good night, Mom. I'll see you in the morning." CC turned toward the room he'd be sharing with her.

Her mother spun around. "Wait, where are you sleeping?" Her gaze zipped to Tuck and back.

CC pointed at the next door. "Right there."

Natalie turned to him, and her pencil thin eyebrows formed an inverted V. "And you?"

"I'll be right—"

"Down the hall."

His head snapped in CC's direction. The pointed widening of her eyes demanded he not contradict her claim. Was she serious? They hadn't discussed what they were going to tell her mother about their relationship but, in his opinion, no explanation was necessary. The whole world had witnessed that kiss earlier today, if not live, then on the newscasts and sports networks. Natalie had seen it as well, or she wouldn't be here.

"Tuck's room is there." CC pointed to the last door at the end of the hall.

He spun his head to follow her finger and bit back a groan. Why couldn't she have picked the other door for his fictitious bedroom? If they were going to play out this farce, the twins' nursery would have been a much preferable choice, but no. That would be too easy. Instead, she'd put him right smack dab in the master suite.

He curled his lips in a smile, but the narrow-eyed stare he pinned on her warned she was going to pay, and pay big. If he stepped one foot into Jake's bedroom, he'd never hear the end of it. His only choice was to stall.

He turned to Natalie and jerked a stiffened thumb over his shoulder. "Yep. That's me. Right down there."

"Well, then."

Like stone statues, no one moved. Natalie wore an easy smile as she stood with a hand on the knob of her opened door. A few feet away, CC looked as if she wanted to drop through the floor. Her lips were pressed tight together, and her gaze bounced from the floor to the ceiling, then down the hall in the opposite direction. Anywhere but at him.

He shuffled his feet, hoping to break the fucked-up standoff they all seemed to be caught in. Nothing. He hiked his chin at CC. If she'd just say good night and go into their room, maybe he could drag his feet long enough for Natalie to give up and close the door. Busy studying the wallpaper as if it were made of gold, CC didn't notice.

Damn it to hell. His shoulders slumped, and he spun around to stalk down the hall.

"Good night," Natalie called to his back.

"Good night," CC echoed.

He raised a hand and resisted the urge to growl. "Good night."

Fifteen long steps later, he hadn't heard the click of one shutting door, never mind two. He glanced over his shoulder as he arrived at the master suite—and wanted to cry. Natalie lifted her hand to wiggle her fingers in a wave. CC wore a pained smile.

Gritting his teeth, he grabbed the knob, opened the door, and slipped inside.

As quietly as possible, he pushed the door closed at his back—and winced. The soft click might as well have been a gunshot. He was going to strangle CC. For shit's sake, they were grown adults. Here he was, sneaking around like a teenager caught after curfew.

A subtle rustling from the large bed across the expansive room made him hold his breath. Fuck. Two minutes. All he needed was two minutes, and then he could slip back out the door with none the wiser. Another rustling and the room flooded with light.

With his arm stretched to the bedside lamp, Jake glared at him over one bare shoulder. Gracie peeked at him from beneath the other and yanked the sheet up over her husband's bare ass.

Tuck shot out his hand like a Heisman winner. "Don't say a fucking word."

Jake slid to the side and Gracie squeaked, pulling the sheet up to her chin. Jake sat up. "You get lost?"

"No, I—"

"Good. Get your ass out of my bedroom."

Gracie pressed a hand to her husband's arm. "What's going on, Tuck?"

He jammed his fingers into his hair and accepted defeat. "CC doesn't want her mother to know we're sleeping together."

"Oh, I hadn't thought of that." Concern puckered her brow.

Jake snickered. "Sucks to be you, but you're not bunking with us. There's a couch downstairs. Scram."

"I don't need the couch. I just need a minute until Natalie settles, and then I can sneak in with CC."

"You've got three seconds."

"Jake." Gracie shook her head.

"Okay, four seconds."

"You're all heart." Tuck turned and opened the door. He peeked out and relief washed through him when both CC and Natalie's doors were closed. Looking back at the naked couple on the bed, he leered. "Nice jammies."

The pillow thumped against the door just before he shut it behind him.

* * * *

"Take a walk with me."

Sitting at the table on the patio early the next morning, CC cradled her coffee cup in her palms and eyed the trees beyond the yard. "I don't know if I can, Tuck."

"Sure, you can. You didn't think you could face down fifty thousand Yankee's fans either, but you did."

"Yeah, and look how that worked out." She touched gentle fingertips to the purple bruising beneath her eye.

He grinned and leaned over in his chair to press a kiss to her lips. "I never realized a black eye could so be sexy."

She laughed and shoved him away. "God, you have a one-track mind." And that track had kept her awash in pleasure for a good portion of last night, once he'd snuck back in to join her in the big four-poster bed. He'd threated to paddle her ass if she ever put him in such a position again, and she'd giggled her way through his telling of how he'd interrupted Jake and Gracie in their birthday suits.

His blue eyes sparkled with teasing laughter as he sat back.

"Thanks for calling your friend at ESPN."

He shrugged. "I owed him one, and he's always been true to his word. He's got an exclusive story, and you'll get your privacy back."

He'd taped the phone interview an hour ago from their bedroom as she listened in. She'd marveled at his ability to say so much and reveal so little. With typical Tuck charm, he played coy, deftly sidestepping the issue of her identity with some good ol' boy teasing about his reputation. Whether by prearranged design or Tuck's skill at the verbal two-step, her name never came up.

The three minute spot would air later this morning, scuttling the hopes of anyone still interested in breaking the story. He insisted the plan would work, and she hoped he was right.

He pushed from his chair and held out his hand. "Come on. Let's check one more fear off your list before the house begins to stir."

Against her better judgment, she placed her palm into his. They crossed the lawn, leaving a path through morning dew, and she breathed deeply as they approached the edge of the woods.

"You doing okay?"

She nodded, though technically it wasn't the truth. The shadowy gloom of the thick timber gave her the creeps and made her palms sweat. She wiped her free hand on her shorts but continued forward. He was right. One less fear weighing her down would bring her another step closer to freedom, and though living in Manhattan, the chances were good she'd never have need to venture into the woods in the future, you never knew.

"When I was a kid, our parents used to take my cousins and me to a state reserve about an hour west of Boston called Purgatory Chasm. How's that for a spooky name?" He gripped her fingers tight and guided her over a small log partially blocking the trail.

She glanced over, suspicious. "Are you making that up just to distract me?"

His teeth flashed in a teasing grin. "Why? Is it working?"

She chuckled. "A little."

"Good, but I'm serious. We'd all squeeze into my uncle's station wagon before the sun had even come up. Once we got there, the adults would cook an incredible breakfast on the outdoor grills while us kids explored the rocks and caves." He brushed a low branch aside so she could pass. "The rock formations had different names like The Coffin, Lover's Leap, and my favorite, Fat Man's Misery."

She glanced at him over her shoulder. "Why was it called that?"

"Because no fat man is getting himself into that crack. There's this huge granite boulder that looks like someone took a giant sledgehammer and broke it down the middle. The gap is about a foot wide and fifteen feet deep. We used to see how many of us could cram inside at once."

Surprised to note he'd let go of her hand and she was now leading *him* down the trail, she waited for the fingers of panic to grab at her throat. When they didn't, she heaved a breath and hurried her steps. "Have you been back? I mean, since you've grown up?"

"Nope, but I'd like to. Jessi has a show in Boston on Friday and the Chasms were always her favorite. What do you say we make a date to go this week?"

To Boston? He wanted to take her to his hometown? Her suddenly racing heart had nothing to do with fear. She shouldn't read anything into the request. They had a week and a half left in their agreement, after all, and there were only so many movies and museums to see. Still, she couldn't help the growing kernel of hope....

She stopped and turned to face him with a cocky smirk. "I don't know. You're not a kid anymore and, well..." She ran her gaze up and down his muscular body. "Fat Man's Misery might mean you. Are you sure you'll still fit?"

His twinkling eyes squinted, and he reached for her. She took off like a shot, laughing as she dodged limbs and hopped over rocks. The thud of his pounding feet behind her disturbed the absolute quiet as she rounded a corner and skidded to a halt. Beneath the spread limbs and heavy foliage of an enormous oak tree, she pressed both hands to her chest and gasped.

His arms slid around her from behind, and he dropped his head to her shoulder. Six feet away, a bubbling spring meandered through the thicket. Wild blueberry bushes lined the opposite bank. A fat raccoon lumbered into the dense shrubbery as a Blue Jay chastised an unseen companion, setting up a racket from a high branch in the distance.

"It's beautiful." Her breathless voice seemed to stir the air and a gentle breeze wafted over them.

His stubbled cheek rubbed against hers in a nod.

Tears pooled on her lower lids, and she turned in his arms. Pressing up onto the toes of her sneakers, she lifted her face until she could brush her lips against his. His familiar scent blended with the tang of tree sap and natural mulch, and her eyes slid shut as she tangled her fingers in his hair.

Gently, as if he too were aware of the serene enchantment of this place and time, he drew her closer. She curled into his body, telling him wordlessly how much his belief in her meant.

The past and all its fears held no sway in this magical moment, and she opened her mouth to him as surely as she did her heart. His low murmur encouraged, and she slid her hands beneath the hem of his loose T-shirt to graph the muscled cords and strong lines of his back with sensitive fingertips. He shuddered beneath her exploration, and her lips formed a soft smile against his.

The power of this place, combined with her burgeoning heart, whispered of sweet, endless possibilities, there for the taking if only she had the courage to grasp at the chance. Hope, bold and irresistible, shimmered through her veins, and she answered the call. She pulled back enough to lock her gaze with his.

"Love me, Tuck."

Whether he recognized the heartfelt plea in her request or not, she knew its depth and opened herself to those possibilities with joyous abandon. The world ceased to exist. There was only Tuck and this serene glade as he took her mouth as if parched for the taste of her. With mouths and hands, they worshipped at the altar of pleasure.

A bed of leaves cradled them as he lowered her to the ground. Shade from the grand oak dappled patterns on the backs of her eyelids. He peeled away her T-shirt and shorts with gentle hands. She followed suit, rolling up to strip the shirt over his head and spread her hands over his chest. Like the healthy animal he was, his hair-sprinkled skin heated her fingers as they slid to his waistband.

He lifted his hips to aid in the removal of his shorts and briefs, and she shifted onto one elbow to admire what she had uncovered. Powerful, muscled, sleekly beautiful, he lay sprawled before her with no hint of modesty. His blue eyes, searing in intensity, burned into hers. Their eyes locked, and he reached out to search through the pocket of his discarded shorts. A condom appeared in his hand.

"Always prepared, I see." She rose to her knees. Laughter gleamed in his eyes and she held out a hand. "Let me."

Her fingers shook as she rolled the latex down his thick erection, and before she lost her nerve, she threw one leg over his hips to straddle him. His sexy, dimpled smile urged her on, and she braced above him. A ragged sigh shimmered from her lungs as she lowered herself and drew him inside. Full, hot, delicious, she savored the sense of coming home.

His hands came to her hips, and he arched his. Yearning, deep and seductive, demanded she move, and their bodies swayed in a timeless flight. High above the treetops, where the air was sweet and clear, they flew on the winds of time. Swirling, falling, only to be tossed upward once again, they traveled to a place out of time. And when, at last, they floated back to earth, she slid to his chest, boneless, depleted, and secure in his arms.

Chapter 22

"I saw the clip from the game and heard Tuck's interview yesterday. Can I help? I could make some calls."

The simple cadence of her father's voice on her answering machine threatened to suck CC back into the horror and confusion of those months following the kidnapping, and her bones ached with the violence of her shudder. Unbidden images and sounds flooded her mind. The frightening glare of camera lights. Her father's voice echoing in numerous concert hall speakers as he played for those cameras. Incomprehensible questions about the kidnapping tossed at her like stones. The internal quivering of her body as she stared into the calculating and oddly excited eyes of strangers.

She shook her head, scattering the hateful memories, and jammed a shaking finger to the delete button as Curt ended his latest message with, *"Let me know."*

"Yeah, I'll get right on that."

For sixteen years, she'd done her best to push the memories to the back of her mind. His absence had allowed her a measure of success, but hearing his voice again brought it all back to the forefront. What did he want from her? Hadn't she given him enough?

No doubt he'd be happy to make a few calls, inserting himself in yet another press bonanza, but as far as she was concerned, the situation was resolved. Just as Tuck had predicted, his interview, while entertaining, deflated interest in the story, and as was often the case with the voracious press, they'd moved on to the next salacious blockbuster. Maybe she should send a thank-you gift to the NBA star who'd been caught with his gym shorts around his ankles as he gave a female reporter her own personal inside scoop.

Come to think of it, she still had that bag of super-duper condoms Kris gave her.

Her cell phone buzzed, and Tuck's face appeared on the screen. Her heart did a shimmy shake, and she blew out a cleansing sigh as she answered the call.

His deep voice caressed her ear. "I'm a block away. You ready?"

"We're walking out the door now. Are you sure Walter won't be a problem? I could leave him with Kris."

"Na. The Tucker madhouse is pet friendly."

His family home. Butterflies erupted in her belly. Okay, so they wouldn't technically be staying at his parents' house, but she'd be meeting them. Buds popped on the kernel of hope planted by Gracie's insistence of Tuck's feelings, which had then gone on to sprout shoots after their walk in the woods.

"Okay, but don't say I didn't warn you."

She thumbed the screen and opened the door just as Tuck, in his red Jeep, pulled to the curb. Four hours later, he exited the Massachusetts Turnpike into South Boston. Like an amateur tour guide, he pointed out the places of his youth. They drove by the stadium where he played high school ball and the pizza shop where he scored his first kiss with Amy Jo Borucki as they scrolled through the selection on the jukebox.

"I grew up right down there." He jerked his chin toward the street on their left. "It was a good neighborhood back then, even if it was a little rough around the edges. It's grown pretty seedy over time. For years, my sibs and I pestered Mom and Dad to move somewhere a little less dangerous. They finally conceded five years ago but didn't go far."

He bumped the vehicle along the cobblestone streets of City Point, a bustling South Boston community at the tip of the harbor. Centuries-old brownstones sat tucked between newer structures of glass and steel, and somehow, the clash of eras worked with charming results.

They pulled to a stop in front of a large brick home. Three stories high, and almost as wide, it overlooked the dark water of the Atlantic. Walter whined for release from the backseat, and as she climbed from the Jeep, the butterflies came fluttering back. As if Tuck understood her sudden case of nerves, he smiled and took her hand.

"Come on. You're going to love them."

He pulled her up the steps and through the unlocked front door, and she nearly tripped over her excited dog. She took hold of his collar. A cacophony of voices rang from somewhere at the back of the house, and Tuck dragged them straight to the sound. At the end of a narrow hallway, they stepped into a large kitchen full of happy chaos.

Three of the eight chairs surrounding the long table were occupied. Open sports pages lay in front of a mountain of a man with a shock of gray hair. From the sound of it, he and the man across from him, who looked similar enough to be his twin, were in the midst of a friendly argument over a blown call at last night's Red Sox game. Tuck's cousin, Jessi, laughed at something a tiny blonde woman said and pulled several wine glasses from the cupboard.

"Get out of that, Tim." A middle-aged woman with a slim build and graying blond hair slapped a hand at a slightly younger version of Tuck. Grinning, Tim dipped his finger into the large stockpot on the industrial-sized stove, then plopped the sauce covered digit into his mouth.

Tuck released her hand and stalked forward. "Hey, punk, save some of that for me."

All heads turned, and the obvious pleasure on his family's faces plucked a chord of envy in CC's heart. Multiple greetings were called out at once, ratcheting the decibel level up to the dangerous zone. Tuck dropped a kiss on his cousin's head, then swung the young blonde in his arms for a sloppy kiss.

CC watched from the doorway in silence, her fingers clenched around Walter's collar, as Tuck wrapped his arms around the older woman in a heartfelt hug. "Hi, Mom."

Tim turned his head, and a shiver raced down CC's spine at the eerily familiar arch of his brow. A surprised smile tipped the corner of his mouth. "If it ain't the Yankee fan. Hellooo beautiful."

Suddenly, the only sound was the ticking of the wall clock. Pressure expanded in her chest and the heat of a blush scored her cheeks as all eyes pinned her in place. Tuck released his mother, wacked a hand across the back of his brother's head, and crossed back to her. He grabbed her hand, but when he dipped his head toward hers, she reared back in dismay.

Kissing her in front of a bunch of strangers was one thing, but these people were his family. His gaze narrowed on her in silent question as she focused on regulating her breathing. She shook her head slightly and dragged in a calming breath.

"Losing your touch, big brother?"

Tim's laughing comment flared her blush to a blaze of embarrassment. Not for herself, but for Tuck. Her horrified gaze flew to his, but instead of wounded pride over her apparent slight, silent laughter gleamed in his eyes.

"Welcome to the madhouse, sunshine." He winked and turned to face his curious family. "Everyone. This is CC." His gaze dropped to her dog. "And Walter."

* * * *

Several hours later, Tuck balanced on the back legs of his chair and watched the action fifty yards away through the kitchen's screen door. His uncle Ryan, Jessi's father, along with Tim and their sister, Patty, were on a packy run for more beer and with dinner still a half hour off, Jessi had commandeered CC for a walk on the beach. Tuck had been banned from accompanying them by his cousin, a squirt barely out of braces, who had proclaimed primly that women occasionally needed some men-free conversation. After a hesitant glance his way, CC had agreed.

What was it with women and girl time?

Down on the beach, Walter performed a perfect dodge and weave pattern. Jessi's laughter could be heard as CC ran in circles, flapping her arms in an attempt to protect her dog from the angry seagull diving repeatedly for his head. Tuck grinned. From where he sat, the dog was the only sane one in the bunch.

Gentle fingers threaded through his hair, and he turned to smile at his mother. She brushed the locks back from his forehead and dropped a kiss there, the way she had when he was a boy. He wrapped an arm around her waist, and she rested her cheek against the top of his head.

"She's very sweet, Kevin."

"And not bad to look at," his father added from the other side of the table.

"I noticed." Tuck shot him a toothy leer.

His mother straightened and moved to stir the pot of sauce on the stove.

He scraped a palm across his jaw. "She was nervous about coming here."

"That's understandable. When a man brings a woman to meet his family, a woman tends to get ideas." His mother turned to drill him with squinted eyes and pursed lips. It was a look she'd perfected long ago. The one that said, *I see right through you so you may as well fess up.* Obviously, the woman she was talking about getting ideas was herself.

The legs of his chair thumped to the floor, and because he wasn't sure how to answer the unspoken demand, he played dumb and hedged. "It's more than that. I'm not at liberty to say much, but life's been tough on her. She doesn't do well around strangers."

His father grunted. "Then kissing her in front of fifty thousand *Yankee* fans was probably a mistake."

Tuck grinned. As far as he was concerned, kissing CC was never a mistake. A lifelong Sox fan, of course his father would be more concerned about his oldest son showing his face in enemy territory. "I'll be sure to make a scene for the cameras next time I'm at Fenway."

"See that you do." Satisfied the hometown field would get its share of the limelight, his father smiled. "Your mother's right. CC's a peach. This bunch would intimidate even the most outgoing of women, but she's holding her own."

Tuck sipped his beer as his gaze slid back to the screen door. Yes, she was. While more quiet than usual, she'd eventually settled down enough to join in the madness with his boisterous family—once that initial flash of panic faded. A small smile tugged at his lips at the memory of the surprise in her eyes after she stiff-armed his attempted kiss.

Her obvious dismay that she'd embarrassed him in front of his family was misplaced. Tucker men were used to strong women who stood on their own two feet and weren't afraid to show it. CC fit the mold perfectly. As prickly as she could be at times, she had a soft and giving heart. There wasn't a cruel bone in her body, and though she'd avoided men most of her life, she understood the male ego more than she admitted.

It had been all he could do to keep from grabbing her up in his arms and ravaging her sweet mouth until she purred in response. Angry? Shit, there was no room for anger in a heart bursting with pride.

Two weeks ago she wouldn't have been able to walk through the front door, much less hold him off in front of his family. Not without the breath backing up in her throat, anyway.

Unfortunately, pride was quickly overrun by alarm. The reality of her progress in reclaiming the natural pluck that had survived nightmares slashed at his gut like his mother's favorite serrated knife slicing through bread. Did his sunshine realize she'd conquered the ability to ward off the attacks on her own? That she no longer needed him?

"Do you love her, Son?" His father's quiet voice shattered his dark musings and he blinked.

Did he? He'd never before told a woman he loved her, but from the day they'd met, the idea of love at first sight had haunted him. The words had been on the tip of his tongue as he and CC made love by the banks of the stream, but had the unexpected and gut-deep need to admit such feelings been a natural byproduct of the sexual haze that fogged his mind or the honest cry of his heart?

The fact that he'd had to bite back the words pointed toward love, but how could a man who'd always been content playing the field take one look at a woman and never again care to explore what or who was beyond the next corner? Did he have what it took to pull off that kind of commitment, that kind of love?

He lifted his head and met the steady gaze of the man who raised him, a man who'd known the love of his life when he found her. "How do you know, Dad? How do you know a woman is the right one?"

"Knowing for sure is impossible, because life doesn't come with guarantees. Isn't that right, Maryanne?" Loving contentment softened the smile his father turned on his wife of thirty-four years.

Tuck's mother smiled, and his father winked and turned back.

"But if you look down the road into the future and can't imagine living your days without her there to share the joys and sorrows, you'd be a fool to let her go."

A fist of denial slammed into his chest at the thought of walking away from CC, but the decision might not be his. Sure, things had changed between them since they'd made their pact, and she melted into his arms whenever he reached for her, but she'd been adamant their relationship was only temporary. Nothing she'd said since indicated that had changed.

"I may not have a choice."

His father's brows crashed together above disbelieving eyes. "I've never known you to walk away from something you wanted. If she's the one, then grab hold of her and don't let go."

He sighed. "It's complicated."

A dismissive scoff flared the older man's nostrils. "Then un-complicate it."

"Easier said than done." Tuck swallowed the remainder of his beer.

"That's enough, boys." His mother tapped the spoon to the edge of the pot. "The girls are on their way back up from the beach."

Tuck turned to look. Sure enough, Walter sprinted toward the deck stairs with CC and Jessi following.

His mother wiped her hands on the towel tucked at her waist and took the seat next to his. "Before they get here, I'll just say this."

He grinned. Of course she'd have one last thing to say. She always did.

She rolled her eyes. "It's the complications in life that make it fun."

A crash and a low grunt had all three of their heads spinning toward the door. The screen hung from its hinges at an odd angle. Beyond the mangled door, the Rottweiler staggered and shook his head.

Tuck and his father burst out laughing.

His mother grinned and crossed her arms. "I rest my case."

Chapter 23

After two blissful nights spent curled against Tuck's side in his Beacon Street condo overlooking Boston Common, they hit the road for Manhattan early Monday morning. CC sighed, recalling their adventure to the Chasms yesterday, which had turned out to be a group event. The moment he mentioned their plans, his family had invited themselves along, and she'd gotten to experience a Tucker family breakfast cookout in the woods. Whether it was the warm and teasing company, or she'd actually put her terror of the forest behind her, she wasn't sure, but she didn't have a moment of unease as they explored the trails and caves of one of Tuck's favorite childhood playgrounds.

With the weekend behind them, Tuck was scheduled for a four PM photo shoot his agent had set up. That worked for CC. She desperately needed some time to think. Though she'd enjoyed herself more than expected, the time spent with Tuck's family left her unsettled.

She waved good-bye from her front door and went inside as he drove off. Ignoring the blinking light on her answering machine, she trudged upstairs to her bedroom. Walter pounced onto the bed as she dropped her bag to the floor. She flopped down beside him and ran her fingers over his thick neck.

"Well, what do you think?"

I think I may have busted my snout on that screen door.

She grinned and rolled onto her back. God, what a disaster. She'd been so embarrassed she wanted to sink into the floor until Tuck's mother explained they were on their sixth screen since moving in. His father suggested they start buying them in bulk. Tuck found the entire situation hilarious, as did the rest of the family.

What would it be like to be a permanent part of that group of looney, loving people and not just a temporary, though welcome, interloper?

She tossed a wrist over her eyes. "Dangerous thinking, CC."

"What is?"

She dropped her arm to her side and stared at Kris in the doorway. "I didn't know you were home."

Her cousin strolled into the room. "Obviously. Move over, mutt." She shoved Walter aside and stretched out on her side, facing CC. "I assume you're talking to yourself over the test stud."

She winced. "Not a good sign, huh?"

Head propped in her palm, Kris shrugged. "Depends."

"On?"

"On whether or not I need to give you more condoms."

She laughed. Despite living together, they didn't see each other every day, thanks to Kris's busy work and social schedule. And with the chaos after the Yankees game, then leaving for Boston, they hadn't had a chance to talk. It would have driven her cousin crazy not knowing what happened the other night.

"Actually, I still have the ones you gave me."

A low groan rumbled in Kris's chest.

"Tuck had his own stash. Who knew?" She giggled and tried to dodge the punch to her arm but failed.

"You're such a bitch!" Kris sprang up and sat with her shoulders slouched, her legs crossed beneath her. "Details. Don't leave me hanging."

She rolled off the bed to her feet and scooped up her bag. "I don't kiss and tell."

"You don't have to. It's written all over your face."

Crap, that wasn't good. Hoping to head off the line of questioning, she changed the subject. "Did Mom get to the airport okay?"

Sly to her ways, her cousin smirked. "I delivered her there personally. She's at home, safe and sound in the world of plastic surgeons and out-of-work actors. One of her kooky friends invited her to a crystal cleansing ceremony last night, whatever that means. She was all excited. Now spill it. How'd the weekend go?"

Clutching the bag to her chest, she fought off the sudden urge to cry. "It was wonderful."

"Then why the long face?"

"I screwed up, Kris." She spun and stalked to her dresser. Slipping the bag to the top, she began unpacking.

"Screwed up how?"

CC turned in time to see her cousin's eyes nearly bulge from their sockets.

"Oh, shit. I thought you said Tuck had his own condoms."

"He did and we used them. Quite a few, in fact."

Kris's bangs ruffled with her released breath. "Don't scare me like that." Her shoulders sagged with relief. "If you haven't had unprotected sex, what's the problem?"

She slid her eyes shut and slumped back against the dresser. "I'm in love with him."

"Well, duh."

Her eyes popped open. "What's that supposed to mean? This is exactly what I was trying to avoid. Some best friend you are. Instead of tossing me a bag of sex supplies, you should have talked me out of going."

"Like I could have. Face it, kiddo, you were toast long before you talked yourself into that booty call."

She crossed to the bed and fell forward, flat on her face. With her mouth mashed into the comforter, her voice was muffled. "God, I'm such an idiot. How could I have let this happen?"

"You don't *let* love happen. It either does or doesn't. You don't have a say in it."

She turned her head to glare. "What are you all of a sudden? The Love Guru?"

A smirk. "I read it in a fortune cookie last week."

Squeezing her eyes shut, she groaned.

A gentle hand rubbed her back. "What about him? Does he feel the same?"

"I have no idea. I mean, guys don't normally take a woman to meet their family if they don't have feelings, right? But this is Tuck we're talking about. He has a reputation for changing women more often than most men change their underwear." Kris snickered and CC shook her head. "I just don't know."

"Have you tried asking him?"

She rolled up onto her elbows. "Are you insane? I couldn't."

"Why not? It can't be any worse than going over to his place and asking him to pop your cherry."

"I did not!" A coughing laugh gurgled up and out.

Kris shrugged a slender shoulder. "When a virgin shows up at a guy's apartment in the middle of the night with a bag of condoms, it amounts to the same thing."

Okay, that was probably true. She pushed herself up until she was sitting. What did it matter, anyway? He'd be leaving for training camp at the end of the week, and that would be that.

"We made a bargain, Kris. Three weeks and we both walk away. In a week, our deal will come to an end."

"You keep telling yourself that, kiddo." A serene smile settled on Kris's lips as she stood and walked to the door. She paused and looked back. "And when that doesn't work, renegotiate."

* * * *

CC gripped the pen and formed his name in big block letters. TUCK. She resisted the juvenile urge to draw a sappy heart beside his name and sat back, staring at the notepad as if it were a snake about to strike. All in all, she should be satisfied. Her birthday promise expired on Sunday, the day before Tuck started training camp, and the list of fears she'd overcome far outweighed those she hadn't. Unfortunately, the remaining items were biggies. Looking at them gave her heartburn and that last one made her want to throw up.

She slashed her pen across the paper, scratching out one of the three. Though she trusted Tuck, she simply couldn't do as he suggested. She couldn't open herself up to Curt again. Whatever was behind his sudden interest, he'd just have to be disappointed. She'd made too much progress, worked too hard at breaking through her self-imposed barriers, to watch her fragile sense of freedom crumble away over a man who'd cared more for his career than he ever did his child.

She glared at the last two items and gnawed on her lip. Maybe it was a massive psychological rationalization, but the need to clear the list and proclaim herself healed, before the deadline of her agreement with Tuck came to an end, burned like a bonfire in her belly. Regardless of her feelings for him, his belief in her and his dogged, sometimes bullying assistance in her quest, were gifts she couldn't repay. The least she could do was see the job through.

With their time together rapidly coming to an end, and his departure for training camp looming, telling him she loved him was the more urgent of the two, but her heart cringed at the prospect. As terrifying as agreeing to the Arts Council show was, it didn't come anywhere close to the thought of baring her soul to a man who'd made it clear from the beginning permanence wasn't in his vocabulary.

Ronald's request she enter *Yearning* into the Art Council's show rankled her since *she'd* insisted from the beginning she wasn't interested, but after everything else she'd accomplished, cowering from the challenge smacked of cowardice. She'd never be truly free unless she tackled this last hurtle, and though Tuck didn't know it, this one she'd face solely for him.

Her palms broke out in a sweat, and she glared at her cell phone. Geez. She'd survived being filmed with her tongue stuck down Tuck's throat in front of millions of people. How bad could a few dozen art snobs be?

Before she could chicken out, she picked up the phone. Ronald answered on the second ring.

"CC, I was planning to call you in the morning."

She wiped a sweaty palm on the thigh of her jeans. "I guess I saved you the trouble then."

He hesitated when she didn't continue. "Have you made a decision?"

Eyes squeezed shut, she plunged ahead. "I'll do your show."

The heavy breath he released sounded in her ear. "Oh, CC. Thank you. You won't be sorry."

"I'd better not be, and before you get all worked up, I have a few conditions."

"Like?"

"First, I remain anonymous. No names. I'll show up and give the council their hour, but in any introductions made, I want to be introduced as *Yearning's* creator."

"CC—"

"Yes, I know. It's stupid, but I have my reasons."

He sighed. "I'll do what I can."

"You'll do exactly what I'm asking for or I'll walk. How do you think that'll look on the agency's resume?"

"Okay." An edge of frustration colored his reply, but it was the best he was going to get. "And two?"

She fought to keep her voice from trembling. She was wrong. Agreeing to throw herself into the public eye, for any reason, sent her heartbeat into convulsions. "You said you'd be there for me. I expect you to honor that promise. As far as I'm concerned, this is *your* show, not mine. I'll shake hands. I'll even make small talk if I have to, but I expect you to control the situation. I'm not interested in getting caught up in a circus."

Chapter 24

CC hefted the small wooden box from the closet and crossed to her workbench, where Tuck leaned his ass against the edge with one booted foot crossed over the other.

He propped his hands on the bench beside his hips. "What are you doing?"

She removed the box's lid and rested it against the bench leg on the floor. "I'm packing up a piece for delivery."

He watched in silence as she crossed the room to take *Yearning* from the top shelf. When she returned to place the sculpture into the box, he slanted his upper body toward hers for a better view. "Nice."

"Thanks."

Studying the clean lines of the delicate form, she couldn't help but agree. Her fingertip traced over the woman's reaching hand and she sighed. Each sculpture held a little piece of her heart, but this one was more. It had come from her soul. Though she hadn't understood as she bent over her workspace the morning she met Tuck and shape had emerged in the twisting wire, the sculpture was a self-portrait. A soul-deep cry for what could be.

As if she'd spoken aloud, Tuck straightened at her side. "Does it bother you? Letting it go?"

She whipped her head around to look at him, but if there was a deeper meaning in his question, it didn't show. Simply curiosity was all she found.

She looked away. "A little." She'd given Ronald her word, and she wouldn't back out now but, in truth, she regretted seeing the piece go. She shrugged and gave her pat answer. "But art is meant to be shared."

Tuck smiled as she twisted open the tie on a bag of Styrofoam peanuts. "I'm sure the new owner appreciates the sentiment."

She poured a waterfall of packing peanuts into the box and dipped her hand inside to spread it around. "It doesn't have a new owner." She added more peanuts and kept her eyes on what she was doing. "Yet. I agreed to do the Art Council's show."

When he said nothing, she turned her head and met his gaze.

A small smile softened his face. "Another fear put to rest, huh? Good for you. I'm proud of you."

She jammed her shaking hand into the box. "Don't be. I'm scared to death."

"But you're doing it anyway. That's what counts."

"Maybe. Unless I puke on Ronald's dress shoes."

Tuck slumped back against the bench with a grin.

She bent to retrieve the wooden lid from the floor, while reaching for her power drill. Tucked beneath the power tool, her fears list skittered across the surface of the bench. He twisted his upper body, picked up the sheet of paper, and scanned her handwriting. "What's this?"

The drill clattered to the bench top, and she snatched the paper from his fingers. "Just some doodling." She folded the sheet in quarters and jammed it into the front pocket of her jeans, but from the way his mouth tweaked in a pleased smile, he'd had enough time to ascertain the contents.

Thank God I refrained from adding that stupid heart.

"When's the show?"

Apparently, he wasn't going to make an issue of seeing his name on her doodle list. That so worked for her. A ragged breath shuddered in her chest. "Friday night."

"Are you going to invite me?"

Shit. She hadn't thought that far. Training camp started on Monday, which meant he'd be gone by Sunday night at the latest. She didn't want to miss a moment of the three days they had left, but after their Yankee stadium fiasco, his appearance at the show would only cause problems.

"I'm not sure that's a good idea."

Disappointment clouded his eyes. "Because someone might make the connection between us? I'm not sure artsy types spend a lot of time at Yankee stadium or watching ESPN."

"*I* did."

"Only because I dragged you there."

When she opened her mouth to make a further argument, he held up his hand.

"The thing is, I leave for Syracuse on Sunday."

Oh God. She wanted to slap her hands over her ears and chant la la la so she wouldn't have to hear him say, *it's been fun, but now it's time to move on.* Not yet, her heart cried. They had several more days left in their agreement and damn it, she wanted them.

Instead of stomping her foot like a spoiled little girl, she nodded. "I know."

He slid his fingers into the front pockets of his jeans. "I've got this team thing tomorrow, but after that I planned on locking you away in my condo and not letting you go until it was time to leave."

"You did?" Relief made her legs go weak. She clutched at the edge of the bench.

He nodded, pulled his fingers from his pockets, then immediately shoved them back in again. "And speaking of my leaving, we need to talk about our…arrangement."

Her heart sunk almost as quickly as her gaze dropped to the floor.

"I think we should renegotiate."

"What?" Her head snapped up, and she stared at him wide-eyed. Geez, was Kris psychic too? She mentally slapped the stray thought aside and clamped down on a slightly hysterical grin by flattening her lips. If he wanted to renegotiate, that meant he wanted more time. A good sign.

He tugged his hands from his pockets once more only to shove them through his hair.

Why, he's nervous. A really good sign.

"I know we were both firm on the three week limit, but I want more."

Oh, so do I. So do I. Her heart leaped, and her sudden loss of breath had nothing to do with panic. Could it be Gracie was right? Had he lost his heart as well? Her eyes slid shut in sweet wonder.

He cleared his throat, and when her lashes fluttered open, she was surprised by the hard slant of his face. He shook his head. "Look, it's no big deal, I just thought if you weren't seeing anyone when I got back, and I'm not seeing anyone, we could get together." He picked up a stray piece of wire from the bench and twisted it in his fingers. "You know, for old time's sake."

He dropped the wire, and it pinged to the bench, the same way her heart fell to the floor.

Oh, God. Tears prickled behind her eyes and she turned, blinking them away. "Sure. For old time's sake."

So much for thinking he wanted more time with her. Why bother taking their agreement into the realm of a relationship, when friends with benefits was so much more convenient? But casual sex with a man who moved on to yet another woman every couple of weeks would never work for her.

Her list crinkled in her pocket, and she pulled it out. She held the folded paper up over her shoulder so he could see, but didn't open it and didn't look his way. "I made a list of everything I wanted to accomplish through our…arrangement. As you probably saw, I hit every goal but one."

The scrape of his boots on hardwood reached her as he shifted his feet. "Your father?"

Not even close, you dipshit. She tossed the list to the bench and picked up the wooden top for the crate. "Yeah."

"Are going to see him?"

"No." She fit the top to the box and scooped up the drill.

"I think you should. What your father did to you was unforgiveable, but this is about you, not him. You'll regret not finishing it down the road."

"Yeah, well, life is full of regrets." The whine of the drill pierced the air, and using more force than was necessary, she sealed the crate. Gritting her teeth, she buried screws into the corners while she imagined staking all four of his limbs to the wall. When she finished, the silence was deafening.

"Are we still on for dinner?"

Surprised by the question, she turned. Though his face had lost some of its tension, his eyes didn't quite hold their usual warmth. Actually, she shouldn't be surprised he intended to continue along with the status quo. From the beginning he'd had one agenda. Obviously, that hadn't changed.

Instead of telling him to go fuck *himself*, as she should have, she nodded. What the hell. As Kris said, the guy knew his stuff. If sex was all he was willing to give her, she'd take it. For now.

She could always put a hit out on him once they were done.

* * * *

Tuck winced as a door slammed shut on the second floor. After cramming her tools into various drawers and calling Ronald to tell him curtly the piece was ready for Putnam's courier, CC stomped upstairs to shower. Tuck slid his gaze to the power drill. Though he'd wanted to, he hadn't offered to join her. No telling what kind of weapons she might turn on him while he was in a vulnerable state.

Her anger made no sense. Hadn't he backed off and played it cool when her eyes slid shut and she started to withdraw? If anyone should be pissed, it was him. He'd never asked a woman for more before—not in the sense he meant with CC, anyway—and she wanted more too, even if she was too fucking stubborn to admit it. A woman didn't melt into a man's arms as if she couldn't get enough of him if she didn't.

He had no doubt he could sweet talk her out of her snit, but he'd have to be more careful about bringing up their future next time. The red checkmarks on her list proved how stubborn she could be. A woman who refused to back down in the face of such adversity would be a tough nut to crack, but crack her he would.

He might be looking at third and long, but he wasn't foolish enough to let her go. That meant he'd have to find a way to keep her. He sucked at his teeth and stared at the empty staircase. An in-your-face offense had put him on the scoreboard earlier in the game, and he wasn't one to screw with what worked. Slipping his cell phone from his pocket, he called in the special teams.

* * * *

"I didn't realize you'd branched out into the restaurant industry."

Tuck slid his keycard through the lock and opened the door to his condo. "I haven't, but trust me, you're not going to starve."

She brushed by him to step inside and he smiled. At her prickly best, Little Ms. Sunshine didn't employ the silent act like most women when they had a man in their crosshairs. No, CC fell back on sarcasm, and he preferred her style.

He shut the door and leaned against it as she stood in the foyer and looked around. When she turned to face him, she bared her teeth in a chilling smile that would have frightened dogs and small children. "What's the plan? A bowl of Cocoa Puffs and then we get naked, or are we eating in bed?"

"Either works for me." He pushed off the door and strode by her, heading for the small dining room off the living area. "But I have something a bit more substantial than breakfast cereal in mind."

He stopped at the panel door. Turning, he cocked his head at her in question. Her smile dripped with imitation sweetness as she stalked toward him and froze comically when he slid the panel aside. She stopped short. He glanced over her shoulder into the room he'd ventured into only once since he'd purchased the place, and raised an impressed brow.

Pure blind luck had found Gracie in the city when he called requesting her help. She'd outdone herself, as had Dominic, the head chef at Reuben's, his favorite restaurant. No doubt they'd both exact a stiff price in payback.

Elegant in its simplicity, the glass dining table gleamed in welcome. An open bottle of wine chilled in a sterling carafe at one end. A fat candle, surrounded by white rose buds and greenery, sat in the center. Matching green linen rested on stark white porcelain dinnerware. The sparkling wine glasses reflected the candle's flickering light.

"Slick." CC stabbed him with a sidelong glance before continuing into the room. She wandered over to the side table and lifted the lid on the first of three chafing dishes. Her emerald eyes cut to his beneath a fan of dark blond lashes. "Elves?"

"Something like that." He grinned and stepped to the table to pull out her chair.

She sniffed, replaced the lid, and slid into her seat. Her napkin snapped crisply as she spread it across her lap. "I hope you don't expect me to serve you. I'm starving."

He eyed the centerpiece and hoped Gracie hadn't slipped a camera into the blooms. Jake would bust a gut laughing. Just in case, he gave his friend something to think about. Dipping his head, he brushed his lips across a spot on the back of CC's neck he'd discovered was ultra-sensitive.

"Me too," he whispered in her ear.

The delicate shudder rolling through her made him smile, and he straightened.

He retrieved the wine and held the bottle before her. At her silent nod, he splashed the golden liquid into their glasses, then turned to the side table to fill their plates. A low growl rumbled in her belly when he placed the plate of tender beef medallions, fluffy lobster pie, and steamed asparagus in front of her.

He chuckled at her blush and slid into the chair across from her. "Dig in, sunshine." *You're going to need the fuel.*

She forked up a portion of buttery shellfish topped with golden breading and slipped the tines between her lips. With a low moan, her eyes drifted shut. He shifted in his seat and picked up his wine glass for a healthy swallow.

Her eyelids fluttered open, and she took several more bites of lobster before stabbing an asparagus spear. Eyeing him, she nipped off the feathery top and jerked her chin toward his full plate. "I thought you were hungry."

"I am."

"You aren't eating." The asparagus spear disappeared in three more crunching bites.

"Oh, I plan to." He set the wine glass onto the table and fingered the stem.

A smirk flattened her lips at his purposeful innuendo, and she picked up her knife. "I appreciate you pulling out the big guns like this," she sliced through a medallion then brought the fork to her lips, "but the whole seduction routine isn't necessary." She popped the morsel of meat into her mouth and chewed. "I think we both know I'm a sure thing."

He grinned and picked up his fork. "That wasn't the case a couple of weeks ago."

"A couple of weeks ago I didn't know what I was missing." Though her words were uttered with a cheeky lightness, resentment was broadcast in her glittering eyes. "And you were worried about despoiling the virgin." She slid another piece of meat into her mouth and shook her head. "The rumors about you were right. I succumbed to your practiced technique with barely a whimper."

His good humor crashed at her biting tone. Jesus, what was it with women? Did they belong to a secret society that taught them how to deliver a dig with deadly accuracy? Yeah, he'd been with a lot of women. So fucking what? Since meeting *her*, he hadn't been able to think about another woman, much less practice his *technique* on one, and it was about time she knew it.

He tossed his napkin onto the table and jerked to his feet.

She jolted and blinked up at him as he rounded to her side. "Oh, are we done?"

"Not by a long shot." He pulled her from her chair, hefted her over his shoulder, and stalked down the hall to the bedroom.

She propped her hands on his ass to lift her upper body but didn't put up a fight otherwise. "Hey, I wasn't finished."

"Too bad. Neither am I." He crossed to his bed, and heaving a shoulder, unceremoniously dumped her onto the mattress. A spread hand to her chest pushed her back when she immediately started to rise. He threw a thigh over both of hers and straddled her. "But first, we're going to get a few things straight."

Retribution glittered in her eyes, and he grabbed both her wrists before she could reach any vulnerable body parts, especially the one jammed up against his fly. He rose onto his knees and leaned over her, pressing her arms above her head. "For the record, I haven't even *looked* at another woman since we made our deal. You knew who I was when we made our bargain. Throwing my reputation in my face now is a low blow."

"I don't see how. Aren't you the one who suggested we continue to hook up *after* you've found your next plaything?"

"That's not what I meant." He pressed her wrists farther into the mattress with a quick shove and let go, sitting back.

"That's how it sounded to me."

"Then you weren't listening." He propped his hands onto his spread thighs.

"Yes, I was." She lowered her arms to cross them at her waist and fried him with a glare. "You distinctly said—"

"I know what I said." What a cluster fuck. He jammed a hand through his hair. "But damn it. What's a guy supposed to say when he tells a woman he'd like to shift their relationship to something more and her only reaction is disappointment?"

"That's not what you said." The sexy wrinkle he loved creased her forehead suddenly. "Is it?"

More for effect than in reaction, he growled low in his throat. Confused and off balance was just how he wanted her. "What the fuck else would I be talking about when I said I wanted more?" Her gaze dropped to his crotch, and his growl was real this time. "Don't even say it."

A mulish twist puckered her mouth. "Well, how was I supposed to know? You made it clear from the beginning, this," she swung out a hand to indicate the bed, "was what you were after."

He leaned forward with a scowl, and she sunk her head deeper into the pillow. With his nose an inch from hers, he made his scowl a leer. "Oh, I'm still after that, but that's not all. Have I made myself clear?"

A twinge of doubt still glimmered in her eyes, but the outrage spitting at him since she'd stomped upstairs from her studio eased, and her body softened beneath his. "Not exactly."

He lowered himself until he was stretched out on top of her. His denim covered thigh slid between her legs, left bare by her skirt. She shivered, and he cupped her face with his hands. "Then let me clarify. I'm not done with you, CC Calhoun."

Her lashes fluttered as she stared into his eyes.

"And you're not done with me. When I get back from training camp, you'll be right here waiting. If I have to come looking for you, you won't like the consequences."

He covered her lips with his, and her honeyed sex taste exploded in his mouth. With a hungry growl, he nipped at her bottom lip, then nibbled his way over her cheekbone to the delicate shell of her ear and bit down gently on the lobe. She squirmed beneath him and sighed.

"Now, say it. Say you want more, too."

Her arms came around him to cling, and she gave in gracefully. "I want more."

Triumph surged through him. The game clock still ticked, but he was back in the red zone. He lifted his head to grin into her eyes, dazed with reawakened sensuality. "All you had to do was ask."

Chapter 25

CC wrestled with the urge to run for her life, an impossibility with her high-heeled feet rooted to the sidewalk. Crap. She should have told Tuck he could come tonight when he asked again this morning, and to hell with the potential consequences.

Her breathing techniques had obviously gone rusty from disuse. Tuck's fault, of course. Lately, the only panting and gasping for breath she'd done had been at his hands. And mouth. And Lord, his magical tongue.

Heat washed through her, and she cupped her hands over her blushing cheeks. As he'd promised, he'd returned from his team meeting yesterday and spent the next thirty hours introducing her to the concept of *more*. It was a wonder she could walk when he finally let her leave his condo to prepare for tonight's event. She still wasn't sure what all the *more* he requested entailed, but his insistence they continue their relationship beyond training camp was enough for now.

A burst of laughter from a group of young people on the corner ripped her from her sensual musings. Glancing around, as if waking from a dream, she sucked in air through her clenched teeth. She could never thank Tuck enough for helping her face her demons and find the strength within to slay them one at a time, but she'd been premature in thinking she'd mastered the art of beating back the attacks on her own.

A band of pressure built in her chest, and she wiped her damp palms on the hem of her pale yellow cocktail dress. *Breathe. Just breathe.*

A glance at her watch proved she was already late, but it was hard to be punctual when you spent ten minutes building up the courage to open your front door. Why the hell hadn't she told Kris about tonight? If her cousin were with her, she'd have no chance to chicken out, but at least she'd have someone at her side for moral support.

Too late to call for reinforcements. She'd just have to suck it up. Tonight was her own damn fault, but she'd given Ronald her word.

Light from the high windows spilled onto the sidewalk and illuminated the inside of the swanky gallery like a human fishbowl. A modest crowd bunched into small groups, lingering over cocktails as they studied the various works of art staged about the room. She spotted Ronald at the bar, schmoozing a tuxedoed a man with steely gray hair. The older man's head stopped a full two inches shorter than that of the big-breasted blonde on his arm, her curves poured into a dark red sheath.

A young couple approached CC, and she took a step back so the man could open the gallery's door. He held it for the woman, then cocked a head at CC. Now or never. Gulping a breath, she mumbled her thanks and rushed inside.

She paused in the small foyer as the couple continued forward into the gallery. As she skulked in the shadow of the unused coat room, occasional twitters of muted laughter punctured the murmur of quiet conversation. Twisting her hands at her waist, she concentrated on regulating her breathing as she waited for Ronald to turn and spot her.

In, out, in again, she slowed her breaths as she glanced around the gallery.

Okay, this isn't so bad. No more than two dozen patrons milled about the room. She faced more than that every week at Parson's Market grocery shopping. Then again, this was New York. None of the shoppers ever actually *spoke* to her, only Wanda, and the market owner spoke to everyone.

Unfortunately, as one of the featured artists, she was not only expected to make an appearance, but she'd also need to make polite conversation. She was here. She'd met that requirement, and maybe if she kept moving, she could keep the verbal contacts down to a minimum. No doubt Ronald would have an issue with her rational. He'd insist she engage with her audience, but if she was going to make it through the allotted hour without passing out, a compromise was in order.

Not waiting for her agent, she skirted the bar and dipped into the crowd.

Dugan McDonald held court in front of his contribution to the show, a life-sized couple in marble, wrapped together and straining passionately in the missionary position. The fifty-something artist droned on about vision and perception in front of a half dozen people who had no idea they'd been trapped by one of his long-winded dissertations. Like most people who looked on his work, CC couldn't help but admire the artist's talent. Classically trained, his creations pleased the eye with their attention to detail while the blatantly sexual tone of the pieces evoked varied and often fervent responses from critics.

Too bad Dugan had the personality of a shoe. She sped up her steps and didn't make eye contact.

For a full ten minutes, she roamed the gallery, making sure to steer clear of anyone who looked as if they might try and strike up a conversation. She rose on tiptoes to see over the shoulders of a crowd gathered in front of a small framed landscape and spent several minutes studying a knot of intricately twisted glass toward the back of the room. As she strolled through the aisles and marveled at the talent on display, pride bloomed deep in her belly. She dismissed the smug stirrings as only natural. Having your work included amongst the crème de la crème of the New York art scene would make anyone a little proud.

By the time she spotted *Yearning*, displayed on a lighted pedestal thirty feet away, her heartbeat and breathing had returned nearly to the normal range. Standing in front of her piece were two men, dressed more casually than most of the patrons in crisp jeans and button down shirts. Curious of what they were saying, she meandered over and stopped a few feet away.

They hovered close together, and the younger of the two turned his head to grin at his taller companion. "Anonymous. How coy is that?"

The older man laughed. "I don't know, but anyone who has the balls to keep their name from the Art Counsel gods is someone I'd like to meet."

"You're in luck."

Busy eavesdropping, she hadn't been aware of Ronald's approach, and she jumped. He grasped her elbow as the gray-haired man and the blonde from the bar came to a stop beside him. Ronald's bright smile was accusing. She rolled her eyes, then stifled a groan when he addressed the two young men.

"Gentlemen, meet, Ms. Anonymous."

The younger man gawked, his mouth twisted comically. Behind a pair of fashionable, dark-framed glasses, his hazel gaze flicked briefly to her agent and the other couple before returning to her. "Oh my God. I can't believe it. *Yearning* is yours?"

The breath clogged in her throat as a crowd started to gather around them. She was going to kill Ronald. She smiled weakly. "Guilty," was the best she could manage.

A huge grin lit the younger man's round face. "Oh, honey. You have nothing to feel guilty about. Why, you're a genius." His long fingers clutched hold of his friend's arm, and he tugged him closer. "I'm Dan and this is Paul. We couldn't believe it when we saw you were showing a piece." He poked Paul's side with his elbow. "Didn't I tell you *Yearning* was by *our* anonymous?" His smile went dreamy and he slapped his free hand to his chest with dramatic flair. "We bought your *Morning Stroll* a couple of months ago from Putnam. It sits in a place of honor on our mantle. We're uber-fans."

"Uh, thanks." Pressure built in her chest as even more patrons drew close.

"CC." Ronald squeezed her arm, and she turned to glare at him. His lips curved at the corners in a sickly smile, and his eyes pleaded with her to play nice. "I don't believe you've met George Truman and his wife, Pam. George is the president of the Art Council."

CC's heartbeat took off like a greyhound out of the gate. She coughed and nodded to the president but slammed her mouth shut. There was no point in speaking, since no recognizable words would come out anyway.

"How lovely." Pam turned from *Yearning* to smile. "What gage wire do you use?"

"I saw a piece of hers at Putnam's last week," someone whispered behind Ronald.

Dan leaned forward and squeezed her arm briefly. "Honey?" He dropped his hand and linked it with Paul's. "We were wondering. Why do you go by anonymous? I mean, it's a brilliant marketing strategy, don't get me wrong. Makes people wonder, but why not use your name?"

"I admit I'm curious about that myself," the council president added.

"I—" Oh, God. "I—" Her gaze flew to Ronald who, as far as she was concerned, was a dead man walking. Her lungs convulsed on a wheeze. *Breathe, CC!*

"I believe that might have something to do with me."

What little breath she had whooshed from her lungs like a tsunami wave, and the hair on the back of her neck prickled and stood on end. Excited whispers broke the sudden silence, and the crowd crushed closer. She turned slowly, sure she must be mistaken. The blood drained from her head, leaving her dizzy, as her gaze clashed with the green eyes she hadn't seen since she was nine.

With his typical entourage surrounding him, Curt stood three feet away. "Hello, CC."

The years hadn't been kind, from what she could see. Live and in person, her father didn't have access to the usual airbrushing at his disposal on those magazine covers he appeared on at every opportunity. Though always on the thin side, his body had slid toward skinny and the toll of his rock 'n' roll lifestyle showed on his aged and haggard face.

What the hell was he doing here? Her mother had no idea she'd consented to Ronald's request, and even if CC had told Kris about the show, her cousin would just as soon spit in Curt's eye then aide him. She'd checked the brochure Ronald had dropped off yesterday. No mention of her name was given. How the hell had Curt known she'd be here?

Confused fury flooded her brain, and her angry gasp kick-started her struggling lungs. "How did you know where to find me?"

"You two *know* each other?" A tinkling laugh gurgled in Dan's throat. "Oh, I can't believe this. I'm standing two feet from Curt Jenson, Paul. Curt Jenson!" His lashes fluttered as if he were about to swoon, and then suddenly, his eyes widened. He slapped a hand to the clip on his waist and whipped out his phone. "Would you mind if I took a selfie, Curt? Oh, my friends will never believe this."

CC couldn't believe it either. Apparently, Dan was a chronic uber-fan. He scurried up beside Curt, grinned, and stretched out his arm to snap several shots. She bristled as Dan cooed over a concert of Curt's he and Paul had been to recently.

The young fan's selfie started a stampede. Cameras flashed as she stared in disbelief at the spectacle of wealthy patrons slobbering all over themselves to be photographed with the rock legend.

A familiar face beyond the melee caught her eye. Bobby Oakley, her father's long-time base guitarist, had been a small beacon of light during those days Curt dragged her around on that hellish tour. Though she hadn't known it at the time, he'd been the one to finally put his foot down and free Kris and her from her father's manic prison. As he had so many times back then, he offered her a sad smile.

Tears stung at the back of her throat as she returned his silent greeting.

"How *do* you know each other?"

CC ignored George Truman's question and turned a pointed stare at Curt. "How, Curt? How did you know to find me here?"

He dipped his head to scrawl his name across a show brochure, then handed it off to a waiting fan. He glanced up with a wincing smile. "When you wouldn't answer my calls, a…friend took pity on me."

A *friend?* What friend? Only Tuck and Ronald knew her schedule and neither of them would.…

Fingers of apprehension danced up her spine. She hadn't demanded Ronald expand on the reason for his odd behavior that day he pleaded with her to do the show. Maybe she should have, but no, that couldn't be. How would he even know about Curt?

She jerked her head in Ronald's direction, but he paid no attention to the mini-drama taking place. He faced the back of the gallery, his focus on something across the room. She followed his gaze and surprise made her blink.

Relief washed through her and left her legs wobbly. Like a modern day knight come to rescue her from the madness, Tuck crossed the room in an easy, loose-hipped gait. The gallery lights fired his golden blond locks with red and blue highlights, and his black-on-black tuxedo rode his wide shoulders and trim hips with the precision only a custom job could achieve.

Uneasiness pricked her relief at his lack of a smile and turned to dread when Tuck's sober gaze locked on Curt and stayed for a long moment before sliding to her. Betrayal slashed at her as his words echoed in her head. *"You'll regret not finishing it down the road."*

Oh dear God.

He slowed his steps, and when he reached her, he held out his hand.

She took a full step back and spoke in a condemning whisper. "How could you?"

Though guilt dulled the blue of his eyes, in typical Tuck fashion, he went on the offensive. "Relax, sunshine. I came in the back door."

What the back door had to do with anything, she didn't know and didn't care. What he'd done was a deal breaker. Before she could tell him so, a squeal pierced the air and she turned. Dan's face was lit up like a child's on Christmas as he stared at Tuck. Amongst the renewed chattering excitement of the crowd, the small smile riding her father's lips confirmed what her heart, even now, cried couldn't be true.

He stuck out his hand to Tuck. "I think my daughter's relieved to see a friendly face."

CC's eyes slid shut briefly as her last hope crumbled along with her heart. When she opened them again, her childhood nightmares had returned in living color.

The room erupted in chaos, with questions flying from nearly every mouth. Dan was beside himself with excitement, snapping pictures as he danced from foot to foot. Pam turned her baby blues on Tuck to ask if he was in the market…for art, she added, almost as an afterthought. Her husband, George, leaned toward Ronald to grumble he didn't like surprises. CC tuned out Ronald's wheedling apology.

Through it all, her father held her gaze. "I'm sorry," he mouthed.

Not sure if his apology was for the current fiasco or for the past, she shrugged. What did it matter? Any affection she'd carried in her heart for the man who fathered her had died long ago. He was a stranger and, surprisingly, his presence no longer had the power to hurt her.

If this meeting had come three weeks ago, she'd no doubt be passed out on the floor. Instead, her heartbeat tripped along at a steady beat and her breathing remained even. As if she were an uninvolved witness to the shambles that was her life, nothing touched her. Not fear, not anger, not even sadness.

Perhaps the shock of Tuck's betrayal was responsible for her numbness, or maybe facing her father again had finally freed her. Whatever the case, she was done. Done with this ridiculous circus and done dreaming of a life she'd never had a chance at to begin with.

* * * *

Tuck kicked his condo door shut behind him and tore at the bow of his tie. After stomping into the kitchen, he paused before the refrigerator, curled his fingers into a fist, and then thought better of slamming his hand into the stainless steel appliance. Jacking up his catching hand two days before training camp would only land him on the injured list.

His cell phone buzzed in his pocket, and he scrambled to retrieve it. "It's about damn time." Expecting CC's return call after the five messages he'd left her over the past hour, disappointment crashed into him like a wrecking ball. Gracie's picture on the screen made him scowl. He thumbed the screen and answered with a curt, "What?"

"Well, hello to you, too."

His shoulders slumped on a sigh. "Sorry. I'm in a shitty ass mood."

"Uh-oh. What did you do?"

"Why do you assume *I* did something?" He clenched his teeth at her soft chuckle. He shrugged out of his tux jacket and tossed it on the back of the couch as he stalked across the condo toward his wood shop. "What's up with you women? A guy tries to do something nice, show a little support, and it blows up in our faces."

"I take it we're talking about CC?"

He tucked the phone between cheek and shoulder before snapping the cufflink from one wrist and rolling the linen sleeve to his elbow. "All I did was show up at her art show tonight. She got pissed and took off while I was surrounded by a handful of autograph junkies. Now I can't find her. She didn't go home, and she won't answer my calls."

A quiet hum sounded in his ear. "Why is she pissed?"

"How the fuck should I know?" He paused in the act of rolling up his other sleeve, plucked the phone from his shoulder, and squeezed his eyes shut. "Okay, so she asked me not to come because she was afraid my presence would draw unwanted attention."

"A logical concern. Did it?"

He opened his eyes and gritted his teeth. "What do you think?"

Her sigh was long and windy. "You should have respected her wishes."

Yeah, he probably should have, but tonight was a huge step for her. He'd needed to be there. Just to make sure she was all right, and he'd taken precautions. Christ, he'd even slipped the security guard a C-note so he could sneak in through the back door and avoid the paparazzi.

His nostrils flared on a wry scoff. "Not that it would have mattered if I had stayed away. By the time I arrived, the place was already a circus. Her father was there."

"Curt Jensen?"

"The one and only. Along with his entourage." The memory of her, standing like a deer in the headlights at the center of the chaos, made his stomach muscles clench with frustrated anger. Guilt scraped at the soft tissue of his mind for his part in her obvious discomfort but, the truth was, if not for the crowd of art lovers crowding the space, her anxiety would have gotten a lot worse. He would have taken great pleasure in driving her father's nose through his famous face to the base of his skull.

"You said they were estranged."

Ripped from his homicidal thoughts, a harsh laugh blew through his lips. "Estranged is too mild a word for their relationship. She hates the bastard. With good reason."

A moment passed. "Then maybe it's not you she's pissed at."

"Maybe, but doubtful." The look of betrayal on her face when she'd avoided his reach had nearly knocked the wind out of him, but she'd pulled a Houdini vanishing act before he could drag her off somewhere private and demand to know what had put the cold steel of finality in her eyes.

Gracie's understanding murmur drifted to his ear. "Give her some time, Tuck."

He picked up a sanding stone beside the bench he'd been working on earlier that day. "I don't have time to give her. I leave for camp in thirty-six hours, remember?"

"Then keep trying to reach her. I'll try, and get Jake and Max on board, too. She's bound to answer one of us eventually."

A band of iron squeezed his chest. What if she didn't? He knew good-bye when he saw it, and her glittering green eyes had practically screamed, "Adios, asshole." He shoved a hand through his hair. "Thanks, Gracie. Do me a favor?"

"Anything."

"Even if she makes you promise not to tell me where she is, call me right away if you talk to her. I'm worried about her."

He spent the next day and a half frantic with worry. CC might have overcome the worst of her fears, but it wasn't like her to go off on her own. She hadn't returned to her condo. He knew because he'd checked every room and closet, twice, much to Kris's consternation, and a call to Natalie proved she hadn't hopped on a plane to go hide out at her mother's home in L.A. As Friday night passed into Saturday, and then Sunday arrived, neither he nor his friends had had any luck in reaching her. Finally, he'd bullied Kris into admitting she'd heard from CC, and she was fine. She simply didn't want to talk to him.

Red-hot fury replaced the worry as he packed his bags to leave for Syracuse. He refused to name the ache below his heart hurt as he climbed into the car service limo, and by the time the private jet touched down in upstate New York, he wanted nothing more than to forget he'd ever laid eyes on CC Calhoun.

Chapter 26

CC dropped her head to her workbench with a groan. "God. Why can't everyone just leave me alone?"

The doorbell rang again, and she slid from her stool to answer the door, grumbling beneath her breath. At least she didn't have to worry Tuck would be standing on the stoop. An improbability after his last, curse-laden message, but one she'd rather avoid just the same.

Apparently, he hadn't appreciated being left at the gallery and liked having his calls ignored even less. Too bad. She'd taken the opportunity to slip out of the gallery without him noticing while he'd been busy signing autographs and taking selfies with his adoring fans. She'd ignored his call five minutes later, and after shutting off her phone and checking into the first hotel she came to, she'd ordered a bottle of wine from room service and cried herself to sleep. The next morning, she'd ignored the dozen voice mails, calling Kris to tell her she was all right, and had spent the remainder of the weekend, including her birthday, feeling sorry for herself, but she was done with that.

With the start of training camp this morning, Tuck's calls had stopped, and she'd promised herself so would her tears. It was time to get on with her life, and if her friends and family would just cooperate, she would. Only Kris seemed to be on her side. Between phone calls from her mother and visits from Max, as well as Gracie and Jake, she was ready to scream.

Walter bumped against her thigh, and she curled her fingers around his collar. She yanked open the door, ready to do some of that screaming, but the sight of her father, alone for a change, made her blink.

"May I come in?"

Her shoulders sagged. "What's the point, Curt? I don't have anything to say."

"But I do. I promise I won't stay long."

Too exhausted and heartbroken to argue, she turned and wandered into her studio, leaving him to follow. As she climbed onto her stool, he stopped beside the couch and eyed Walter. The dog gave him a smile.

Curt shoved his fingers into the pockets of his low-riding jeans. "I had a Rottie once. Smartest animal I ever had."

She shot the dog a sidelong glance. "Yeah, well, Walter's still working on finding his intelligence. Aren't you, buddy?"

Smart enough to get you to follow me around with a baggie to pick up my shit.

She cleared her throat, and her mind of Antonio, and turned back to Curt. "As you can see, I'm working. What is it you wanted to say?"

He dropped his gaze to the floor. "First. I'm sorry, CC."

She arched a brow. "So you said at the gallery."

"And you didn't believe me."

"Whether or not I believe you doesn't matter."

He lifted his head, and his eyes were intense when he met her gaze. "It does to me."

"Why?" She sighed when he flinched. "I'm not trying to be mean, or even rude. Honestly. We don't know each other and that's okay. It makes no difference to me one way or the other. Why, after all this time, are my feelings suddenly important when they never have been before?"

He lowered himself to the edge of the couch and sat with his hands dangling between his knees. He stared at the floor. "Because I'm dying." He glanced up and tears swam in his eyes. "And I don't want to go without telling you how sorry I am for what I did to you."

Stunned, she stared. He was dying? "Does Mom know?"

He nodded. "Why do you think she's been trying to get you to talk to me? For some reason, she still cares."

"She loves you."

"I know. I just don't understand why."

CC did, but she didn't bother explaining that some hearts, once given, could never turn back.

"I was a shitty father, CC." A mirthless laugh flared his nostrils. "A shitty man, when it comes down to it. I still am." He slouched back on the couch. "I let blind ambition run my life, and I ended up missing it."

"What's wrong with you?" she asked quietly.

"Cancer. My pancreas is riddled with it." He scraped a palm over his jaw. "Until a few months ago, I didn't even know what a pancreas was." A sardonic smile twisted his lips. "Anyway, what I wanted to say is, you're right not to have anything to do with me. I'm no good. I wasn't a kid when

I met your mother and you were born. I was a grown man, greedy for the spotlight, and I did unspeakable harm in my quest to stay in it."

"I'm sorry." And she was. As numb as she was to him as a father, the man was suffering.

"Don't be." He sat up. "And once I'm dead, don't ever blame yourself for not having a relationship with me. That's on me. No one else. You deserved better."

She had no idea what to say. Tears stung her eyes and distorted the wire in her fingers when she looked down.

"Oh, shit. Don't do that." He jerked to his feet. "I've said what I came to say, and I want to apologize for upsetting you the other night at your show. When Bartolini contacted me and told me you'd be there, I figured it might be my only chance to get you to listen."

Her head jerked up, and her heart did a crazy flip in her chest. "*Ronald* told you where I'd be?"

"Ronald's your agent, right?"

She nodded and struggled to control her breathing.

"He left a message at my hotel Friday morning, saying he had information regarding you I might be interested in. When I called him back, he gave me the address and time of the showing."

Her fingers clenched even as her stomach sunk. "Tuck didn't tell you I was doing the show?"

Confusion beetled his brows. "No. I'd never met Tuck, much less spoken to him, until he walked into the gallery."

She tossed the wire to the bench and sat up straighter. "But you smiled at him when he got there. I saw you."

He shrugged his shoulders and a smile played on his lips. "I caught that kiss between the two of you at Yankee stadium on TV. Who would have ever thought my little CC would snag herself a superstar?"

Oh, fuck!

The yoke of despondency that had ridden her shoulders for the past three days slid away, and a grin grabbed at her lips. A hiccup of hysterical laughter bubbled up from her lungs. She hopped from the stool, and in three long strides, threw herself at her startled father. His arms came around her hesitantly, and his slim musician's hands patted her back as if he wasn't sure what to do with them.

She pulled back, pecked a kiss to his cheek, and smiled. "Thank you."

"For what?"

"For giving me back my dream." She palmed his cheeks in her hands. "And for finally being the man I always wanted you to be."

His smile was cautious and she grinned.

"But now, I've got to go!"

* * * *

"I need your help."

CC stood on the porch of the Malones' farm, unsure of her welcome. She hadn't been particularly agreeable when Gracie and Jake stopped by to plead Tuck's case. The sour expression on Gracie's face didn't bode well.

"Please, Gracie."

"He's my friend, CC. You hurt him."

"I know I did. I screwed up, bad, and you can hate me if you want, but I'm hoping you won't."

Tuck's friend crossed her arms. "How, exactly, did you screw up?"

Okay. Good sign. Her sigh was breathy with relief. "Can I come in? This might take a few minutes to explain."

Gracie opened the screen door. Five minutes later, after shooing the twins out the back door with the dogs, she paused as she poured CC a glass of wine. "I'm so sorry."

"Me, too." CC picked up her glass. "Curt and I were never close, and I guess we won't ever be now." She stared into the glass. That was okay. She might not have the loving memories other women had of their fathers, but by showing her he cared enough to make sure she didn't blame herself, he'd given her a gift she'd always treasure. "But that's not why I'm here. It's a long story, but I thought Tuck had betrayed me by sending my father to my art showing the other night."

"Why would he do that? He knew about the kidnapping and the way you felt about your father."

"Like I said, it's a long story." She sipped her wine. "Anyway, my father said Ronald is the one who told him where I would be."

"Your agent?" Gracie sat across from her with her wine.

She nodded. "A couple of weeks ago, Ronald mentioned he'd stopped by my studio one morning and Tuck was there. It hadn't dawned on me that was the day Tuck overheard my father's message and realized who I was. When I saw Curt at the showing, I assumed Tuck had told him where to find me because I didn't think anyone else knew about Curt. Obviously, I was wrong. Ronald must have heard Curt's message as well that morning."

Gracie swirled the wine in her glass. "And he didn't tell you?"

"No, he didn't, but it makes perfect sense that he would jump on the chance at some extra publicity by inviting Curt." She gulped a swallow of cool wine, then lowered the glass. "I'm so stupid. I didn't want to do the show in the first place, but Ronald convinced me. He told me he was having some financial issues and the show would help."

"How?"

"Having a client in such a prestigious show increases the agency's visibility, which means he'll get more clients, and knowing him as I do now, he'll no doubt charge a higher percentage for his cut."

Gracie lifted her glass. "That sounds like normal business."

"It might be normal, but an ethical businessman doesn't use romance or a woman's family to increase his bottom line."

"Romance?"

She grimaced. "You know Tuck and I started dating because I wanted to test my theory, right?"

Gracie nodded encouragingly.

CC cleared her throat to cover her embarrassment. "Well, Tuck wasn't the first man I asked. I approached Ronald first."

"Hmm. Tuck didn't tell me that. Does he know?"

"Definitely. He was there when it happened."

"Oh, our boy must have loved that. Ha!"

They shared a grin.

"Anyway, Ronald turned me down flat. He claimed he was seeing a new woman."

"And Tuck stepped in to save the day."

CC snorted a laugh. "Something like that. Then a week or so later, Ronald shows up and says he wants a do-over, with me."

Gracie blew a raspberry. "A do-over? Guys are such dorks. Did he know about Tuck?"

She nodded. "He must have, since he was there that morning with Tuck when Curt called. Apparently, Ronald didn't see my relationship with Tuck lasting. He said Tuck had a reputation for using women and didn't want to see me hurt."

Gracie's eyes glittered with fury on Tuck's behalf. "What about the new woman he was supposed to be seeing?"

"Exactly. He *claimed* that didn't work out." CC held out her glass when Gracie picked up the bottle. "I turned him down, of course, and he had no choice left but to come clean on how his financial mess was the reason he was so anxious I do a show."

A growl rumbled in Gracie's throat. "What a dick. Is his number in your phone?"

Confused, CC nodded.

Gracie held out her hand. "Give it here." CC complied and Gracie scrolled through the contacts, then tapped the screen and held the phone to her ear. "Hello. Is this Ronald Bartolini? Yes, this is Gracie Malone. I represent CC Calhoun, and I just called to tell you you're fired." She thumbed the screen and handed the phone back.

CC giggled. "I don't think that was technically legal. Unfortunately, we have a contract."

Gracie ginned and held up her glass. "Who cares? It was fun." Their glasses clinked. "How else can I help you?"

"You can tell me how to get in touch with Tuck. He's not answering his phone, and if the messages he left over the past couple of days are an indication, he's written me off. I don't want to wait three weeks to talk to him."

Gracie swirled her wine. "His phone is shut off."

"Because of me?" CC hated her whining tone, but she was desperate.

"No, not you, although knowing Tuck, he'd be willing to let you sweat a little before he answers. No, it's off because Coach Timmins has a rule. No cell phones at camp. He likes to intimidate the rookies and, unfortunately, the older players get caught up in his tough guy net."

She dropped her forehead to the tabletop.

"But I have an idea."

CC lifted her head to peek across at her friend. Gracie wore a determined grin as she pushed back from the table and announced, "Road trip!"

* * * *

The big SUV rolled to a stop at the gate, and Gracie offered the uniformed guard a dimpled smile. "Hi, Teddy."

Teddy, a balding man, who had to be pushing seventy, rubbed a finger over the beak that passed for his nose and returned a shy smile. "Hey there, Mrs. Malone. Does Jake know you're coming?"

"He will in a few minutes."

Teddy chuckled into his hand and waved them through the gated fence surrounding the Marauders' Training Complex.

CC twisted her hands together in her lap. "This sounded like a good idea five hours ago, but now that we're here, I'm not so sure."

Gracie wheeled the big vehicle into a parking space right in front of the large building. The sign read *Reserved for Coaching Staff.* She twisted the key in the ignition and turned in her seat. "You are too sure. You're just scared Tuck will refuse to listen."

CC dropped her head back on the headrest with a groan. "I thought you were supposed to be helping?"

"I am."

"Could have fooled me."

Gracie's quiet laughter didn't help.

"Listen up, because I know what I'm talking about. Guys have their good points but basically, they're dorks. That doesn't mean they can't be tough, especially when they're hurt. You hurt Tuck, CC. Badly. I've never seen him look so lost as when he couldn't reach you. You owe him an apology."

CC shifted her head to look at Gracie's serious face. "Do you think I don't know that?'

"I think you're scared shitless he won't react the way you hope he will once you do."

"What if he tells me to fuck myself?"

Gracie arched a challenging brow. "We're talking about Tuck here. Why would he tell you to go fuck yourself when he'd much prefer to do the task himself?"

"What if he doesn't?" She squeezed her eyes shut for a moment. "You didn't hear his messages. He's really mad."

"What if he does?"

"What are you, the devil's advocate?"

Gracie grinned but sobered quickly. She sighed. "I'm going to tell you something I shouldn't, and if you tell him I told you, I'll call you a big, fat liar."

"What?" she grumbled.

"He told me you take his breath away."

She sat up straight, hope radiating from her heart to her smile. "He said that?"

"Yep. Of course, he likened you to a tick in the next sentence, but that's beside the point."

"A *tick*?"

Gracie waved a hand and pulled the keys from the ignition. "My point is, the man loves you. The question is, do you love him?"

Geez, a tick. What did that mean? She shook off the internal question and nodded. "Yes, I do. I never thought I'd ever meet a man who could make me yearn the way Tuck does, heart, mind, and soul."

"He sounds like a man worth fighting for."

"He is."

Gracie opened the door and hopped out. "Well, then, we've got a battle to fight."

CC hurried to keep up as Gracie sped her through a series of hallways as if afraid CC would change her mind if she had a moment to think. A distinct possibility. The thought of facing him made the saliva in her mouth dry to the consistency of sawdust.

Sawdust. A sardonic smile curled her lips. She'd experienced plenty of emotional wounds in her life, and here she was, standing on her own two feet and marching forward to heal the most important one of her life. Mom would be so proud.

The bright light stung her eyes as Gracie punched open a utilitarian gray door and the practice field came into view. Gracie headed straight for the random section of scaffolding on the sideline. Players grunted and slammed into one another on the grassy field beyond. CC's steps slowed to a halt as her gaze searched for Tuck's tall form. Gracie had to retrace her steps to grab her hand and drag her along.

"You can do this," she said without slowing down. "You owe him. Remember."

CC bit her lip and tried not to stumble, a difficult task considering Gracie's long strides. Slapping her free hand to her chest over her thundering heart, she fought against the fear threatening to suck her under. What if he refused to listen? What if she'd blown the best thing to ever come her way? Mentally shoving aside the doubt, she kept moving. She'd come so far, ticking off every last item on her fears list with one very important exception. Without Tuck, every victory she'd achieved over the past three weeks would never have been possible, and she'd be damned if she'd go on without him.

When they reached the scaffolding, Gracie shaded her eyes and looked up at the bulky man in shorts and a Marauders T-shirt who stood by himself on the ten-foot-tall platform and called out instructions on a megaphone.

"Hey, Coach." She smiled when he turned to look down at them and cocked her head in CC's direction. "This is CC Calhoun. She has something she needs to say to Tuck."

The big man's piercing gray eyes burned into CC. "Is she the reason he's been two steps behind since he showed up?"

Gracie grinned. "Yes, I believe she is."

He scowled. "Is she going to fix him, or make things worse?"

Gracie turned to CC with an arched brow. CC swallowed and nodded. Gracie looked up at the coach once more. "Fix."

Coach Timmins tucked the megaphone under one arm and propped his hands on the metal railing. "Then climb up here, young lady. Tuck is the best wide receiver in the league, but the way he's playing today, he won't make the practice team."

"Up there?" CC gawked at the high metal scaffolding. There weren't any stairs.

Gracie leaned close to whisper in her ear. "Is he worth the fight?"

CC grabbed hold of the first bar and started to climb. Swinging her leg over the top railing, she sent a tentative wave at Jake as he jogged to his wife's side.

"I don't believe this," CC heard him say. "Does Tuck know she's here?"

"He will in a second." Gracie looked up and gave her a thumbs-up. "Now or never, sweetie."

Coach held out the megaphone. CC wrapped her fingers around the handle, sucked in a bracing breath, and depressed the trigger. A piercing squeal echoed off the complex's high walls. Every head on the field whipped around, and she almost dropped the thing, trying to make it stop. Coach reached over and depressed a small button on the side.

"Press the red button first, then pull the trigger and speak."

"Oh, thank you." God, what the hell was she doing? She followed his instructions and spoke into the mouthpiece. "Kevin Tucker."

Close to sixty men turned at the sound of her voice. Panic exploded in her chest, and she staggered back a step. *Suck it up, CC. Tuck is out there somewhere. If you want him, you'll have to stand your ground.* Dragging in a calming breath, she raised her chin and stepped back to the rail.

"Hot damn. I think somebody wants you, Tuck," a male voice called out, causing a round of laughter.

"Son of a bitch."

She couldn't tell which uniformed body was his, but that angry voice was Tuck's. She stared at the crowd looking her way, and her heart lodged in her throat as one big body pushed his way through the others to stalk toward the sideline. As he ripped the helmet from his head, Tuck's sweaty blond hair gleamed in the sunlight, and her racing heart did a summersault in her chest.

He didn't even look her way, stomping up to Gracie with a snarl. "Get her the hell out of here, Gracie."

CC cued the trigger, and the returning squeal made her, and everyone else, wince, including Tuck. She scrambled to press the red button, then held the machine to her lips. "I'm not going anywhere until you answer a question."

His furious gaze switched to Jake. "Can't you control your wife?"

Gracie smiled serenely. Jake looped an arm over her shoulders and shrugged. "My wife doesn't seem to be the problem."

Disbelief hardened his face when he looked up, but he still didn't look at her. He glared at Timmons. "What the hell's going on, Coach?"

"The girl has something to say." Timmons spread his hands wide as if to say, what am I supposed to do?

"Not to me, she doesn't."

CC's heart dropped to her stomach as he jammed the helmet back onto his head and spun around to jog back onto the field. Righteous anger fired her temper. From the beginning, she'd tried to avoid him, but would he let her? No. He'd pushed, cajoled, and seduced her into losing her heart, so he'd just have to suck it up, the same way she was. She slammed her finger to the red button, cued the trigger, and held mouthpiece to her lips. "Stop right there, stud."

He stumbled to a stop and turned slowly. Even through his helmet, the stunned disbelief shone in his blue eyes.

She swallowed, but this was her one chance. Gracie was right. She wasn't about to give up without a fight. "You heard me, Kevin Tucker. I said I have a question to ask you."

He turned his back and continued on at a more leisurely pace.

His teammates shuffled their feet until someone called out, "I'll answer your question, darlin'." Snickers and outright laughter rose from the men.

She poked the button and cued the trigger. "Thanks, but my question is for Tuck, and Tuck only."

He ignored her, shouldering his way through the scattered men as he continued toward the middle of the field.

She dragged in a breath and took a chance. "Twice, I asked you what you wanted, but you didn't answer."

That stopped him cold, though he kept his back to her.

"So, I'll tell you what *I* want."

Catcalls and whistles filled the air, and she squeezed the trigger. The nasty squeal brought blessed silence.

She held the megaphone to her mouth. "I want *you*, Tuck, and not just for old time's sake."

The silence on the field was complete. He turned slowly and, at last, his blue gaze gleamed at her from beneath his helmet. When he took the first step in her direction, the breath lodged in her throat. When he tore the helmet from his head and started to run, tears stung her eyes. She leaned over the railing as he started to climb. A smile curled her lips, and when he vaulted onto the platform and swept her into his arms, her heart beat so hard she was afraid it would burst from her chest.

He held her tight as the cheers and laughter from his teammates sounded from below. He dipped his head and pressed his forehead to hers. "*Now* I'll tell you what I want. I want you to love me, the way I love you."

A tear tumbled from her lashes, and she pulled back to look into his eyes. "I do."

Dimples popped in his blinding grin. "There. That wasn't so hard. Was it, sunshine?"

Epilogue

"It's time!" Jessi Tucker's face beamed with excitement as she skidded in through the doorway. The staggered hem of her raspberry haltered bridesmaid's dress swished around her lower thighs.

CC swallowed and turned from the mirror, a hand pressed to her belly. Kris gulped her champagne as CC's mother fussed with the fall of CC's ankle-length wedding dress of cream crinkle chiffon and lace. Gracie handed each of the twins a small basket, and they danced from foot to foot, unable to contain their excitement at being a part of Uncle Tuck and Aunt CC's big day.

Exactly one month had passed since that day at training camp when she'd crossed the last item from her fears list and proclaimed her love for Tuck. To her surprise, he'd ignored his teammates' catcalls by dropping to a knee right there on the high platform to demand she marry him.

Twenty minutes later, Coach Timmons had regained control of his training camp, and Gracie led a stunned CC back to the SUV with Tuck's Super Bowl ring hanging by a chain on her neck with his promise to replace it with a proper engagement ring the day he got back.

She glanced at the sparkling solitaire on her left hand and smiled. If she'd been dreaming of a long, leisurely engagement, she quickly discovered that wasn't the case. Despite Coach Timmons's rule, Tuck must have gotten his hands on a phone somehow because hers began ringing off the hook the next morning.

His mother, Maryanne, woke CC before the sun had finished rising, and after apologizing for the early wake-up call, explained they needed to get to work immediately if they were going to have everything ready for her son and new daughter-in-law's wedding in thirty days. Considering Timmons's scowl as he attempted to bring order back to his team, CC dismissed the idea of returning to Syracuse to set Tuck straight on the concept of mutual decision making, but they'd had that conversation before she consented to let him slip his ring on her finger at last.

Both Gracie and Jake had insisted their home's sweeping back lawn was the perfect location for a late summer wedding. CC agreed, and though she didn't share why, suggested the vows should be exchanged at the edge of the magical wooded path. She couldn't think of a better place to publicly declare their love than where she'd officially lost her heart.

Kris linked her arm with CC's as they followed the others downstairs to pause inside the open kitchen doorway. Music swelled, as if on cue, and Jessi stepped out into the sunlight to begin her march. Through the window, CC scanned the wedding guests seated near the edge of the woods for the short ceremony.

At least a dozen of Tuck's teammates were peppered throughout the crowd of fifty guests, their superior height and broad shoulders drawing the eye. At the end of the grass aisle, Tuck stood with his back to her, strong and straight in his dark tux, with Jake and Max by his side. Tuck's parents, his brother, sister, and multiple family members sat several feet away in the front row.

A joyful sigh eased from her lungs. So much had happened since that day in the coffee shop. Beyond losing her heart to her very own *player*, she'd been embraced by a large, raucous, and sometimes crazy, extended family. Her heart pulsed with more happiness than she'd ever dreamed was possible.

Tears pricked CC's eyes as Gracie bent to give the twins last minute instructions.

"Stop that right now." Kris squeezed CC's arm. "You'll make me cry, and a bunch of Tuck's friends are out there. How can I bag my own hunky player if I have raccoon eyes?"

"I'll put in a good word for you," Gracie promised with a wink as she stepped outside to follow Jessi and gave them a clear view of the yard.

"Oh my God." Kris released a shivering sigh. "It's a warrior hunk convention."

CC laughed as her mother stepped to her side to take her free arm. There had been tears and smiles when she'd asked both her mother and Kris to walk with her, even before Curt had sent his condolences, saying he wished her happiness and didn't want to intrude on such a day. They'd been there, loving her and walking beside her, as she fought to find her way back from the darkness. She wanted them at her side as she finally arrived.

Her mother nodded at the twins. "Now remember, girls, walk slowly and take a pinch between your fingers, like I showed you, then sprinkle the dust to the ground before taking another. All the way to Uncle Tuck, okay?"

Twin heads of jet black curls nodded as they moved outside together.

CC arched a brow as a light, powdery substance floated to the grass from the twins' fingers. "What are they sprinkling?"

"Sawdust, of course."

Her mouth dropped open. "You've got to be kidding?" She turned her head to meet her cousin's laughing gaze.

Her mother's smile was smug as she tugged CC and Kris out onto the deck. "Dreams are nothing to trifle with, baby. I'm just making sure yours come true."

Kris snickered and rolled her eyes.

"Scoff all you want, but Tuck agrees with me." Her mother patted CC's hand. "Where do you think I got the sawdust?"

CC's head snapped forward, and her gaze locked on her groom's. His grin stretched, as if he knew exactly what was being said, and love gleamed in his eyes. She answered back silently with a grin of her own and hurried her steps toward him and their future.

Her mother was right. Dreams were nothing to be ignored, especially when they were about to come true.

THE END

Meet the Author

Wife, mother and *really young* grandmother, **Mackenzie Crowne** shares her home with her high school sweetheart husband, a neurotic Pomeranian, and a blind cat. She calls Arizona home because the southwest feeds her soul. Her love of the romance genre has been a lifelong affair, both as a reader and a writer. A bout with breast cancer sharpened her resolve to see her stories shared with others. Today, she's an eight-year survivor, living the dream. Her friends call her Mac. She hopes you will too. Visit her website at mackenziecrowne.com, find her on Facebook, or follow her on Twitter at twitter.com/MacCrowne.

Keep reading for a sneak peek at Book Three in the Players Series

To Win Her Heart

In order to protect her, they'll both have their guards down...

Country music's It Girl Jessi Tucker is fed up with her family's stifling security measures. The threat of a dangerous stalker has gotten the men in her life—including her football star cousin, Tuck Tucker—monitoring her every move. To get the freedom she yearns for, Jessi hatches a plan to recruit Max Grayson, Tuck's sexy brawler best friend, to play the role of her new boyfriend. But if her scheme works, will she be forced to hide her true romantic feelings for the sake of her independence? Or will she finally steal the heart of her dream man?...

Max has been pining for Jessi for years and would do anything to protect her, but a professional cage fighter with too many skeletons in his closet has no business being with one of America's sweethearts. Yet while Max does his best to keep Jessi at arm's length, the Tucker family persuades him to accept her offer.

Max believes he can keep Jessi safe from danger, but can he shelter her from his own dark secrets, the media's unforgiving spotlight—and a mutual desire that's harder to resist each day...

Available April 2016

Learn more about Mackenzie Crowe at
http://www.kensingtonbooks.com/author.aspx/31681

Chapter 1

Jessi Tucker needed a man. One with sharp edges. Some bite. Someone who projected the perfect mix of toughness and respectability—with a little bad boy thrown in for good measure.

Lucky for her, she knew right where to find him.

Slipping the designer sunglasses from her eyes, she scanned the half dozen occupants of the brightly lit fight center. A pair of men squared off on one of three large mats while several others called out encouragement to the combatants inside the netted octagon ring in the back corner. Bare, well-developed male chests seemed to be part of the dress code, but Max Grayson's muscled body was nowhere in sight. A hum of feminine disappointment vibrated in her throat.

"Can I help you?"

Jessi turned to face the approaching woman. Short, spiky, pink hair covered her head over an angular face. At least a head taller than Jessi's five-four, her slim build didn't detract from the buff and toned arms, legs, and bare midriff between her cut off T-shirt and spandex shorts.

Her big, brown eyes grew wide. "You're Jessi Tucker! Wow. I mean, wow! My boyfriend and me are huge fans. Your cousin, Tuck, got us tickets when you and Spence were in town last year for your Country Thunder tour." Her teeth flashed in a grin. "Oh, man. Eddie's gonna be so jealous when I tell him you were here. I'm Tina." She stuck out her hand. "I'm the junior self-defense instructor. Are you here to take a class?" Pumping Jessi's hand, excitement increased the volume of her voice with every word. "Oh my God. I can't believe this. You'd want something private, right? I'm available at the moment. The ring is booked for the next two hours, but there's a mat open."

"Actually"—Jessi tugged free and cut in before Tina could catch her breath—"I came by to speak to Max. I guess I should have called first to see if he'd be here."

Tina's smile cooled, and Jessi eyed the painful looking bar piercing her left brow. The thirty-something instructor didn't look anything like the string of Barbie Dolls who clung to Max's arm whenever he appeared at one her family's frequent gatherings. Then again, according to Tuck, *women* were Max's type.

Jessi wouldn't know, since he mostly ignored her.

"No problem. He's upstairs in his condo."

"Oh." Jessi's gaze flicked to the staircase climbing along the back wall to the second floor. "Is he alone? I wouldn't want to disturb him if he's... ah, busy."

Wry laughter danced in Tina's eyes. "The coast is clear, honey. Max has a way with the ladies, but he keeps things strictly professional during business hours."

She wanted to ask about after hours but thought better of it. If Max agreed to her proposition, she'd be doing her best to find out for herself. After thanking the woman, and promising to send along a signed copy of her latest CD, Jessi crossed to the stairs. The echoing thuds from below quieted as she reached the second floor landing and rounded the corner. A set of double doors beckoned from the end of a short hallway.

She stalked forward, stopped before the doors, and frowned at Spence's voice echoing in her head. *When are you going to stop acting like a scared little girl, afraid to do anything unless Daddy says it's okay?* Irritation simmered, but while her partner's sneering insult pissed her off, the underlying truth in his words rankled. A derisive sniff fluttered her nostrils. Her father would have a conniption if he knew what she was up to, but damn it, Spence was right. It was time she took a stand.

Breathing deeply, she refused to consider what she'd do if Max laughed and slammed the door in her face. Positive thinking was in order. She sucked air through her nose and closed her eyes to visualize the next few seconds, the way she did whenever she was about to step on stage.

Excitement raced through her as the giddy scenario played in her head. Max would open the door. Surprise would light up his long-lashed, gray eyes and one side of his mouth would lift in that sexy, crooked smile that made her toes curl. He'd take her hand and tug her inside, and he wouldn't be able to wait until the door was closed before he kissed her. He'd wrap his muscled arms around her, tuck her close, and...

Her eyes flashed open, and she slapped a hand to her belly. Anticipation and panic tumbled together in a hot mess, wrestling for the upper hand. She was going to throw up.

No, I'm not!

She swiped her damp palms over the thighs of her jeans, and rolling her shoulders, she knocked briskly. No sound came from within. She knocked again. Nothing. The silence taunted her, but she couldn't chicken out now. This was too important. Pressing her ear to the door, she listened intently—and choked on a strangled squeak when the door suddenly swung inward.

Off balance, she stumbled forward and shot out her hand to keep from tumbling over the threshold. Heavy muscle covered by taut skin arrested her fall and scorched her palm with delicious heat. Her fingers tingled with the desire to investigate further, and she might have done just that but for the deep clearing of a throat.

She snatched back her hand, and focusing on the sight in front of her, nearly swallowed her tongue.

Shirtless, Max's broad shoulders and chest filled the doorway. Her heartbeat took off in a racing gallop, and the breath stalled in her throat. She blinked at the black tribal tattoo riding one well-developed pectoral. The bold design swirled over his left shoulder and ended in a half-sleeve.

Her gaze flew up, past his face, to the water gleaming in the cropped, ebony hair covering his skull. Helpless, her eyes followed as a droplet trickled down the side of his cheek and jaw to hang from his stubbled, square-cut chin. The translucent bead plopped onto the center of his chest and slid through the thin line of short, black curls stepping down the ridges of rock hard abs until it disappeared beneath the towel wrapped around his trim waist.

Her throat clicked on an audible swallow and kick-started her breathing. She dropped her gaze to his bare feet before making the return trip to his face. If the surprise she'd been expecting had been in his eyes, she missed it. By the time her gaze locked with his, wary disbelief darkened the slate gray orbs.

Arching black brows slammed together. "What the hell are *you* doing here?"

She stifled a wince. Not exactly the greeting she was hoping for. So much for her fantasy. She shrugged inwardly. Knowing Max, that wasn't going to happen anyway, at least not today, but if she pulled this off, she'd live her fantasies soon enough.

Cocking her head, she offered him a friendly smile. "Hello, Max."

He leaned forward and turned his head to look down the empty hallway. His lips were flattened in an unhappy line when he straightened and faced her again. "Where is he?"

Confused, she blinked. "He who?"

"Your idiot cousin." He raised his voice as he double checked the hall. "Tuck. If you've got a camera running, I'm gonna kick your ass." He straightened once again and pinned her to the spot with a steely-eyed stare. "Look, Squirt, whatever punk he's got going, don't let him suck you into it."

She ground her teeth at the annoying nickname, but was nonetheless relieved. Preoccupied with Tuck's supposed prank, Max was less likely to realize how crazy her plan was. All she had to do was get him to agree before he did. She crossed her arms. "Are you going to invite me in?"

His brows shot up comically. "Hell, no, I'm not inviting you in." Suspicion narrowed his eyes as he shot a quick glance over his shoulder. His head whipped back around, and he fisted his fingers around the knot of the towel. "Did he sneak a camera into my condo?" He dipped his head around the doorjamb once more to shout, "Forget kicking your ass. I'll kill you, Tuck."

She grinned. Talk about paranoid. "There are no cameras. In fact, Tuck has no idea I'm here. There are, however, several people downstairs who are bound to come running if you keep shouting, so I suggest we move this inside."

"Forget it." He gripped the towel tighter and flicked his other hand toward her in a shooing motion. "Go away. Whatever you Tuckers are up to, I don't want any part of it."

"Fine. We'll have this conversation right here in the hallway, but don't blame me if—"

"Max! Is everything okay?" Feet thudded as one of the men from downstairs took the steps at a run.

She smirked and didn't bother to finish her warning. Ha! As if this six-foot, two hundred pound bruiser needed protection from her.

"Shit." She bit back a smug smile as at least part of her fantasy came true. Max grabbed her arm and yanked her inside.

After gripping her elbow, he shoved her behind him and held her there as he spoke to the unknown man. "I'm good. I'm expecting an equipment delivery at two. Make sure Tina goes through everything before she signs. They stiffed us a half dozen sets of gloves last time."

"Sure thing, boss."

Max shut the door on the unseen man and immediately released her arm. He moved several steps away and pierced her with a narrow-eyed glare. "Don't move an inch."

As he stalked across the room in a long legged stride, her greedy gaze catalogued the muscled expanse of his back. She swallowed, her attention snagging on the adorable set of dimples peeking just above the low-slung towel. Heat simmered in her belly, and she bit down on her lip to prevent an appreciative sigh.

He disappeared through a doorway and slammed the door shut behind him. Her cheeks puffed out on a blowing breath, and she tugged the scarf from her neck. Yeah, that hadn't exactly gone as planned, but at least he hadn't sent her packing. Her shaking fingers fumbled to slip open the buttons of her coat as she glanced around Max's inner sanctum. Having never been invited to his home, she'd been curious at how he lived. She planned to take full advantage of the opportunity to poke into his private space.

After shrugging out of her hip-length, woolen, houndstooth coat, she draped it and the scarf over the back of an oversized leather couch. For a bachelor, he had a good eye. A long, black granite island separated the modern kitchen from a comfortable living area. Floors of old-wood planks, aged brick walls, and exposed ceiling beams gave the open floor plan of the converted warehouse a warm, yet masculine, air.

The creamy, smooth, mahogany hide of the couch was luxurious under her skimming fingertips as she meandered deeper into his lair. Opposite the couch, orange flames licked at several logs in an inviting brick hearth below a huge, flat screen TV. Beneath the far wall of high windows, a built-in bookshelf caught her attention. Tossing a glance at the closed door where Max had disappeared, she crossed the room and bent to study the titles.

Considering his career, the many health and fitness books made sense, but there was also a wide selection of novels. She plucked one hard-bound title from the shelf and scanned the back blurb. A smile tugged at her lips. How about that? Max had a taste for fantasy fiction. Replacing the book, her gaze fell on the heavy bag hanging from a beam in the far corner.

Her heels clicked on the hardwood as she approached the fat, leather cylinder. A vision of Max, sweaty and intense as he worked the bag with fists and feet, honing his fighting skills along with the hardened plains of his athlete's body, flashed in her mind. Her belly muscles did a happy dance at the idea of a private demonstration. With a hum of anticipation, she balled her hand into a fist and threw her best punch. The bag didn't budge.

"I told you to stay put."

Startled, she jumped and whirled around as Max stalked by her into the kitchen. The towel was gone, which was too bad. The man certainly knew how to wear white terry cloth. She shook off her disappointment. For the coming conversation, the casual jeans and T-shirt covering his muscled frame were probably better than mostly naked and sexy as hell.

"Yes, well." She cleared her throat and trailed after him. "An aversion to orders is why I'm here."

"Meaning?" He wrenched open the refrigerator door, and his head disappeared inside.

She slid onto one of the island's four high stools. An alliance with Max, whether real or farce, was her best hope of breaking the chains her family had wrapped around her so tightly she couldn't breathe.

And she was sick of Max looking through her as if she wasn't there.

She'd been in love with the big jerk since the first time she met him, and since she was determined to shake up her world, she meant to do something about his habit of giving her the cold shoulder.

She folded her hands in her lap. "Meaning, I have a proposition for you."

His head popped up, and a wary frown pulled down the corners of his lips. "I don't like the sound of that." Straightening, he closed the refrigerator door and propped his hips against the counter to unscrew the cap on a water bottle. "Listen, I don't know what your cousin promised you to help him with his game, but I'll make it worth your while to forget it."

A hot wash of excitement coursed through her veins in a beeline straight for the juncture of her thighs. Oh, *she* liked the sound of that, but she wasn't about to *forget it*. She propped her elbows onto the counter and leaned toward him. "Worth my while, huh?" Pursing her lips, she dropped her voice to a flirtatious tease. "How would you do that?"

His Adam's apple bobbed on a swallow, and she could have sworn his gaze dropped to her mouth—before he scowled. "Does your father know you're here?"

"Nope." She fluttered her lashes. "There are some things a woman's father doesn't need to know about."

He jerked straight, and the wariness in his eyes slid back into suspicion. "Cut that out."

"What?" She blinked and played dumb. If nothing else, she was going to make Max Grayson finally see her for the woman she was.

He bumped out his chin. "Don't try using those baby blues on me. It won't work. I've watched you work your wiles to get your way too many times. What's going on?"

She sat up straight. He'd watched her? That was news. From her perspective, he did his best to ignore her most of the time, but he was wrong about her getting her way. If she did, she wouldn't be here. Okay, that wasn't quite true. If not today, she would have worked up the nerve to approach him eventually. Whether he knew it or not, Max held her heart in his hand, and he was either going to hold it properly, as he did in her dreams, or give it back once and for all.

Bold truth was called for, or at least as much truth as she could afford without tipping him off to the personal side of her agenda. If he agreed to help her, there would be time enough later to ease him into the concept of exploring a real relationship between them.

"I'm here because I need your help."

"With what?"

"With getting my family off my back."

"How am I supposed to do that?" He shook his head and pulled a long sip of water from the bottle.

She fidgeted with the hem of her blouse and had to take a deep breath before she could force the words out. "By pretending to be my boyfriend."